Return To Dixbury

by

Maxine Sinclair

Cover illustration http://www.andrewdelf.co.uk

Visit the author's blog at https://maxinesinclair.com

In memory of
Kathy Lynn Elrick.

Sunshine, love, laughter.

For everyone who read Dixbury Does Talent and wants to know what happens next...

Chapter 1

I stand with my bowl of cereal, eyes on stalks, gawping at my television.

"Joshua, Joshua! Come here!" I yell to my live-in boyfriend of three months. He comes running into the room, wet curls hanging over his eyes, wearing my baby-pink bathrobe.

"Whoa, whoa, where's the fire?"

I point to the television. "Look!" Then I glance sideways at him. "Are you ever going to get yourself a manly bathrobe?" He laughs, wrapping it further around himself, turning his attention to the screen.

"Amy – I've told you not to watch this rubbish – it's not good for you." He screws his face up at Jeremy Kyle.

"It's Steve and Justine!"

I haven't seen Steve, my estranged husband, since I told him on Christmas Day that there was definitely no going back, that our marriage was beyond salvageable. He'd told me that my timing stank (he had a point) and then, without much fuss, he left. I didn't know whether he'd returned to Justine, the floozy he'd originally left me for, but now my television confirms that he clearly had.

"So, darlin', you were pregnant and you told Steve here that the baby was his, right?" Jeremy Kyle cross-examines her.

She flicks her lifeless iron-flat blonde hair out of her eyes. "Yeah."

"And then, Mitch shows up and tells Steve that the baby's his," he goads as the camera pans to 'Mitch' sitting around the back.

"Yeah," she says again.

"Yeah," Jeremy repeats. "So whose is it, Justine? Do you know?"

"It's Steve's. I love 'im," she says.

"You love him – that's doesn't guarantee he's the dad though, does it?"

She looks down. The camera cuts to a downcast, awkward looking Steve.

"Oh My God, Josh, what is he doing on there? Has he no self respect?" I ask, not taking my eyes off the screen.

"Not much that I can see."

Jeremy continues, "So, Steve – do you love her?"

"Yeah."

Oh my – has he also lost the ability to use more than one word at a time?

"And you want that beautiful six week old baby girl to be yours?"

"Yep I do. I love her. I just need to know for sure if she's mine."

Camera switches to behind the scenes to show Mitch, muted, shouting aggressively, jabbing his finger at the camera.

"Whoa - he's tough to lip-read." Joshua jokes.

"OK guys," Jeremy says, slapping his card in his hand. "We need to bring out the third person in this, everybody please welcome Mitch to the stage."

Justine sits in the middle of the two prospective fathers. What a sorry bunch. Clearly angry that he may not be the father, Mitch, replete in faded tracksuit bottoms, white reebok trainers and a t-shirt sporting the words 'Who's The Daddy', fidgets, smacking his knuckles into his palm.

"So Mitch," Jeremy says. "Tell us your side of the story."

"I met 'er last summer and she was proper my girl, y'know. She dumped me when this ******** showed up," he says, nodding towards Steve.

"Ooh choice language – but, hey - quite accurate." I say. Joshua snorts a laugh.

"The dates work out, man," Mitch says. "She might've slept wiv 'im after – but the kid's mine. Any anyways – she weren't interested in 'im..." He jerks a thumb in Steve's direction, "...when he legged it back to 'is missus."

I raise my hands to my face, "Oh My God!"

“Crikey, Amy, thank goodness they didn’t get you on there.” Joshua says, placing a reassuring arm around my shoulders and pulling me to him.

The three participants all start shouting at the same time. It seems that Steve is telling Mitch that it’s nothing to do with him, Justine is emphasising to Mitch that it’s not his baby and that she loves Steve, and Mitch is making the bleeper man work for his money.

“OK, OK, OK,” Jeremy shouts them down. “Now this is what we do here on The Jeremy Kyle Show – we settle disputes like this. That gorgeous baby there…” camera pans to sweet baby, head to toe in pink and frills, “...has a mum who can’t be sure who the father is and there’s only one way to find out. Join me after the break when we’ll have the results of the DNA tests. Don’t go away.”

I stare, glazing over at the commercials. It’s so difficult to believe that Steve is humiliating himself in this way. Going on television as part of this seedy ‘love’ triangle and revealing himself as an adulterer to boot are not the actions of the man I loved.

“Cup of tea?” Joshua says in my ear. “Might make the next part easier to bear?”

“Yes please,” I say, dropping down onto the sofa. I really don’t know how I feel. I was truly heartbroken when Steve left me for Justine, and the news of her pregnancy only cut me deeper. But when it transpired that he might not be the father, we attempted to reconcile. Even though it didn’t work out and I’ve since moved on, I’m feeling strangely torn about whether I want him to be the biological father.

Joshua returns, sits beside me, passing a builder’s strength mug of tea as the programme resumes.

Recapping all that has gone before, like we have the memories of goldfish, Jeremy is then passed an envelope.

“Right, the DNA results are in. Steve – you want baby Beyoncé to be yours, right?” Steve nods.

Joshua turns to me and mouths, ‘Beyoncé?’

"Mitch, you want Beyoncé to be yours too, don't you?" He nods. "Justine, you say you know she's Steve's – but, let's be honest, love, you can't be one hundred per cent as you slept with both these geezers, didn't you?" She stares blankly at him. "Whatever the outcome of these tests," he says, moving closer and staring her in the eyes, "I want you, Justine, to promise me that you'll devote your time to loving and caring for this little girl. One of these is her dad but don't ever forget that *she's* the most important person in all of this. Got it?" She nods agreement. "Are you ready?" he asks them all.

They all stare at him as he opens the envelope and pauses.

"I can confirm that the DNA test shows that……the father is…...Steve."

Cue audience gasps, profuse swearing from Mitch, and Justine in tears of relief. Steve, looking slightly stunned, rises from his chair and pulls out a ring box. He lowers on to one knee. The audience gasps, chorusing a collective 'woo.' Justine weeps and puts a shaking hand over her mouth.

"Jussie – I love you, marry me," he says.

I am agog, spitting out my tea.

"You'll have to bloody divorce me first!"

Chapter 2

"Mornin' boss!" Gina's Essex twang rings out as she arrives for work at Hip Snips.

"Morning G." I call from the small staff room.

With multi-coloured backcombed hair and red bodycon dress, she totters the length of the shop. By the wary look in her eyes, I can tell that she saw it too.

"So, what did you think? Did you know they were going on there?" I ask, knowing of Gina's association with Justine through the darts team.

"Nah – they kept it quiet. Almost peed me pants when I saw 'em! Woz funny though, weren't it?"

"I just can't believe he'd go on Jeremy Kyle!"

"It's his though, ain't it? The nipper. Ain't you glad you dumped 'im?"

Gina's complete disregard for subtlety is one of the things I love most about her.

"Yes, little *Beyoncé* is his. And what about him proposing to her? He's still technically married to me!"

"Short memory 'ain't 'e!" she laughs.

The phone rings. Gina pulls a face and teeters off to the reception.

I attend to the coffee machine thinking how I should probably expect to hear from Steve any day. He may have his faults but I'm guessing that bigamy isn't one of them - I'm sure he'll want a quickie divorce, and then we'll have to decide what to do about Rose Cottage. Being up for sale and having had little to no interest has suited me fine – I'm happy living there with Joshua. It's all homemade dinners, snuggly lie-ins, lazy Sundays and long walks with Basil, our now jointly parented Cocker Spaniel. I honestly can't remember a time when I've felt so grateful for my lot.

Gloria, my friend and fellow ballet dancer, breaks my reverie. “Hello there, Miss Dreamy.” She smiles, poking her pristine head around the staff room door.

“Gloria, lovely to see you.” I get up to kiss her cheek. “You haven’t got an appointment today, have you?”

“No, no, I was just passing. Just wanted to let you know I’ve a few errands to run before ballet class tonight and wondered if I could pick you up a little early?”

“Oh don’t worry – I think Josh has to go there anyway – he’s still helping out until they can find a new caretaker so I’ll get a lift with him.”

“OK, that’s fine then.”

“Did you see it?” I ask, and then inwardly rebuke myself – of course Gloria didn’t see Jeremy Kyle – she wouldn’t watch such a programme, she’s the epitome of class.

“See what, dear?”

“My ex, Steve, on Jeremy Kyle.”

“Jeremy Kyle?” She looks puzzled.

“Morning talk show. Some call him Jeremy ‘Vile’?”

Gloria registers a look of recognition and simultaneous horror.

“Oh My Lord! I know who you mean - what on earth possessed him to do that?”

“DNA testing to find out ‘Beyoncé’s’ paternity.” Gloria grimaces. “Hold on, I haven’t told you the worst part yet.”

“There’s something worse than calling a child ‘Beyoncé’?”

“After he found out that she’s his, he whipped out a ring and proposed to Justine right there on national TV.”

“Good grief – sounds like a ratings grabber. How do you feel, dear?”

“I was stunned. I just can’t believe he’s the same man I married. Thank goodness I’m happy with Joshua otherwise it’d really sting. I’m expecting to hear from him soon, I’m guessing he’ll want a hasty divorce.”

"Well, dear, if you're looking for a good solicitor I can highly recommend Simone Bletchley – she works at Wood and McMillan's - I've used them for years."

"Thanks, Gloria. Hope it won't get nasty."

"If it does, Simone's your woman." She smiles kindly.

"Anyway how are you and Brian? Is love still in the air?" I tease.

"We're fine." She smiles and then looks down. "However, my daughter, Fliss, is coming to stay – it seems she's had a falling out with her husband; all very concerning. I don't know how long she'll be staying." She takes a deep breath. "I've decided to introduce her to Brian but I'm not sure how it'll go."

"Oh Gloria, I'm sorry. Hope your daughter's ok. I shouldn't worry too much about them meeting. I mean, it's Brian – what's not to love?"

"Yes dear," she says, sounding anything but sure.

The door opens and I hear Gina greet Mrs Plumb, a dear old loyal customer, who must be in her nineties. A snail could beat her when she moves from basin to chair, but, arriving for her weekly shampoo and set, she is the bread and butter of my business.

Gloria and I have moved on to discussing the latest tricky ballet steps we're trying to master when Gina rushes into the staff room, her shoulders shaking, eyes brimming with tears and legs crossed in the event of an accident.

"What on earth's tickled you?" I ask.

"Mrs Plumb asked me to do summat different to 'er 'air…" she says, barely able to get the words out.

"What's funny about that?" asks Gloria.

Gina is fit to burst.

"Spit it out." I say.

"You know 'er 'usband died just before Christmas?"

I frown. "Still can't see the joke."

"Well…her son is takin' 'er picture this afternoon."

We stare blankly.

"It's for 'er profile pic… on Tinder!"

We all wind our necks around the staff room door to look at sweet old Mrs Plumb.

"Well well," I say in wonder, "Mrs Plumb – my new role model."

Chapter 3

Entering Dixbury Village Hall changing rooms I find Lucia telling a bawdy tale of her previous evening's exploits with her boyfriend, Geoff.

"Lucia!" Josie half-laughs. "Can you please remember that my fifteen-year-old daughter is present?"

"Mum, really!" Catherine protests, blushing.

"Yes, we don't need to know the finer details," huffs Julay, as she admires her haughty figure in the slightly corroding mirror.

"Aw – you're just jealous, Fancy Pants," Lucia retorts.

Gloria smooths her wrap-over cardigan and exchanges a smile with Marion who is changing quietly in the corner.

"Locker room banter, I think it's called," Sam says to me out of the corner of her mouth as she adeptly clips her hair into a high bun.

I smile, happy to be around my dancing friends. As I pull on the black ballet garb that most of us tend to favour, I think about how ballet bonds us. With the exception of young Catherine, who has every chance of going on to professional training, none of us will be prima ballerinas, but, nevertheless, our hearts and souls are devoted to the art of the dance.

Gathering in the hall, Brian, our only male dancer emerges from the men's changing room to join us. We all start warming up individually.

"You know Helena told us she was looking for our next ballet competition?" Marion says. "Well, I saw an advertisement in the post office for one in Afton."

Before anyone can reply, the door opens and we turn to see our beloved teacher, Helena, in a wheelchair, being pushed by a tall, handsome, olive skinned man. Tearing our eyes away from him we see her purple plastered foot and gasp.

"OK, OK, don't worry, folks." Helena says waving her hand. "I stupidly fell at the allotment and broke my ankle - I'm temporarily out of action."

"Oh no!" Gloria says. "You poor thing."

Murmurs of concern rumble around the room.

"Sorry – I should introduce you to my partner, this is Uri." She says, half turning to look up at her fine-looking man. He dazzles a smile and nods to us. I think I see a trickle of drool from Lucia's lips.

"Anyway, I'm sorry, I'm not going to be teaching for a while." Helena continues. "I've thought about it and I could get here and talk you through the steps but I don't think it's the best way for you to learn. So I've asked another teacher to temporarily take over your classes." If any of us were hoping the replacement teacher was Uri, she immediately bursts that bubble by adding, "And he'll be here shortly."

Was that a collective sigh of disappointment?

"Aw, that's a shame," Marion says. "I was just telling everyone about a competition in Afton and wondered if you'd enter us. But maybe not now, eh?"

"Well, the doctors say it'll be six weeks before I'm walking again – when is the competition?"

"End of April."

"Well, that would give us a couple of months. Are you all keen?" Helena looks round the group.

"What kind of competition?" Samantha asks.

"Pretty much the same as Dixbury Does Talent, just a smaller local one," Marion answers.

"I can find out more about it and then register you, if you'd like me to?" Helena says. "It'd give me something to do. It's only been a few days and I'm getting bored already, aren't I?" She looks up at Uri.

"Yes, she's not one for sitting still," he says and the room dissolves into girlish giggles.

"So if you're all agreed? I'll look into it and get back to you, OK?" Helena says.

We nod enthusiastically. With our transport breaking down and not being able to take part in last year's Dixbury Does Talent, we're now all raring to compete.

Just then the door flies opens and an older imposing looking man strides in. He smiles broadly at us over his small half moon glasses, revealing perfect white teeth. His flamboyant style of dress certainly catches the eye; not many men can get away with a silk scarf, frilled cuffs and a long green velvet coat.

"Is that a syrup?" Lucia murmurs to me.

"A *what?"* I whisper.

"Syrup of fig, wig!"

"Shhhh." I say, stifling a giggle, clocking his thinning-at-the-sides grey hair and thick dark ginger mop top.

"People, this is Bendrick Henderson." Helena says, as he bends to kiss her hand. "Bendrick is an ex-dancer and highly experienced teacher…" she turns to him, "...and, for many years, you ran your own school in Birmingham, didn't you?" He nods. "Let's hope you're up to teaching The Dixbury Dancers!"

After a smattering of laughter he opens his arms wide to address us. "My dahlings! I am so utterly honoured to be your guide, your imparter of wisdom, your
teacher for the foreseeable future." He smiles. "I have taught for numerous years both here and abroad, I held the coveted seat of residency at the BALA Academy, and was an advisor to RAB but, for now, I am on hiatus. I have moved to this gloriously verdant part of the land and am seeking out new opportunities…" He continues talking, closing his eyes and turning his face upwards, enunciating each syllable and tossing his silk scarf over his shoulder. It's like watching the opening of a play and we are transfixed. The word 'theatrical' was created for him.

When he concludes with an exclamation of being 'at our service', Helena explains to him our ritual of 'Prayers and Pains' where, at the start of class, we each state what we hope to achieve and inform of any injuries.

"Marvellous, my dahlings - please proceed." He says, rocking on his heels and folding his hands over his large round stomach.

"I'm Marion. I want to improve my turn out."

"I'm Samantha and I want a deeper plié."

"I'm Amy," I say, frantically trying to think of what I want to achieve. "Er, I just want to enjoy the class." He smiles and nods.

"I'm Brian, sir, and I would like to concentrate on my thumbs as they insist on sticking out." We all laugh.

"My name is Gloria, I wish to achieve the double pirouette."

"I'm Josie and I want to jump higher!"

"A noble deed indeed." Bendrick replies.

"And I'm Catherine,' she says shyly, exposing her braces. "I want to build strength for pointe work." He smiles kindly at her.

"Name's Lucia," she says, winking at him. "Just wanna dance!"

Finally we all turn to our last dancer, Julay.

"Dear man," she starts, matching Bendrick's dramatic flair. "I wish to work on my élongé and improve my lines as is the way of the true danseuse."

I have no idea what that means.

Their eyes meet and they smile, half bowing in respect to one another. I have a feeling I'm witnessing the coming together of kindred spirits.

"Right then," Helena says. "For now, my work here is done. I'll look up that competition in Afton and pop in again when I've got news. I'll literally hop off and leave you in the capable hands of your new teacher. Be gentle with him!" We all giggle.

"Thank you dear lady," he replies.

"Bendrick," Helena says, pausing for thought. "Maybe after a few sessions you might be able to match the talents of my dancers to a classical piece for the competition? I'd certainly value your input."

"Yes, of course, marvellous. It would be my utter pleasure."

"You'll come by from time to time, won't you?" Samantha asks Helena.

"Of course, wild horses couldn't keep me away. I hate being far from the barre – you've no idea what an injury like this does to an ageing dancer!" We make sympathetic noises. "As soon as this pot comes off." She nods to her leaden foot, "I'll be seeing the physio and getting back in shape."

"Are you going to Philip?" Sam asks.

"Yes." A look of recognition crosses her face. "Oh yes, I believe you know his son?"

Sam blushes. "Yes, Jason."

"And getting to know him better aren't you, Sammie!" Lucia says with a salacious wink and in return receives a scornful look.

"He's helping me with my studies," Sam says, steering the conversation away from her fledgling love life. "And one day I'll be the physio for The Dixbury Dancers!"

"Then we'll be a proper professional troupe!" Gloria chips in.

Helena proudly beams at us all. "In my eyes, you already are."

Chapter 4

Returning home from 'Throwback Thursday' when we charge hairdressing prices from twenty years ago and consequently have an onslaught of custom, I'm exhausted. I open the front door to find a large note on the floor.

Take off shoes and coat and follow your nose.

I love Joshua – my life is all the more fun for having him in it. I obey instructions and deeply inhale the smell of cooking. As I'm nearing the kitchen I spy a glass of wine on the hall table and another note.

Pick up, sip, and head to the room where we dine.

Smiling, I obey, once again. Mmm, Merlot, my favourite – he knows my taste. I survey the dining room bathed in soft flickering candlelight. The table is set with my prettiest flowered patterned plates and twinkling crystal glasses. The glistening hanging chandelier diffuses light and casts shadows on the walls, floorboards and white voile curtains. The Beatles' "The Long And Winding Road" plays quietly and I feel my heart squeeze at the exquisite perfection that surrounds me.

Pinned to the back of a chair is another note.

Please sit your pretty derriere here and await service.

At that moment the adjoining door opens and Joshua walks in, smiling, carrying dishes of olives and bread.

"You're lucky that said 'pretty' and not 'pretty large'!" I laugh, looking up at him. He leans over, places the dishes and kisses me.

"You know I like your rump."

"Well I like yours too." He sits opposite me. "So what's the special occasion?" I ask, unfolding my napkin.

"It's Thursday."

I pause to puzzle. "Am I missing something?"

"Nope – and neither am I – we're not missing a thing, we have everything we need."

"Ooh Mr. Cheesy!" I laugh.

"OK then, tell me one thing you want that you don't have."

"OK, well this'll sound shallow – but I'd like to stay in this house, with you. I don't want to move but I'm guessing Steve is going to need the money soon."

"Don't sweat it, Amy - we could be happy wherever we are."

"True enough." I say, picking up a hunk of bread. "But tell me honestly, would you rather a fresh start in a new place? Does it bother you being in what was my marital home?"

"Nah – I love it here too." His handsome face turns serious. "I mean it though, Amy, home is a feeling – and that feeling for me is with you."

I tilt my head and sigh. "Aw, that's beautiful,"

"Well what a coincidence, 'cos you are too."

He reaches across and takes my hand. I will never tire of looking at him – that beautiful face, soft smile and mad curly hair with a mind of its own.

"Hey, bet you can't do this though," he says, picking up an olive, throwing it in the air and adeptly catching it in his mouth.

"How much?"

"This week's ironing."

"You're on, mister!"

I grab a fat green olive and toss it in the air. It bounces off my chin and rolls onto the floor, where Basil, the ever-hungry hound, races to retrieve it. By the speed in which he expels it I'd say they're not to his taste.

"Ha, right, I've a few shirts hanging up that could do with an extra press." Joshua teases.

"I'll sit on them with my perfect derriere"

"Whatever floats your boat, my love," he says as he takes the lid off the casserole dish to reveal a bubbling Coq Au Vin. Devouring it amidst bubbly conversation he then he proves his culinary expertise further by producing the lightest, fluffiest chocolate mousse. He's a keeper.

"Nine and a half out of ten!" I award him, consuming each morsel and wiping my mouth with a napkin.

"What did I lose half a point on?"

"Nothing – just don't want you getting a big head."

"Ha! Fair enough. Clear up and then watch a film?"

"Yeah!"

"We can watch Grease if you like?" He knows how much I love musicals and his offer is all the more magnanimous, as I know he doesn't.

"Really?"

"No."

We laugh and I throw my napkin at him. That's us, – sharing an easy wit – I can't imagine a time when we'll stop laughing. Even through all the years with Steve I didn't feel as relaxed as I do when I'm with Joshua. Successful relationships are often touted as something couples have to work at but, as far as I can tell, we seem to be sailing along buoyed by a calm breeze. It might be fair to say that we're still in the honeymoon period – but Joshua always jokes that we're the 'supermarket couple' because we simply 'click and connect'. I tell him that it's 'collect' but he waves me away claiming I'm too picky.

Snuggled up on the sofa, with my favourite fluffy pastel throw over us, he accedes to watching West Side Story, claiming it's more of a 'manly musical'. I'm not sure such a thing exists but if it gives me the chance to watch it again, I'm not going to argue.

As the final tearful scene plays out, I lift my head from his chest to find him fast asleep.

"Joshua, Josh." I nudge him awake.

"Uh?" He squints through bleary eyes. "Oh no – did I miss it?"

"Have you ever seen it?"

"Nah."

"And I can tell that that upsets you deeply."

He smiles, pushing the heels of his hands into his eyes to rub them awake. "C'mon then sleepy head," I say, ruffling his hair. "Let's get you to bed." A phone beeps. "Me or you?"

"You – mine's charging."

I ferret around in my bag pulling out my phone. My picture perfect evening concludes as I read the message from Steve.

Hi. Need to meet soon – we need to discuss stuff. When are you free? S.

Chapter 5

"Come in, dear," Gloria opens her front door to welcome her daughter, kissing her on both cheeks. Felicity 'Fliss' Arnold, not one for hugging, rubs her mother's arm and smiles. "Here, let me take that." Gloria holds out her hand to take the Louis Vuitton case.

"It's okay, I can manage."

'Mmm, still the independent one,' Gloria thinks. At the age of seven when Fliss was learning the piano, Clair de Lune had vexed her. Gloria, an experienced pianist, had sat on the stool next to her daughter and offered help. Fliss had thrown a temper tantrum of epic proportion, screaming at her mother that she would never learn if her mother always did it for her. Gloria quickly learnt how to walk on eggshells.

"Ok then, darling." Gloria says, retracting her arm. "Your room's still in the same place. Why not unpack and then come down for a nice cup of tea?"

"Thanks, OK."

Gloria watches as Fliss struggles to hump her huge case up the stairs and wonders just what is going on. A phone call from her late last week merely informed her that she would be returning home for 'a while'. Gloria worries that all is not well in her feisty daughter's marriage.

Five minutes later, ensconced on the comfy sofa in the corner of the kitchen, Gloria passes her daughter a cup of tea. She notices how Fliss's dress is hanging on her, and, despite the clever use of make-up, dark circles peep around her eyes.

"How are you?" Gloria asks.

"Been better." Fliss says, her mouth turning down.

"Is everything alright with Tim?"

Fliss sighs deeply. "Not really. I'm conducting a little experiment – see if he misses me."

"Oh I see – so how does he feel about you being here?"

"Between his job and golf I doubt he realises I've gone."

"Of course he'll miss you, Fliss. You've been together eight years, and the last I heard he loved you very much."

"Mum," Fliss takes a slow breath. "You don't know what you're talking about. He's not the saint you always make him out to be." Her eyes flash a tiny spark of anger.

"OK darling. Look, I don't want to pry –"

"-But you're going to anyway."

Gloria sighs. She knows there's no use talking with Fliss when she's in this mood – better to leave it for another time. Her daughter has come home, this is her chosen safe haven, and that's good enough for now. The rest can wait.

Fliss stares into her tea.

"You know you can stay for as long as you like." Gloria says.

"Thanks Mum." Fliss flicks a piece of cotton from her dress. Her gloomy expression reminds Gloria of something she once read about how a parent can only be as happy as their unhappiest child. "So, Mummy Dear." Fliss brightens. "Enough about me. When am I going to meet your fancy man?"

"Now, now darling, let's not call him that. He's my friend."

"Friend eh? Friends with benefits?"

"I'm still not completely sure what that means but I'm going to say no." Fliss laughs. "Anyway," Gloria takes a deep breath. "I've invited him round tonight for dinner."

Fliss's face drops. "Oh, I thought it'd be just us two tonight. But that's fine if you've already made the arrangements."

"I can postpone if you like?"

"No, no, it's your house, it's up to you."

"Fliss," Gloria says in a warning tone.

"No, Mum, really, it's fine."

"OK then, if you're sure, I'll cook for both of you tonight. I'm making your favourite. Want to help with some chopping?"

Fliss shakes her head. "I'll just sit here if it's alright with you? You know I love just being around when you're in the kitchen." She smiles. "Remember when we used to make cakes for Daddy?"

"Ha! Yes, most of the mixture went in your tummy! He used to laugh at his 'bite size' cakes." The two women laugh. "OK, right, better get on." Gloria rises, taking the teacups with her, leaving Fliss to blankly gaze out at the garden.

Gloria peels and chops whilst keeping an eye on her daughter. Fliss has always been a prickly one, but this seems different, and getting her to open up is going to be a mighty task indeed. Wiping her hands on her apron, Gloria sighs at the thought of how Fliss's father would have known what to do and say. Stanley, in his calm, caring way would pacify and cajole Fliss into talking and the conversation would end with their daughter in an altogether lighter mood.

Hmm, thinks Gloria, that's the problem when 'Daddy's girl' is left with only Mummy.

Six o'clock on the dot the doorbell rings and Gloria rushes to the door to greet their guest. Returning to the lounge she shines from every pore as she positions this kindly looking man before Fliss.

"Fliss, this is Brian."

"Hello Felicity." Brian smiles.

"Oh, oh, she prefers 'Fliss," Gloria intercedes.

"No, 'Felicity' is fine," Fliss says.

"Well, it's a pleasure to meet you, whatever your moniker," he laughs. "Your mother's told me all about you."

"I'm not sure that's a good thing." Fliss smiles.

"Hush now, darling, of course it's good." Gloria soothes. "Right, can I get anybody a drink?"

"Please let me do the honours." Brian says. "Felicity, what can I tempt you with?"

"Gin and tonic please."

"Ooh good idea, let's all have one!" Gloria says.

Brian makes his way to the old-fashioned oak drinks trolley in the corner of the lounge. The hairs on the back of Fliss's neck stand up as she watches him open the lid and take out the long cut glass tumblers and green gin bottle.

"How do you like it? More gin less tonic?" he jokes.

"As it comes is fine."

Gloria's body tenses. She wants their meeting to be amiable. Brian is a lovely man, a constant companion and a staple of her life, and Fliss, despite her scratchiness, needs her mother's love and support at this time. Gloria's heart pulls in opposite directions - although her immediate pull is to the kitchen to ensure that an overcooked dinner doesn't contribute to an already precarious evening.

Fifteen minutes later Gloria carries the platter of a roasted chicken to the table to find Fliss and Brian trying their best at small talk.

"Your mum tells me you have quite a job?" Brian says.

"Mum exaggerates greatly, but, yes, I've recently been promoted to manager of a top wine bar in the centre of London – very popular with the after-work crowd."

"Sounds wonderful. Your mum says you get quite a few famous folk in there too."

"We've had a few, but we sort of have an unwritten confidentiality policy."

A slight hurt registers on his face. "Of course, of course, totally understand - very professional."

Shifting uncomfortably in the silence, Gloria turns to Brian.

"Would you be so kind as to do the honours, please?" she signals to the chicken.

"Of course, my darling," he says, getting up.

‘*My darling’*, the words echo in Fliss’s ears and her heart picks up a pace. She looks up to see Brian sharpening the two long knives, smiling down into her mother’s fluttering eyes. Her mind flashes back to her father standing in that very spot and anger grips her gut. How can her mother move on so quickly? It makes a mockery of their marriage. Look at her, she thinks, old enough to know better, fawning over this man. Fliss suddenly becomes aware that Brian is asking her something.

“Leg or breast?”

“What?”

“Chicken.” He points with the knife. “Leg or breast?”

“I’m sorry, Brian, I don’t want any chicken,” Fliss says. Gloria looks up sharply. “I want my dad to carve the meat, I want a drink poured by him – not you!” She may sound like a small child, but she just can’t do it – her father’s funeral was only a couple of months ago. Shakily, she rises from the table.

“Fliss –“ Brian starts.

“Please don’t call me that, my friends call me Fliss, you can call me Felicity.”

“Felicity!” Gloria shouts. “That is quite enough! Brian is our guest.”

“Your guest, Mother!”

“I haven’t said this for a very long time, young lady, but you can mind your manners and go to your room!”

To match such an order Fliss flounces out of the room slamming the door, the reverberations of which are felt all over the house.

Chapter 6

"Ok my dahlings, I'd like a grand rond de jambe finishing in arabesque. Eye lines lifted, legs elongated and toes pointed. In the grand rond, keep the leg level – if we start at ninety degrees we maintain ninety degrees, then fondu on the supporting leg, bringing the working leg into retire on a straight supporting leg, follow through to extend to the front once again on fondu, bring back again to retiré. Lower into fifth and pirouette. Do not lower the leg and keep a balance in retiré. When the music stops, lower the heel first and maintain fifth position."

What??? Bendrick is a madman!

And judging by my classmates' expressions, I think everyone agrees. Lucia is sweating so profusely that there's a visible puddle at her feet; Gloria's usual cool façade is replaced with spikey hair and running make-up and poor little Marion is visibly trembling. Not even halfway through the class and we are lined up here, at the barre, in collective bewilderment.

"Sorry, Bendrick," I raise a hand tentatively. "Could you go through that again please?"

"Certainly, my dear." He starts off again, and although the words are familiar, I just can't follow. It dawns on me that Helena always demonstrates and explains at the same time, leaving us in no doubt what's required. Bendrick's stand-on-the-spot-and-bark-instructions method just doesn't wash.

"All clear?" he asks, scanning the room.

Nobody answers – fright does that to people. Taking silence as affirmation, he leans towards the stereo, starts the music and we begin.

"Higher legs…don't look down…point the toes…sharper into the retiré…deeper bends into the fondu…stretch like soft elastic…don't show me the effort…show me your smiles, danseurs," he commands over the music.

"I'll show him something…" Lucia gasps, looking fit to burst a blood vessel. A quick scan of the room finds Brian struggling to raise his leg to even nineteen degrees let alone ninety, Marion turning blue from holding her breath in concentration and even Sam looking flushed and flustered. As the music finishes, most of us bend over, hands on hips, trying to catch our breath.

"Right, dancers," Bendrick begins. "Let's move to grand battement, the sweeping of the legs –"

"Benny, c'mon, give us a break!" Lucia says, wiping the sweat from her cleavage. "We're not the Royal flippin' Ballet!"

Bendrick looks taken aback. "Nonsense – you're all doing marvellously well. I want to stretch you all, give you exciting challenges, let your inner ballerinas shine forth!"

"Benny, some of our inner ballerinas have been sitting on sofas for the past few years, love."

"It's just a tad above our station." Marion gasps.

"A notch or two down, sir, might be appreciated." Brian chips in.

Only Catherine, our promising dancer, is benefitting from this level of teaching, but as she only joined our group for extra practise, she shouldn't be the yardstick for the whole class.

"OK OK, let me think," Bendrick says. "Right, instead of the grand rond let's do it à terre, and instead of balancing in retiré just hold it in fifth. OK? Right, starting positions please."

Not really the simplifications we'd hoped for…

*

"I'm cream crackered," Lucia gasps, as we make our way to the changing room.

"My little legs are done," Marion says. "They actually buckled near the end in there."

"If we carry on like this we'll be needing oxygen masks," Gloria says, placing her hand on her heaving chest.

"My poor thigh muscles," I groan, trying to rub some life back into them.

"Hey guys," Samantha says. "Might be as good a time as any to tell you that I have to collect hours as part of my physio qualification. I'm looking for guinea pigs. So who fancies a treatment, massage, or just general advice - any takers?"

"Can you inflate my lung?" Gloria asks.

"Put me down for an all-body jobby," Lucia says, slumped over the changing room bench.

"Hey," I say, sidling up to Sam. "Talking of 'all-body jobbies', how's it going with that mentor of yours?"

"Urgh, Jason, what a slow starter! I love a geeky, awkward type, but this is ridiculous. I don't know how else to make it clear that I'm interested," she moans.

"Now then, Samantha, not that I'm in a position to offer romantic advice, but why don't we go for a drink and mull over your options?"

"That sounds like a plan." She smiles. "But don't go getting me ratted like last time!"

"Ha! Can't promise that." I laugh. "Actually, thinking about it, Joshua is away with his college students on a residential next week, why don't you come over and stay the night? We could get a takeaway? Crack open a bottle?"

"A bottle, yes."

"Ha ha ha, some folk just can't hold their drink."

"..And I would be one of them." She points to herself.

A loud knock at the changing room door gets our attention.

"Ms Gathergood please!"

I smile recognising Joshua's voice. "Hold on a minute, Josh, just coming," I call out. "That's my cue," I say to Sam, sweeping past her, throwing my large dance bag over my shoulder. "See you all next week."

To a chorus of 'goodbyes' I exit the changing room and into the arms of Joshua, planting a big kiss on his mouth.

"Oooh nice," he says.

"I missed you." I say, putting my arms around his neck.

"I didn't miss you…"

"Eh?"

"I looked through the window and couldn't miss you."

"Oi!" I say, punching his arm. He turns to run away from me and, laughing loudly, we fall out of the village hall doors. He then swoops me up and spins me around squealing. As he plonks me down I see Steve, arms crossed, leaning against his van in the car park.

Urgh, what's he doing here?

He walks towards me. "Amy."

"Steve." I feel like we're squaring up, and I'm suddenly aware of Joshua next to me. "This is Joshua."

Steve grunts a hello.

"I'll wait in the car, OK?" Joshua leans into me.

I touch his arm. "Thanks."

Steve watches him walk away. "So that's your fancy lover boy who you told me had buggered off to New Zealand and wasn't coming back and there was nothing between you?"

"I don't think you can be righteous here – you left me for Justine."

"I never lied to you."

"Yes you did! Every time you went out of our house and met her, every time you were late in from work and didn't tell me what you were doing – you lied to me all the time." I battle to remain calm.

"You told me there was nothing between you and Sheep Shagger…"

"Oh for pity's sake, Steve! He went to New Zealand, but unlike you, he couldn't live without me so he came back for me."

"Very romantic," he snaps back.

"Yes it was!"

Steve looks to the ground and then lifts his eyes.

"Anyway, you're not answering my texts."

"I'm still reeling from your classy TV appearance."

He has the decency to flush. "Right, I'm looking into whether I can buy you out of Rose Cottage."

"I see," is all I can say as I fight the rising bile; the thought of Steve and his new little family ensconced in *my* beautiful cottage cuts me to the bone.

"And the other thing..." His eyes fail to meet mine. "I miss Basil and I –"

"Oh no, Steve," I spit. "No! I'm keeping Basil – he is *not* up for grabs."

"Why? We bought him together."

"Wow, Steve, you leave the marriage, you want the house *and* you want the dog! You planning on leaving me with anything?"

He sighs like I'm the unreasonable one. "Basil is both of ours."

Am I really about to say that I'll see him in court for a lazy Cocker Spaniel who leaves mucky paw prints all over the place?

"You live in a flat – he needs a garden," I say.

"But after we've sorted Rose Cottage I'll have a garden."

"Aaargh!" We fall into silence and I take a grounding breath. "As we don't know what's going to happen with Rose Cottage there's not much point discussing this now, is there?" I say tightly.

He nods. "OK. We'll talk about it nearer the time." He glances at Joshua and gives him the once over, before turning back to me. "Right, I'll let you get on then."

"OK."

He starts to walk away but then stops and turns back. "Oh and I'm seeing a solicitor."

"Does Justine know about that?" I say before turning and walking back to Joshua.

Chapter 7

"Mum," Fliss says, flouncing into the lounge and plonking herself on the large armchair.

"Felicity," Gloria says, looking up over her newspaper.

Fliss chews her lip. "Look, about last night."

"You were rude to Brian," Gloria says. "He was my guest and he was only trying to be friendly."

"I'm sorry, Mum."

Dressed down in sweat pants and t-shirt, with her hair tied back and no make up, Fliss looks vulnerable, fragile even. Gloria would love to rewind to a time when a motherly cuddle would 'make everything better'. If only.

Fliss sighs deeply. "He was at the drinks cabinet, standing at the top of the table, carving the meat – those were Daddy's jobs! I'm just not ready to move on."

"Oh darling, I'm not asking you to. Brian is a very good friend to me. Can't you just be happy that I have a companion?"

"But it's not just companionship, is it?"

"Fliss, you're never going to have another father – but you could have a happy mother who has a kind and caring friend."

"Yes I know, I know." Fliss plays with the tassels on a cushion. "It's just so soon – Daddy only died at Christmas."

"Darling, Daddy was in that home for a long time – he didn't know what day of the week it was. You know that I visited him every day I could. I didn't betray him."

Fliss bites her tongue and only the clock ticking fills the silence between them. She clears her throat. "Tim called me."

"Did he, darling?"

"Yep, seems he finally realised I'd gone."

Gloria gives her a square look. "Can I ask what he said?"

"He was asking if I'd be back for the Spring Ball in April, apparently tickets were one hundred and fifty a shot. Guess he doesn't want to waste his money."

"Ah, I see. Any plans to meet up before then?"

"Pfft. He asked to see me, but didn't sound like he meant it. He thinks I'm being petulant as he's got a 'lot on at the office' and has to 'put in the hours' so he can 'snag that promotion.' I'm sick of it."

"Maybe you two need to sit down and talk about it?"

"I would if he could tear himself away from..." she stops.

"From?"

"Oh there's this woman at his office; Lexy. I hear a lot about Lexy; 'Lexy said this, Lexy did this, Lexy did that,' Urgh, I can't tell you how sick I am of that bloody name!"

"Is she a colleague?"

"No, unfortunately, she's his new boss."

"Have you met her?"

Fliss nods. "A couple of weeks ago. We went to a works thing and she was there. She's young." Fliss shivers.

"Darling, I'm sure there's nothing to worry about. I know you don't like me saying it, but Tim is devoted to you."

"Then why doesn't he want to spend time with me? Why is he always either in the office or playing golf?"

"Maybe he's got his priorities in a bit of a muddle, dear. Why don't you contact him and make a date? You know, you two really do have the rest of your lives together." Fliss rises quickly and walk to the kettle. "Fliss?"

Fliss's shoulders slump. "That's just it, I don't know if we do have the rest of our lives together."

"What?"

Fliss turns slowly to her mother. "Mum, I can't have children."

"What?" Gloria walks to her daughter and holds out her arms. "Oh darling."

"No, Mum, please," Fliss says, holding her palms up. "Don't."

Gloria's arms fall to her side. "How do you know?"

"We've been trying for a while and ended up going for tests. Turns out it's a bit of both of us, but more me."

"Oh darling, I am sorry."

Fliss shrugs. "Well, seems nothing can be done, my fallopian tubes are well and truly messed up. So we're considering IVF, but I don't know…" She trails off in thought before shaking her head. "Anyway, I'm hopeful that this time apart will strengthen the bonds and all that, plus I get to catch up with the girls this weekend."

"That'll be lovely. It'll give you something to look forward to. Yes, absolutely, go and have some fun this weekend." Gloria rubs her daughter's arm.

Fliss looks at her mother curiously. "Why? Where are you?"

Oh no, now is not the right time.

Gloria smooths her skirt and gently touches her hair. "I'm going up to the coast for the weekend. It's Madame Butterfly at The Regency."

"Oh let me guess who with…" Fliss rolls her eyes.

"Fliss, don't start..."

"Mum! What are you doing?"

"Fliss, really! I'm not breaking any laws."

"No, just my father's heart!"

"YOUR FATHER ISN'T HERE ANYMORE!" Gloria clasps one shaking hand on top of the other. "Fliss, maybe you're just going to have to come to terms with me having a life after your father."

"Yes, and eventually I might." Fliss fixes Gloria with a stare. "But this is too much too soon."

A cold impasse fills the room.

Gloria exhales deeply. "Fliss darling, don't you think your father would want me to be happy?"

"After a period of grieving, yes."

"A period of grieving?"

"Yes. A year or so."

Gloria feels tears burning. "You want me to put my life on hold for 'a year or so'?"

"Well, not your whole life. But if you wait you'll know whether this new relationship is right for you. I mean, what if he's not the right one? I'd hate to see you get hurt. Given time your mind'll be clearer and you'll feel you've done the right thing by Dad. Don't you feel any guilt?"

Gloria looks away sharply. How many times has she had those exact same thoughts? Yes, of course she feels guilty – up until now she had assuaged it by telling herself that Stanley would want her to be happy. But has it all been a bit too quick? And even if the days and evenings with Brian make her feel alive again, shouldn't she wait? Let the dust settle?

"Mum?" Fliss says, waiting for an answer.

Gloria looks to her daughter. "Hmm?"

"Just wait a while? For me, Mummy, please?"

Chapter 8

"Cheers!" Sam says, clinking my glass.

"Salud," I say, taking a glug of red wine. "How's life then?" She puffs out her cheeks. "C'mon then, spill the beans. How's it going?"

"Aw, Jason's such a nice guy, and we definitely get on well but, I don't know, he just doesn't make a move." She pulls the bowl of nibbles nearer. "I mean, what does a girl have to do?!"

"How about asking him out?"

She blanches. "Oh I could never do that! Imagine the humiliation if he said no."

"But you're getting vibes that he likes you, right?"

"Er, kind of, yeah, I think so."

"So why not give it a whirl?"

"And if he doesn't like me I've lost my mentor – he's *really* helping me with my studies - it's not an easy course."

"OK. Hmmm." I pause for thought. "How about inviting him to something but not making it a date?"

"Like what?"

"A concert? Do you know what bands he likes?" She looks blank. "His hobbies?"

"Apart from being passionate about physiotherapy I really don't know."

Just as I'm trying to think of a physio related social event she squeals.

"Oh, oh! Why didn't I think of it before? There's a physio conference next month." I look at her quizzically. "It's in Basingstoke!"

"The epicentre of romance?"

She pulls a face. "We could travel together, eat meals together, stay at the same hotel…" She grins mischievously.

"Oh yes! I'm liking it – I'll drink to that!" I raise my glass.

Sam takes a swig of wine and reaches for a handful of peanuts. "I saw your ex."

"Where?"

She grimaces. "On the TV."

"Oh God, yeah, I know. Unbelievable, wasn't it?"

"Mmm, are you OK?"

"Honestly? I don't know. Don't get me wrong, I love Joshua, he is the love of my life, but Steve, well, he was the first love of my life. You know what I mean?"

"He was supposed to be your 'forever person'."

"Exactly. Not some moron who leaves me for a bit of fluff from the pub. And, you know, I was really keen on having children and he made it clear he wasn't, and now, here he is with little Beyoncé. It hurts."

"It hurts that they've called her that."

I laugh. "Yeah, he turned out to be such a disappointment. D'you know, he turned up after ballet the other night?"

"Really?"

"Mmm. Joshua and I were just leaving and he was there. He told me he wants to buy me out," I say, gesturing around. "And he's started the divorce."

"Urgh, what you gonna do?"

I rake my fingers through my hair. "I'm looking into whether I can afford to buy him out – but I kind of know the answer already. Hip Snips isn't making what it used to; when money gets tight, having your hair done is one of the first things to go. I need to talk to the accountant and see what he says and I also need to talk to Joshua."

"Yeah maybe together you and Josh could afford it? Or maybe you'd both like a fresh start somewhere new?" she says. I look around wistfully at the pale pink walls, pretty antique framed pictures and bare floorboards and my gut tells me that I'm just not ready to leave here yet. I love this cottage – and that's despite the marital disharmony of recent times. "Hey Amy," she says, gently touching my arm. "I've told you before, wherever you live you'll make it beautiful."

"Yeah, I know. You're right." I look at my glass. "Gosh, this is going down far too quickly; better order some Chinese or we'll be bladdered."

"Yeah, took me days to get over it last time."

I laugh. "Lightweight. OK, I'll get the menu, you get another bottle open."

"Deal."

*

Sam tries to lift herself from her reclined position on the sofa. "We haven't drunk a bottle each, have we?"

"Nah, we spilt some."

We both cackle, which is a sure sign we have, once again, drunk too much. A phone buzzes in the room.

"Whose is that?" she asks.

Like newly born blind kittens we start trying to track down the vibrating noise. Sam is convinced her phone is in her bag, although tipping out the contents proves fruitless and I'm clueless as to where mine is.

"Sam, my bottom's wobbling," I say with some alarm.

"No time to talk diets."

I roll my eyes, laughing, and reaching underneath me I retrieve her phone and hand it to her. She squints, trying desperately to read who is calling, when it falls silent.

"It was him!" she says, lurching into an upright position.

"Who?"

"Oh My God! Jason! Why's he phoning me?"

"To ask you out?"

"Do you think?"

It's a good question – what *do* I think? I frown, trying to think straight amidst the Rioja that's sloshing around my brain. Yes! Why not? She's a lovely person, with a pretty face, long wavy hair, ballerina slender, and fun to be around – why *wouldn't* he want to go out with her?

"Sam, my friend," I say, leaning into her, looking meaningfully into her eyes. "You need to grab the horn by the bulls."

Sam bursts out laughing. "I need what? To do what?"

"Carpe deem! Grab the man. You know," I say, wagging my finger in her face solemnly. "Throw his specs to the wind, ruffle that ginger hair, plant a big one on him – why not? It all could be over tomorrow. Life's too short – you have to go for what you want."

Her glazed eyes blink as she nods at my words. "OK. Shall I call him?"

Even my alcohol-addled brain knows that's a bad idea. "Hmm, I'd text."

"OK." She pulls herself together and shakes her head. "I'm gonna do it."

I watch as she hits buttons, tuts, deletes, hits buttons, deletes, hits buttons again and then holds it out to read.

"Go on then!" I say, eager to hear the words that will woo him.

You called? You wanted me? How cnn I help? I'm at your disposable ;-) I really like you – what do you think about going out sometime? With me? This is def not a drunk text lol ;-) ccxx

"Erm, I'm not sure about the…" I say just before Sam punches 'send' and, with a victorious smile, reclines back on the sofa. "Okaaaay, guess it was good to go."

She places the phone on the small side table and we both sit and stare at it in silence, willing it to buzz and bleep.

Ten minutes later we're still staring…

Chapter 9

I open one eye, vaguely aware of a ringing noise. Where am I? This doesn't feel like bed. Trying to focus, I see Sam curled up at the other end of my sofa. Where is that ringing coming from?

I drag myself up and then have to steady the sway. Urgh, did we really finish that third bottle? Or did we fall asleep possibly in mid conversation? Or should I say, mid-stare at Sam's ever-silent phone? Ouch! Ouch to my head and ouch to how Sam is going to feel when she wakes up and remembers. Think I might let her sleep on a while…

There it is in the kitchen, the offending ringing phone. I lift it carefully to my ear.

"Mmm?"

"Amy? It's me, babe."

Even through the banging in my head there is no mistaking Gina's elongated vowels. "Hi Gina."

"You alrigh' babe?" she asks.

"Heavy night."

"Oh blimey, you ain't gonna like this then. I got the raging squits."

"Eh?"

"The trots, Delhi Belly, the shi –"

"Got it, got it." I put my hand to my forehead.

"I can't get into work – well, not wivout me brown trousers and bicycle clips."

"Ah."

"Sorry babe."

Then, like a blow to the head, the realisation of what she's saying hits me. *I'm going to have to go into work!! Oh My God - I can barely function, let alone cut anyone's hair.*

"Are you sure?" I say.

"Sure? Abou' me bum being glued to the bog? Yeh, babe, I'm pretty sure."

"OK Gina." I massage my temples. "What time is your first customer?"

"Julie P at nine-fir'y and then it's one after annuver 'til Mrs Licky-Licky at four for'y-five."

"OK, I'll cover." I stifle a sigh.

"Fanks. Sorry, babe."

"OK, no problem." *There's my lie of the day.* "Get better, Gina, soon!"

"Fanks, babe. Uh-oh, gotta go."

The phone goes dead.

I flop back onto the kitchen stool and run my fingers through my matted hair. Nine-thirty, mmm, that means I've got just under an hour to become human and be there. No one can control illness...but why today? Why on my day off? Why me? Aargh!!!

Twenty minutes later I'm showered, dressed and downing paracetamols. I can't even think about breakfast – a coffee at the shop will suffice. I look in on Sam who is still out for the count. Fetching a blanket, I throw it over her, and then write a note, explaining my absence. In record time I'm out the door and sitting on the bus feeling mightily bilious. In a 'different ends but same problem' sentiment, my sympathies fleetingly go to Gina.

Arriving at the shop I find our apprentice, Karen, organising the combs and brushes with Kanye West blaring out. With her head down, dreadlocks swinging in time to the beat, she doesn't hear me enter. I propel myself to the staff room and turn the volume down which prompts her to look up.

"Sorry Amy, didn't hear you come in."

"Clearly."

"You OK?"

"Gina's got a stomach bug and isn't coming in and let's just say I haven't had a lot of sleep."

Taking in my appearance, she giggles. "Tired and emotional, are we?"

I scowl at her. "You could say that."

"Shall I put the coffee on?"

"That would be lovely. Can we leave Kanye on low too, please?"

"Maybe a bit of Radio 2 might be better?"

"Very funny – I'm hung-over not deaf."

She laughs, clomping past me in freakishly modern platform shoes. I rest against the wall and marvel at her ensemble today – not everyone can get away with tartan, leather, a forearm of bangles and a floral necktie. But Karen can.

We turn to the ringing of the door. First customer is early. *Darn it – can't I get a break today?*

Karen catches my look of despair. "You go and sort the coffee and I'll shampoo Julie…slowly."

"Thank you."

***

"So, you see, that's when Frankie told Helen that it wasn't going to happen. I mean he'd only just got the job and didn't want to move. But she thinks her career is important too. Wasn't always like that – not so long ago she wanted a little one, you know, so anyway I told them…" Mrs 'Licky-Licky' Lichtenstein is filling me in on her son's latest drama but, even this late in the day, all I can hear is 'blah blah' against the backdrop of a loud pulsing. Every fibre of my being wants to say, 'I don't care. I have no interest in your family. I don't and never will know them and it doesn't matter to me where they live, what they do for a living, or whether they procreate now or at any future date!' But in reality, I murmur, 'mmmm, yes, no' and 'oh dear' in random order. It's not exactly inspiring, but it's all I've got today.

Putting Mrs Lichtenstein's coat on I bid her farewell and turn to see Lucia, resplendent in shocking pink, heading into the shop.

"Hello you! What you doing here?" I say, pecking her on the cheek.

"I was kind of passing, but also wanted to tell you something."

"Oooh sounds intriguing – want a coffee? I'm just finished."

"Why don't we go for something stronger then?" She clocks my involuntary wince. "Not a good idea?"

"I had a bit too much last night. We could nip to the wine bar though, there's no law that says I have to have alcohol."

"Nah, you will though!" Lucia cackles and her voluptuous frame jiggles.

"You're a bad influence," I laugh. "Give me two tics."

•

Lucia orders a large gin and tonic, and I, with a nod to my hangover, opt for a white wine spritzer, before we plonk ourselves down in a corner booth of Websters Wine Bar.

"Go on then, what's the goss?" I ask.

"Well, I wanted to run this by you," Lucia says, taking the gum out of her mouth and looking around for somewhere to put it. I fish out a tissue. "Thanks," she says, wrapping it and then still not knowing what to do with it, places it on the table. "So, here's the thing, you know my fella, Geoff?" I nod. "Well, he has a regular contract with The Dixbury Tribune, drives the big bod around plus some of the others and he got chatting with a journo who wants to do a piece on older dancers. With Darcey on Strictly they're thinking about focusing on ballet dancers and Geoff mentioned us."

"Wow! That sounds interesting."

"Geoff's asking me for a contact person, and as Helena is off I didn't really know who to suggest. Don't know if ol' Benny is the right person."

"Well, I guess as Bendrick is taking the class it'd be him."

"Mmmm, OK. I think we should run it by the others too – some might not want to be on show."

We both have the same thought. "Marion," we say in unison.

"Do you know if Jack's out of prison yet?" I ask.

"Nah - ah. But if he is, I'm sure she wouldn't want him knowing she's still local. Evil bastard."

"Marion's come a long way, much stronger these days, but we definitely have to check with her."

"Right, let's ask the dancers first," Lucia lifts her drink.

"Agreed. Cheers." I raise my glass and as it nears my lips my stomach takes a nauseous flip. "Not sure I can do this."

"Hold your nose and down it in one."

"What are you? Fourteen?"

"Amy, love, you just gotta go for it!"

"And if I puke?"

"I'll be grand jeté-ing out that door quicker than you can say 'white wine spritzer coming up.'" She cackles wildly.

I grimace and raise my glass. "Cheers."

Chapter 10

Sam blinks her eyes open and takes a few seconds to recognise her surroundings. Ah, yes…Amy, bottles of wine, Chinese food, much laughter, staring at a phone…staring at a phone? Oh no! Staring. At. A. Phone! The sheer dread of realisation hits her stomach, forcing her up from the sofa and straight to the toilet. Resting between vomiting bouts, she wonders when she'll learn not to drink with Amy? Or at the very least stop at one bottle?

Sam plods back to the lounge and slumps onto the sofa. Picking up her phone from the side table she flicks through her text messages. Holding it at arm's length and with one eye closed, she rereads her text.

You called? You wanted me? How cnn I help? I'm at your disposable ;-) I really like you – what do you think about going out sometime? With me? This is def not a drunk text lol ;-) ccxx

Oh how could she send that!? Forget the sentiment, just look at the mistakes! She puts her head in her hands and is inwardly wailing when a moment of wild hope strikes: in her state of extreme inebriation, did she actually manage to send it?

She scrolls again to her messages, hoping….

Aw crap, it sent.

'Why doesn't someone take phones away from drunk people?' she thinks, momentarily filled with indignation. Then sinking into a sigh she accedes that she is the idiot who texted drunk and is now therefore the idiot who has to pay the price. Aaargh! Why did she do it? He was so nice - such a good guy! This could've been something great! What on earth will he think of her now? Some lush who goes around drunk-texting and asking men out. A fresh wave of nausea hits her stomach as she makes another dash for the bathroom.

Devoid of food and desperately dehydrated, Sam splashes water on her face, applies make-up in an attempt to appear human, and then sets about clearing up the lounge. Spraying a little air freshener to cover wine and chow mein fumes, Sam then kisses Basil on the nose and lets herself out of the cottage. Not wanting to return to her draughty one bedroom flat, and with fervent need for water, coffee and a bread product, she heads for Expresso High.

Pushing through the frosted glass door she stops dead in her tracks when, sitting at a middle table with his head in a newspaper, she sees Jason. Aaaargh! A quick decision is needed; does she bite the bullet or make a run for it? Brazen it out or skulk away? Just as she's deliberating, he looks up and spots her. *Ah, no escape.* He then beams a smile and enthusiastically waves her over.

"Sam, good to see you! You're not working today?"

"No. Thought I'd use today as a study day, but..." she trails off, realising that she has no study materials about her.

"Ah, I see. Never mind, we all lose motivation at times." He smiles.

Oh I'm going to miss that smile.

"Join me for a coffee?" he asks.

"Er, yes, that would be lovely."

He's not acting like a man who's received an unwelcomed text...

The waitress appears and Jason orders himself another soya latte.

"Skinny latte please. Double shot," Sam says.

The waitress smiles and leaves the table.

"Double shot? You do know the effects of caffeine on the heart and the nervous system?" he says.

"Are you testing me?"

He grins. "Sorry, no. I just can't help myself sometimes."

"Yeah I do know," Sam says. "But my need is great this morning." She gives him a knowing look.

"What's so special about this morning then?"

There isn't a flicker of pretence.

"Erm, had a couple of drinks last night. Just needing an injection of fuel now."

"Ah I see."

He keeps his gaze on her face and she wonders if the creases are still visible from the large corduroy cushion she was face-pressed against all night.

"So what are you doing today?" she asks, briskly changing the subject.

"Gotta head to see those 'Geniuses' in blue shirts," he says, picking up his phone and waving it. "It started going mad last night and now won't work at all."

IT'S ON THE BLINK!! HE DIDN'T GET MY MESSAGE! I AM SAVED!

"Oh dear." She feigns solemnity. "When did that happen then?"

"Yesterday."

"Ah, I see."

The waitress brings the coffees.

"Just need to nip to the loo," Jason says, jumping up. "Coffee goes straight through me."

"OK," she says, thinking how he's so uncool, he's actually cool.

As he hops away she puts a couple of sugars in her drink and, stirring it, she thinks how she's got away with it – he hasn't seen the message! What a victory! She sits back in her chair feeling smug. Taking a sip of coffee her smile slowly fades - hang on a minute - when those Apple store people sort out his phone her message will ping up and then he'll see it and she'll be back to square one. Nooooo!

Her eyes fall to his phone left on the table. She needs a plan. But what? How can she stop him seeing her drunken missive?

"You look deep in thought," Jason says, returning to the table.

"Erm, yes, I was just thinking that I need to go to the Apple store too. I could save you time and take your phone in?"

"Oh thanks, but they'll need my passwords and I'm not sure I trust you with them," he teases.

"Ha ha. Of course."

Darn it...

"But happy to go together if you like?" he adds.

"OK, yes, let's do that."

Jason smiles and takes a sip of his coffee whilst Sam's mind races to invent a reason why she needs to visit Apple, plus a plan for intercepting that message. Not being of a devious nature, and handicapped by a killer hangover, she has no idea about either.

"Shall we go?" Jason asks, downing his coffee and getting up from his chair.

"Absolutely."

Chapter 11

As they walk side by side to the Apple store Sam pays him glib attention whilst simultaneously trying to hatch a plan. Hmm, delaying tactics, that's what she needs! Yes, that way she can get there and explain the situation to a 'Genius.' Right, so she's going to waylay Jason, then go to the store to tell a blue shirted employee that a man will be coming in with a broken phone, and when they've got it working she doesn't want the man to see his messages as, drunkenly, she sent said man a text and now regrets it? Is she mad? Are Geniuses paid enough to deal with this kind of stuff? No, this isn't going to work.

Before long they are entering the brightly lit, headache inducing shop. Once inside they make a beeline for the chief blue-shirt who stands poised with stylus and iPad. He greets them with a perky smile.

"I have a problem with my iPhone – it's messing about," Jason says.

"No problem. Name?"

"Jason Lee."

"Cool man, take a seat, bro," the Genius says or something similar – Sam is far too busy formulating a plan to hear. She zones back in to find Jason and the heavily bearded blue shirt looking at her.

"Did you want to see someone too?" Jason asks.

Oh damn, yes, I said I needed to come here.

"Oh yes, no," she says. "I just wanted to…er…marvel at the laptops. Touch them and you know, feel the quality." Colour rises in her cheeks.

Both stare at her before the guy turns back to Jason and says something along the lines of, "Cool, righteous, wait here at the desk and another bearded blue shirted guy, probably with tattoos and a bald head, will be with you in a mo, dude."

Jason hops up onto a stool and turns to Sam. “Hey, you don’t have to wait with me. Please, go, touch the Macbooks.” He grins.

“Oh no, it’s OK, I’ve plenty of time,” she says with a small shrug.

“OK. So, tell me how’s the studying going?”

“Not bad. Some parts of the latest module are really tough, but with your help and some nose-to-the-grindstone working I should be okay.”

“How did you do in that last module? Did you get your score?”

Sam grimaces a little. “Yeah.”

“And?”

“Seventy-two out of one hundred. That’s not great is it?”

“Well…”

“All the work you put in to help me and I get seventy two! I know I could’ve done better. Bet you hate me.”

“No, I don’t hate you…”

“Well I wouldn’t blame you if you did.”

“Well I don’t.”

“But if you did –“

“Samantha, I don’t hate you…I quite like you actually –“

“Right, who has the prob with the iPhonio?” asks a multi coloured haired girl with too many piercings to count.

Jason turns from Sam to hold up his phone.

Sam drifts away on his last sentence; *‘no, I quite like you actually.’* Did he really just say that? Wow! That is quite an admission from a man of so few meaningful words. So he *does* like her. She smiles to herself, enjoying the warmth his words have created in the pit of her stomach. Dreamily she looks at him only to be jolted back to reality by Ione, the pierced wonder, working away at the phone. Gosh – they certainly don’t mess about! She’s going to have it fixed in no time and those messages will be popping up quicker than lightening. And now that he’s professed to liking her she doesn’t want him changing his mind – *that text* really doesn’t present her as girlfriend material.

"Right, yeah, this doesn't seem to be working," Ione states the obvious as she twists her tongue piercing around, studying the phone.

"So what does that mean?" Jason asks.

Let it mean that he can't take it home today. Let it mean that I have more time.

"I'm going to have to restore your phone. Is it backed up?" He nods. "OK, should take about an hour. You can leave it here and go for a walk if you like, or you can pick it up tomorrow?"

Jason looks at his watch. "Hmm, I have a client in fifty minutes. I'll have to leave it with you."

YES!

"OK fine. I'll just get the form for you to sign and then you're free to go." Ione wanders to the back of the shop.

"Right, that's it then. I'm phoneless for a day."

"I'm sure you'll survive," Sam replies.

An awkward nerve-tingling silence fills the air between them.

"So, see you Friday for our tutorial?" he says, his long lashes blink against his glasses.

"Yep, library at three?"

"Great. I'll see you then."

"Great, see you then."

Sam turns on her heels and heads for the Macbooks. After a few moments of pretending to be utterly absorbed by them, she looks up to see Ione returning with a plastic tray. She hands Jason a form to sign, places his phone in the tray, chats a little more and walks away. Sam resumes her interest in the sleek laptops as Jason passes by.

"See you Friday."

Sam turns to smile. "Yep, yep, see you then."

Sam returns her attention to the equipment for a few moments more before tiptoeing to the front of the store to see his tall lanky frame disappearing from view down the mall. She takes a deep breath and returns to the back end of the store.

Loitering near the man with the iPad she cranes her neck to find Ione. Where is she? She can't personally be restoring the phone right this moment, can she?

"Can I help?" asks iPad man.

"I was looking for Ione. I was just in here but forgot something."

Not exactly a lie...

Just then Ione appears around the tall metal door that doubles as a wall.

"Ione! You got a mo?" iPad man calls.

"Hi, remember me?" Sam asks as Ione saunters over. "I was just in here with a guy." Ione looks blank. "So high, ginger hair, glasses?" Ione's memory clicks into action and she nods her recognition. "Well, I wonder if you could help me?

"What's that then?" Ione asks, flicking her tongue stud around.

"I sent a text message to that guy, a really dumb message. I was drunk. You know what it's like, with a friend, having a few glasses, and you drink before you eat and you feel really tipsy and then you plough on and end up drunk?" Ione raises one of her perfectly pierced eyebrows. "Well, maybe you don't, but I do. And I sent that lovely man a text asking him to go out with me and it was the wrong thing to do that. We're not at that place yet, but we might be soon. And I would really like to ask you, well, beg you really, to let me delete that text before he sees it!"

"Sorry girlie, can't do that. It contravenes data protection."

"Really? It's only a text message, I'm not plotting treason."

"How do I know what the text said?"

"Well you don't, but you can read it if you like?"

"Sorry, no can do."

"Is there any way I can delete the message?"

"Did you send it on iMessage?"

"I think it went through on RingADingMe"

"OK...give me your phone."

Sam passes it to her and watches as she brings up the settings menu, makes a small affirming noise and then shows the screen to Sam.

"There, see that? If you hit that button there, your message will be retrieved."

Sam hits the button and watches her inebriated words disappear.

"Ione, thank you so much, you have literally saved my bacon," Sam gushes.

"S'cool."

"I'll definitely remember that little trick from now on."

"On point."

Sam is pretty sure Ione isn't referring to the art of going on tippy toes in ballet, so she brazens it out with a smile. "On point indeed."

"Later."

Yep, that's an easy one.

"Laters dude," Sam says, and skips merrily out of the store.

Chapter 12

"Ladies and gentleman," Bendrick says. "Before we begin with our pliés and tendus, I believe one amongst us has something to announce." He signals to Lucia.

"Not exactly an announcement, Benny, more of a question," Lucia says. Bendrick half bows. "So, you know my Geoff?" Everyone nods. "Well he does a lot of work for The Dixbury Tribune. He chauffeurs the staff around and long story short, the other day this journo was talking about writing a piece about adults learning ballet. You know, with Darcey being on Strictly and people getting interested in ballet, and all that. Anyway, Geoff mentioned us and the journo asked him to sound us out – if it's something we'd like to do?"

"What would it entail?" Julay asks.

"Guessing someone would interview us, take our picture. It could be a laugh?"

"It could be rather magnificent," Julay says, lightly touching her hair.

"Lucia already told me about it and I wondered if we're all up for it?" I say, not wanting to catch Marion's eye.

"I think we'd like to do it," Josie says, checking her daughter, Catherine, who nods in agreement.

"Bet they'd love the 'mother and daughter' angle," Sam says, smiling. "And me too, I'm in."

"And me," says Marion.

"You sure, Marion?" I ask, narrowing my eyes.

"Why on earth *wouldn't* Marion wish to be a part of it?" Bendrick asks. "She's most essential and, might I add, a beautifully graceful part of this group,"

The tips of Marion's ears turn red as she giggles. "Thank you."

"Right, well, we were just thinking of your old man," blurts Lucia.

"Old man?" Bendrick asks.

Marion fixes on Lucia who, with her shoulders up to her ears, exclaims, "What?!"

"Erm," I say, desperate to divert attention. "So, in the main, are we up for it?"

Everyone murmurs agreement.

"Fine. Is it okay to tell Geoff to get the journo to contact you, Benny?" Lucia asks.

"Absolutely fine. Marvellous. Right then, if we may proceed, ladies and gentleman, please take your places at the barre."

Marion's head lowers as she stands next to me.

Guilt nips. "Marion, I'm so sorry," I say. "I didn't mean for it to go like that, I just wanted to make sure you were OK with being in the paper."

"That's alright, dear," she says, water forming in her sad blue eyes. "My past is always going to be there, and you're right, maybe I shouldn't do it. Jack's still in prison - they said they'd let me know when he's released - but maybe it's better not to tempt fate. I don't want him in my life again."

"Look, you don't have to do this – I mean it won't be the same without you, but you've got to think of yourself - what's best for you."

"You know, dear," she says thoughtfully. "He controlled my life for many years, but I shouldn't still be looking over my shoulder, should I? I don't want to miss out on the fun, I think I did that for years…you know what, count me in." I nod and she smiles.

"Ahem," Bendrick coughs to get our attention. "Left hand on the barre, let's begin."

I give Marion another little smile as she rubs my hand and we take our positions and prepare to dance.

•••

"Ah, it's great to be home," I say, sitting on the sofa with Joshua as he rubs my aching leg muscles.

"Great to be home too. A couple of nights in a hostel with an unruly group of teenagers is kind of fun in a challenging way, but there's no place like home." He leans over to kiss me.

"Don't stop." I indicate to my calves.

He grins. "How was your twinkle toes class?"

"Bendrick is getting better, but he still pushes us hard – wish he could remember we're not kids though. He wants our legs up round our ears!" Joshua's eyebrows do a dance. "Oi!" I playfully smack him in the ribs. "Not in that way!"

We laugh and he pulls me in and kisses me gently. "I've missed you," he says.

"Me too."

We laze against each other, happy to just be. With my head resting on his chest I look around at the softly lit lounge and a lump forms in my throat.

"I've arranged to meet Steve tomorrow after work. Got to talk about this place," I say with my gaze fixed on the pine cones and chunky logs in the open grate.

Joshua shifts to face me.

"How d'you think that's gonna go?"

"Well, I can't afford to buy him out so I guess he'll be buying me out. That's unless…" I chew my lip. "You don't want to pitch in with me, do you?" I pause. "Just an idea."

"I do have savings from when I was supposed to go to New Zealand, but I was kind of earmarking them for a rainy day."

"Without a roof over our heads it will be a rainy day."

"Yeah, but supposing I need the money – it's my back-up plan," he says thinking aloud. He then sees my face change. "No, no, that came out wrong…"

"No, no, you're right – you don't want to hitch your wagon to mine and then it goes wrong and you have no money. That's perfectly understandable." I try sounding light but the edge in my voice cuts through.

"I didn't mean it like that, Amy…"

"Honestly Joshua, you don't have to explain. I'll sort it out with Steve and then I'll find a place to rent somewhere across town."

"We, WE will find a place to rent. I didn't mean it to sound how it did. I know what I want, Amy. I want to be with you."

...but not enough to invest your nest egg.

I use every ounce of might to control the burgeoning tears. This just isn't how we are; ours is a simple, uncomplicated relationship filled with love and laughter. We don't cross swords, hell, up to this point we didn't even have swords! I feel the bubble bursting around me. All this time I thought we were on exactly the same page, at exactly the same moment, but now it seems I'm in deeper. He's not confident enough in 'us' to truly commit. If I had a nest egg would I spend it on a house with him? Yes I would.

I heave a sigh and take in his anguished face. Am I over-reacting? A small voice in my head tells me not to throw the baby out with the bathwater, and looking at his sad, desperate-to-be-believed-eyes, I can't keep my resolve – it'd be like kicking a puppy. I choose to push down the hurt.

"Amy?" he says, looking me square in the eyes. "In the words of the great Mr Travolta, 'you're the one that I want'." He risks a smile.

"Yes, of course, I know that, " I say quietly, patting his hand.

"Come here," he says, pulling me to him and kisses me softly. "I love you, you know that, don't you?"

I nod. Yes, I do. And I love him too. So he's not ready to commit? He needs more time? Then I'll just have to dig deep for some patience; it can't all be plain sailing, can it? Our living arrangements can be sorted, there's no rush. And, ultimately, if I have to walk away from Rose Cottage, then so be it.

"Cup of tea?" Joshua asks, rubbing my leg.

"Yes please."

As he leaves the room Basil, from his fraying tartan bed, opens his sleepy eyes and looks dolefully in my direction. Poor Bas, does he know what just happened? Does he sense a shift in the dynamics here? There's no need for him to worry - we'll work this out one way or another. And as if he can hear me, he rests his head on the edge of the bed and blinks his eyes shut again.

Chapter 13

My toast is halfway in my mouth as I read the letter. *He couldn't wait to discuss this with me tonight?* Our plan is to meet after work to talk about the whys and wherefores of finances and divorcing, and yet I'm now holding his divorce petition! What a bastard.

"You okay?" Joshua asks, sauntering into the kitchen.

"Look." I thrust the letter at him and finally take a bite of toast.

He frowns, reading the opening lines. "Ah, he doesn't waste any time, does he?"

"No, he doesn't."

Passing me the letter, Joshua moves to put his arm around me. "But maybe getting it over and done with is for the best, eh Amy?" he says, nuzzling my neck. "Like an execution, one sharp blow?"

I pull back, with a dubious look. "But it's not one sharp blow, is it? It's the start of rearranging everything in my life. And with a divorce petition that's citing I behaved unreasonably –"

"What?"

I pass the letter back to him. "See?" I point to it.

"Eh? He has the affair and you get divorced for behaving unreasonably!?" Putting down the letter he pulls me close and I soften into his scent and comfort.

"You know about you and me buying this place together?" he says.

"Shh shhh, I don't want to talk about that. I'm sorry, I shouldn't have expected you to do that," I say. "I think we've been full steam ahead in quite a short space of time, and maybe we do need to put the brakes on."

He touches my cheek. "No, Amy, I don't want any brakes. I'm very happy. You just took me by surprise, that's all. Didn't think we'd have to deal with all this so soon."

"By the speed my ex is going I don't think we have much choice."

"You're meeting him tonight, aren't you?"

"Yep." I sigh. "Expresso High after work. I'm dreading it even more now."

"You'll be fine," he says, kissing my forehead. "Just keep calm and remember to breathe."

I look up at him. "Where would I be without you?"

"Standing here talking to yourself."

We laugh softly and then I watch as he heads for the bathroom. I really don't know what I'd do without him, especially now I'm on the official divorce path. Working in Hip Snips I hear countless tales of 'horrid divorces' and I often wonder if a 'pleasant divorce' is a genuine oxymoron? Chewing the last piece of toast, I glance back at the letter and curse my miserable soon-to-be ex husband.

***

Staring blankly at the staffroom wall, I'm playing out scenarios of my scheduled rendez-vous with Steve when Gina's head pops around the door.

"Uh-oh look sharp – slimy rep incoming."

Urgh, I'd forgotten that the Richard Worth rep was due in today – just what I need! A suited and booted, hair gelled, smarmy young fella trying to flog me products I don't want.

"Amy, how's it going?" he asks, wafting a pungent aftershave into our cramped staff room.

"Good thanks, Dave. How are you?"

"Oh you know, rockin' and a-rollin."

"Mmm."

"You got ten?"

"Er…"

I turn to the sound of Mrs Licky-Licky's voice at reception. "I'd like to see Amy please."

"Ooh, sorry Dave, won't be a mo, wait there," I say, skipping off to the desk.

"Mrs Lichtenstein, how can I help?" I smile sweetly.

"Look," she says, holding down both sides of her straight bob, with one side brushing her chin and the other hovering somewhere above.

"Ooh, let me take a look at that for you," I say, quickly ushering her to a chair.

"At first I thought it was me," she says. "But my daughter said it is definitely uneven. If I might say, you didn't seem quite yourself the other day, dear."

I lean over conspiratorially. "I'm so sorry, Mrs Lichtenstein, but I had a terrible migraine that day." *Not an outright lie...* "And even though I'd taken tablets it was still affecting me - I was suffering." I add a forlorn expression for effect. "Please let me straighten this up for you and then your next appointment is on the house."

"Fair enough, dear. Thank you." She smiles.

"Let me get you washed." I look to the end of the shop. "Karen!"

I turn to find Dave still lingering around like a bad smell, which, when you consider his aftershave, he rather is.

"Got time now?" he asks.

"Sure, but let's make it quick – you've got as long as it takes for a hair wash."

He follows me to the staffroom where we sit opposite each other and draw the battle lines. "We've got some fabulous new multi-tonal colours, Amy," is his opening pitch. "All the rage. All the big London salons are using them. You'd be ahead of the game around here." He lays out promotional materials galore for me to peruse.

"No thanks."

"Tinted setting lotions…"

"Already stock 'em."

"These extra length bendy rollers are new on the scene."

"I don't think so."

"Semi-permanent colours for that one off look?"

"Not really my clients."

"How are you finding the Permanent Wave 400?"

"Hate it - I'm just using up the stock."

"Thinking of branching out into eyebrows?"

"Nope."

"The Elite Scissors are discounted at the moment and the more pairs you buy the more discount you get."

"No thanks."

"Need any towels?" I turn to the shelf at the end of the staff room piled high, bulging with towels. He sighs in defeat. "Lovely to see you, Amy. Same time in two months?"

"If you like. Or I could call you if I need anything?"

He packs his wares into his case, smiles a sigh, and with heavy shoulders, heads for the door.

"Amy," Karen whispers, her head around the door. "Licky-Licky is ready-ready."

I get up. "Right. Thanks."

"You didn't buy anything from Rep-tile Dave then?" she asks.

"Do I ever?"

"Not that I can remember. Doesn't stop him trying though, does it?"

"Isn't that just so male? They just need to have their own way and don't care who they hurt in the meantime. Male pride and ego – huh!"

She frowns. "Are we still talking about Dave?"

"You have so much to learn, my little one," I say, and then picking up my scissors, I shake on a sweet smile and serenely drift into the salon.

***

Arriving early at Expresso High and finding a quiet corner table (in the event of a slanging match no one wants to be centre stage), I order a skinny latte. I'm re-reading the divorce petition and anticipating the likely conversations when I look up to see him approaching. How can he look so familiar and unfamiliar at the same time?

"Hi," he says, sweat visible on his brow.

"Hi."

Taking a seat, he spots the divorce petition and by his wince I would guess that he didn't think I would have received it yet.

"Er, just need a coffee," he says, his eyes wide searching for the waitress, who he waves over and places his order.

"So, Steve, let's talk."

"Look Amy, sorry about this," he says, gesturing to the paper between us. "We just need to move on, don't you think?"

"It's all about bloody 'moving on', isn't it? Jesus! It's been five minutes since we split, and yes, I do agree we need to 'move on' but couldn't we have at least agreed the plan of action before you sent that?"

"Well I…"

"And tell me, where do you get off accusing ME of unreasonable behaviour? What the hell did I ever do to you? Except be a loyal wife whilst you were out schtupping your barmaid?"

"I…"

"Tell me how was I being unreasonable? When was I unreasonable?"

"Can I get a word in?" he says, and gives me an exasperated look. I snort. "Look," he starts. "If we divorce before the two years are up – which we should – then we need to give reasons. They won't allow irrecontionable, irrecon –"

"Irreconcilable." I tut.

"Yeah that. We can't do those differences. It doesn't alter how we divvy up our money and stuff – it's just words."

"Just words? You mean just lies."

"So the complete breakdown of the marriage was all my fault, was it?" he says defensively.

"You were the one who went chasing skirt!"

"Only because you weren't interested in me anymore!"

"And what led you to that conclusion?"

"Come on, Amy, admit it, we were plodding. We weren't going anywhere."

"It's funny, I thought I'd got to where I wanted to be."

He looks away in silence and then lowers his voice. "My solicitor just said that I have to name reasons."

"S'funny, I thought you hire a solicitor to do what *you* want, not the other way round."

I can see that he's tossing up whether to fire off another round of ammunition or to let it go. I take a sip of my coffee, trying to hide my shaking hands.

"Look, I didn't come here to argue," he finally says. "I just think we need to sort out finances. If we can do it between ourselves then the court will be pleased and the divorce will be quick."

I nod. "OK."

"Justine and I went to the bank to see if we could buy Rose Cottage…" Just the thought of him and his little family living in my beautiful home makes my heart thump painfully in my chest. "But we can't quite manage it."

"I see." A rush of relief escapes in a sigh. "What are you suggesting then?"

"Dropping the price now for a quick sale?"

"OK. By how much?"

"Say, down to £150,000?"

"That's quite a drop! £160,000."

"£155,000?" he shoots back.

"OK. Done."

He holds out his hand and cracks the tiniest of grins.

I roll my eyes. "OK, next on the agenda. Who gets what?"

"To be honest, I don't really want much; my grandmother's chair and the picture you bought me for our anniversary that year. Apart from that there's nothing really." Sadness forms in his eyes.

"OK. Fine."

"And can you separate out the savings?" he asks.

"Do you want me to transfer it to your current account?"

"Yes please. And what happened to that ISA?" he asks.

"We cashed it in, remember? When the washing machine, boiler and car all ceremoniously died."

"Oh God yeah! The hat trick of death!" He pauses, drumming his fingers on the glass table top. "Good times, Ames."

"Sure Steve. No hot water, no clean clothes and no car to take us to the launderette - it was a bag of laughs."

"You know what I mean. Us. *We* had good times."

I shift in my seat. I know that look. We tried reuniting once before and it just didn't work. We can look back with the rosiest of tinted specs but it doesn't change anything; the life we had and the feelings we shared are things of the past.

"Right, are we done here?" I ask, dredging the remains of my coffee.

"What about the divorce? Will you agree to those terms?"

"Honestly? I don't know, but I'll think about it." I get up and wriggle into my coat. "See you later, I'll be in touch."

He looks up and touches my arm gently. "I know you don't like it, but you and I will always know how it was between us and if you can just agree we can be divorced quickly and move on with our lives."

I sigh deeply. I don't want a long dragged out divorce with back and forth solicitor letters, bad feelings and pistols at dawn. Why suffer more pain than is necessary to uncouple ourselves? Maybe Joshua is right – rip off the band aid and be done. "Okay, I'll think about it."

"Oh and one more thing, please think about Basil – I really would like him."

"Yeah Steve," I turn to look at him head-on. "I've thought about that, and the best you're gonna get is shared custody. And on that point there is no moving."

And with that I throw my bag over my shoulder and walk straight out of the door.

Chapter 14

Gloria is ready and waiting for Brian outside the Theatre Royal clutching The Nutcracker tickets that she had given him for Christmas.

"You look after them," he'd said to her. "I have a habit of losing tickets. I'll put them in a safe place…"

"And then forget where the safe place is," they'd said in unison, and laughed.

So Gloria had put them in her dressing table drawer, eagerly awaiting this date to come around, and now it's arrived she wants to be anywhere but here.

Shielding under the canopy from the rain, she fiddles with her scarf. She watches the umbrellas bobbing around with people racing towards the theatre. An older couple catch her eye as they saunter arm in arm, without an umbrella or seemingly a care in the world. Making their way through the rain with their heads thrown back in laughter, Gloria twinges with envy.

"Hello," Brian appears before her and pecks her on the cheek.

"Hello." She gives a watery smile.

"You OK?"

"Yes fine, fine. Come, let's go, let's get in the dry." She curbs the automatic reflex of linking his arm, and instead marches ahead into the foyer.

"Gloria, would you like an interval drink?" he asks from behind her.

She stops and turns. "Oh, er, a white wine would be lovely."

"Very well. Why don't you find our seats and I'll put in the order."

"Thank you," she says, passing him one ticket.

Leaving him to queue at the bar she enters the auditorium and, exhales deeply into her seat. Looking around her all she sees are grey haired couples, either laughing or chatting excitedly, enjoying the anticipation of the curtain going up.

"Oh, just in time," Brian says, joining her just as the lights go down. Gloria quickly shifts from the armrest and places her hands in her lap. Keeping her eyes firmly forward she attempts to breathe evenly. At one point when the lead ballerina performs the most exquisite combination of lighter-than-air steps Gloria naturally leans in to Brian to comment, but stopping herself quickly she straightens back in her seat. Brian turns and offers a small smile.

As the curtains close on Clara and the Snowflakes for the interval the audience applaud and break into soft chatter.

"Shall we?" Brian rises, holding out his hand. Gloria looks down sharply to avoid his touch – she can't be cruel. As gentlemanly as ever Brian steps back to let her pass and follows her out of the auditorium.

Gloria heads for a high table with bar stools whilst Brian goes to collect the drinks. Returning after what seems like half the interval he passes her a glass. "Here you go, my dear."

"Thank you."

He hoists himself up onto a stool. "Gloria, pardon my asking, but is something troubling you?"

"No..I mean..yes..well..I suppose so."

"My dear lady, whatever it is, I'm your friend; you can talk to me." Heavy creases line the kindest eyes she's ever known and his brow furrows with concern.

"Brian, I'm so sorry, but I think we should see less of each other. It's not you…" she says, painfully aware that she is about to use the biggest cliché in all relationships.

"I see," he says.

Looking into his eyes she already feels remorse for inflicting one iota of pain on him. "I am so sorry," she says.

"I don't mean to be un-gentlemanly to enquire, but is there a reason? I know I'm not the best catch, but I thought we were rather fond of each other?"

"We are, I am, I just…I just think it's too soon after Stanley."

He exhales and looks down. "I see, I just…"

The tannoy's crackle interrupts. "Ladies and gentlemen, please take your seats. The second Act of The Nutcracker shall begin shortly."

"Dear Gloria, I hope you'll forgive me but suddenly I don't feel very well. I think it's the wine," he says, looking at his twice-sipped drink. "Would you excuse me please?"

It's the least she can do. "Yes, of course. I understand."

Reaching for his coat he smiles weakly. "I'll see you soon. Enjoy the rest of the ballet, my dear. Goodnight."

"Goodnight," she says, the word catching in her throat. She remains perched on her high stool and watches him leave. She gazes into the middle distance, unable to move, tears smudging her eyes, threatening to spill over. She swigs back her wine and is grateful for the buzz. She eyes his abandoned glass and reaches for it - what the hell – tonight, numbness is better than feeling.

With people chattering all around her, Gloria looks down at the friendship ring he gave her for Christmas and sighs. Why did Fliss have to make this unreasonable demand? And why did she accede so readily? Was it out of sympathy for Fliss' precarious marriage and the added heartache at not being able to conceive? Is it guilt from becoming close to Brian whilst Stanley was still alive? Probably. But hadn't she made sure that her brain-damaged husband was comfortable and that all his needs were met in that marvellous care-home? She couldn't have done any more! '*Except stay faithful to him*,' she can hear Fliss say.

Gloria takes another large gulp of Brian's wine and stares out at the almost deserted rainy street. Lamplight reflects back in the puddles and it reminds her of the night The Dixbury Dancers were supposed to compete in Dixbury Does Talent and their limousine had broken down in the rainy countryside. On the trudge back to Dixbury, Brian had chivalrously carried her costume and when they'd arrived at the venue too late to compete he had said it 'didn't matter' as he felt they were 'already winners'. A tear escapes and trickles down the side of her nose.

"Gloria?"

She looks up to see Julay with Bendrick in tow.

"Oh hello." Gloria quickly dabs the tear and attempts a smile.

"Hello dear lady. How marvellous to see you." Bendrick says.

"Yesch, you too," Gloria says, a little alarmed by her wine-affected speech.

Julay's eyebrows rise. "Who are you with?"

"No-one, just me," Gloria replies, and then blushes as she follows Julay's gaze to the two glasses. "But," she sniffs a little. "I'm not feeling too good. I think it's the start of a cold. I might just call it a night."

"Oh what a pity! You'll miss the marvellous second Act!" Bendrick says.

"I know. Might be better off at home in my bed though."

"Of course, of course. Hope you feel better soon. Well, we'll see you in class?" Julay asks.

"Hope so. Goodnight."

"Goodnight," they both chime and then turn to join the excited throng milling back into the auditorium.

Deciding it's probably prudent to leave the rest of Brian's wine, Gloria picks up her belongings and heads for the door out into the blobby rain again. Hailing a cab she climbs in the back and with a pounding head and heavy heart she wants nothing more than this day to be done. Tomorrow is another day, she thinks, although it'll be the first of many without Brian, and that thought alone makes her want to crawl under her duvet and stay there until long after the rain has passed.

Chapter 15

With Julay out for the evening Marion decides to do some batch cooking; lasagne, meat pie and chilli that she can divide into portions and put in the freezer for the coming weeks. On a quiet evening Marion likes nothing more than to tie on a pinny and get cooking, and, as Julay won't take a penny in rent, Marion feels that this is her contribution.

As she opens the cupboard she realises she's lacking a few basic ingredients. Putting on her shoes and grabbing her purse, she heads for the local supermarket. It's a shabby little shop – one that looks like it needs a good clean, but as it stocks basil, oregano and stock cubes, it's fit for purpose. Standing in the aisle, comparing the sizes and prices of the herbs she feels a pair of eyes on her from across the way. As she looks up she recognises Iain, vicar and ex-neighbour, who used to be quite friendly with her now imprisoned husband.

"Marion, I thought it was you!" he says, walking over, smiling benignly. With his stereotypical apparel of socks and sandals, neat checked shirt and loose trousers, Marion is once again reminded of her long standing suspicion that he doesn't wear underwear.

"Iain, how are you?"

"I'm very well, thank you." He gives her a deep meaningful look and touches her arm. "And how are you?"

Instinctively she flinches. "I'm fine, thank you."

"I was sorry to hear about all that business," he says, looking over the top of his glasses.

"Mmm." Isn't it funny, she thinks, how a man beating his wife can be swiftly euphemised as 'all that business'.

Iain looks to his shoes. "I've visited him a few times, you know. He's a man in need and the Lord doesn't turn his back on the sinner."

"Yes, indeed."

"And you know, Marion, there would be nothing improper about you wanting to know how he is. Despite what's happened over recent times you have been married to him in the eyes of God for many years."

Marion sighs, thinking that no matter what, Iain definitely wants to let her know how Jack is. She reluctantly succumbs, "How is he?"

"He is asking the Lord for forgiveness."

"Is he getting it?"

He chuckles. "That is between the Lord and Jack. I do know that we, as humans, should not be the ones to judge. Only the Lord can."

"Right." Marion looks down the aisle for a possible escape route. "I'd better get on."

"Marion," he says, half blocking her way. "Your forgiveness could facilitate Jack's rehabilitation in a more expedient manner. He talks about you often. Would you consider visiting him?"

More than anything, Marion wants to say, 'No, Iain. That man beat me black and blue and mentally bludgeoned me day in and day out for most of our 'in the eyes of God' marriage', whereas what actually comes out is, "I'll think about it."

"Please do," he says, placing his hand on hers. "God be with you, Marion."

"Yes, thank you. Please give my love to Penny."

"Of course."

Marion scurries down the aisle but reaching the checkout she finds she's only picked up one of her required items. Checking Iain's whereabouts, she turns on her heels and rushes back down the aisle, grabs the remaining ingredients and hurriedly checks out and leaves.

Retracing her route back home the knot in her stomach twists and she's suddenly reminded of a dog she had as a child. This dog had lived on their street with people who used to beat it endlessly. It used to break her mother's heart to hear the dog howling in the garden in all weathers, and one day, having had quite enough, she went and knocked at their door. She told them that her shy daughter, Marion, was an only child whom, she thought, needed a pet for company and wondered if they were looking to rehome their dog. The owners were taken aback but with minimal persuasion handed over their dog. The first thing her mother did was to insist that Marion renamed the dog; 'a new name for a new life', she said. Marion picked 'Daisy' and she remembers those early weeks when the wee mongrel would flinch from her and bark for seemingly no reason. As the weeks progressed Daisy grew to know that she was loved, but the scars of the abuse never completely disappeared. Loud noises, or tall men would have her running and hiding under their sideboard. Marion wishes for a sideboard right now.

She lets herself in the house, heads straight to the kitchen and makes herself a strong cup of tea. Sitting at the table she thinks how this is the first person to mention Jack since all the drama of the court case. As a couple, they didn't really have friends and The Dixbury Dancers don't tend to mention him much these days, so Iain, with his vicarly ways, visiting Jack in prison and talking about her forgiveness, has reopened old wounds.

Returning to the kitchen she ponders the idea of forgiving him. How can she? And why would she want to? Isn't Jack a closed chapter in her life? She's so much happier now, why would she want to revisit the man who robbed her of her dignity and crushed her spirit? Mind you, she thinks, he wasn't always a nasty man. In fact when they first met he was the on-trend, charmer of the local disco. Who didn't want to go out with Jack Travis? Handsome, cool, witty – everything a girl wanted. And Marion was stunned and delighted in equal measures when he picked her. Before you could say 'bell bottom trousers' they were living in marital bliss.

Although they both enjoyed a tipple, their bliss slowly faded as Jack's intake increased along with his black moods. Somewhere along the way Jack lost his lust for life and he brought it all out on the woman he loved. Mental and physical bruises covered Marion until that final evening when she ended up in hospital. Enough was enough.

As she spoons the meals neatly into Tupperware containers she thinks about Iain's words, 'He is asking the Lord for forgiveness'. She guesses that Jack won't be drinking in prison and maybe his sobriety has seen a return to the man she fell in love with; a man capable of remorse. Could he be that same man underneath all the angst and anger of recent years? And if he is, should she kill two birds with one stone by granting him the forgiveness he's seeking and, at the same time, get the closure she needs?

Closing the freezer door she's not clear about anything except for the pang of regret for having bumped into Iain tonight.

Chapter 16

Gloria blinks her eyes open. By the heavy golden drapes letting in tiny shards of light and the birds in full chorus, she senses it's too early to get up. Her bedside clock confirms it's only four thirty and she rests her head back on the pillow. Like a bad dream, the events of the previous evening return and the image of Brian's crumpled face causes her to wince. To top it all her upper back is aching – it's either her shoulder or back these days – and lying in bed doesn't help. She throws back the covers and heads to the kitchen for a remedial cup of tea. She has nothing to do today so returning to bed later could definitely be an option.

Wrapped in her thick dressing gown she curls up on the chair with her tea and gazes out at the garden through the windows. Feeling like the only soul awake, she muses how beautiful it is at this time in the morning. Apart from the birds fluttering and the neighbour's cat plodding home from a night on the tiles, all is calm.

A tear rises and she shakes her head.

No, no more tears. I made my decision to honour my daughter's wishes. Now I have to live with it.

Fervently needing to escape her thoughts, she reaches for her book and loses herself in the world of cosy crime until, much later, she hears the sound of footsteps above, first padding to the bathroom and then coming down the stairs. When Fliss doesn't appear, Gloria lays down her book and leans forward to the sound of her daughter talking on the phone. Knowing she shouldn't eavesdrop but incapable to resist, Gloria sits still, her ears pricked.

"…Yes please. I would like an initial consultation….erm, well as soon as possible please….I have a time limit….next Thursday? Yes that would suit me fine…..yes, could you tell me where you are exactly?….right got it….so the clinic entrance is at the front? OK…..thank you, that's great. See you Thursday sixteenth at ten o'clock. Thanks again…bye."

Gloria has a sense of unease. What is her daughter planning? Is she having more fertility tests? But why would there be a time limit? And whatever she's doing, shouldn't she talk to Tim first?

Hearing footsteps heading to the kitchen Gloria quickly picks up her book and buries her head in it.

"Oh!" Fliss jumps a little. "Morning Mum, didn't see you there."

"Everything okay?" Gloria asks, peering over the top of her book.

"Yep, great!" she says, putting on the kettle. "More tea?"

"Not for me, thanks." Gloria shakes her head.

"You're up early."

"Couldn't sleep. Those darn birds woke me up."

"Ha, you love the birds." Fliss turns to look evenly at her mother. "You really okay? You don't look yourself."

"Darling, this is how I look at this time in the morning – just wait until you're my age." They both smile. "So what are you up to today?"

"Thought I'd get my hair and nails done. What about you?"

"Not a lot."

"Not seeing Brian?"

Gloria sharply turns her eyes away to the garden. "No."

"Oh?"

"I thought about what you said. I talked to Brian last night and he understood – he's a good man," Gloria says, her eyes fixed on some flowers swaying in the breeze.

Fliss nods. "Right," she says softly. "I'm sure things'll work out for the best, Mum. I think it's the same with me and Tim: a bit of distance will do the trick."

"Mmm mm."

"I'm going to take this upstairs to get ready," Fliss says, raising her mug of tea.

"OK dear."

As Fliss disappears Gloria's thoughts return to the phone-call and the clinic consultation with a pressing time limit. It just doesn't make sense. She sighs thinking how things are never easy with her daughter, and as much as Fliss may present as worldly wise and in control, there's vulnerability behind the façade. And now with the news of her inability to conceive, Gloria can't help but feel an even stronger tug on her Achilles heel. Any doubts about not following her daughter's wishes are pushed aside as whatever this clinic thing turns out to be, it is most definitely Fliss who needs her full support and attention right now.

•••

'Ah, marvellous,' thinks Bendrick, as he reads the email from The Dixbury
Tribune telling him that a journalist by the name of Leanne Cork will be coming to Wednesday's class. It's been a long time since he was featured in a newspaper and he's thrilled by the thought of it – even if the piece will mainly be focusing on the dancers.

Ah – those dancers, his dancers, how very proud he feels of them. He devises classes that would make many dancers run for the hills, but, apart from a few grumbles, his lot all gamely throw themselves into it. He couldn't wish for a better bunch to teach.

He replies to the email and then, carefully considering the strengths of his dancers, prepares his lesson plan for the coming week. Mixing up different steps, turns and jumps, he plans to challenge and develop them in every way he can. He remembers setting up Surrey Ballet back in the nineties, and how he took a sloppy, yet talented, bunch of dancers to become the acclaimed company it is today. In fact, he thinks, his career is peppered with these 'rags to riches' type stories and he inwardly glows at his achievements.

Shutting down his laptop he reaches for his phone and types in the names of each of The Dixbury Dancers. He relays the details of Leanne Cork's planned visit and then chuckles to himself as he tells them to prepare themselves for 'greatness!' He hits send and then resting back in his chair, he envisages their names in lights with all the accompanying credit and glory being shared with him.

Chapter 17

As soon as each Dixbury Dancer received the news they had set about a frenzy of group texting.

Lucia - *Oh My God, Oh My God – what do we wear?*

Marion - *I know! My shoes are so old – I can't be photographed in them.*

Me - *I seriously need a new leotard.*

Julay – *I'm in need of a new bun net, ouch pouches and ribbons.*

Josie - *Well ladies, (and gent if you're there, Brian?) what we need is a trip to Chappelle!*

Lucia - *That is EXACTLY what we need. Saturday?*

Me - *Aaargh, I work ☹*

Lucia - *OK, how about after work at 4.00pm?*

Me - Suits me. All up for it?

And most of us were and are now crowded into the dancewear shop, browsing the rails of leotards, skirts and tops. As Dixbury isn't a town known for ballet dancing, I often wonder how this shop keeps afloat and I would suspect a lot of its custom is crammed into it right now.

"Oooh, look at this," Josie says, holding up a sheer cerise romantic wrap-around skirt.

"Mum! You can't wear that colour," her daughter, Catherine, grumps. "It's embarrassing!" Marion and I exchange a knowing look.

"What other joys do I get in life other than embarrassing my beautiful teen?" Josie laughs, holding the skirt up to her body. Catherine baulks and heads to another rail. "Kids eh? Can't live with them, can't kill 'em." Josie shrugs.

We all laugh.

I'm browsing the leotards when I find a beautiful teal one in cotton Lycra with a lace yoke, it's perfect, but holding it up to my short frame I can tell it would be far too long in the body.

"Julay, I think this would look stunning on you," I call over.

"Oooh yes I do like that," she says, joining me. After browsing the price tag she adds it to the collection of garments over her arm. "Thank you very much, I'll try that too."

"So, what angle do you think the newspaper'll take?" Marion asks.

"Bendrick thinks it'll be about the benefits of learning ballet. It'll be aimed at encouraging people of any age to give it a go. He has high hopes it'll also give us some great exposure and create a fan base. Can you imagine?" Julay says.

"Oh yeah? What else does ol' Benny say?" Lucia asks with a demon twinkle in her eye. "Getting cosy with our teacher, eh Jules?"

Julay sniffs. "No Lucia."

"Well, not wanting to rat on you," Marion grins. "But you did go out with him the other night, didn't you?"

A chorus of 'oooohs' goes up.

"Marion! You make it sound like a date, which it wasn't – just two balletomanes taking in a ballet."

"Two ballet-to-whats?" Lucia asks.

"Two kindred spirits who appreciate the ballet. Anyway, don't send the gossip mill into action as there's nothing to report."

"Yet," Lucia teases.

Julay sighs with exasperation. "We're perfectly happy as we are. And anyway if we need to gossip about anyone, you might want to think about who's not here."

"Yes, where is Gloria?" I say. "I didn't expect Brian…"

"- No, he's got enough tutus," Josie jokes.

"But I did expect Gloria."

Lucia eyes Julay suspiciously. "Go on then, Jules – what do you know?"

"Well," Julay leans forward lowering her voice. "When Bendrick and I were at The Nutcracker we bumped into her. She wasn't with Brian, and I might add she looked a little bedraggled."

"Bedraggled? Gloria? She always looks pristine," Marion says.

"Not that night she wasn't; she was bleary eyed and a little messy – definitely not herself at all."

"Oh dear, I wonder what's happened," I say more to myself than to anyone else. I know things aren't good with her daughter and I also know that Gloria was due to go to The Nutcracker with Brian. I make a mental note to contact her.

"So she wasn't with anyone?" Josie asks what I'm thinking.

"No, completely alone, well…apart from two glasses of wine," Julay says with raised eyebrows and, having successfully diverted attention from herself, heads to the changing room.

"Talking of affairs of the heart," I say, sidling up to Sam. "How's it going with that young man of yours?"

"Urgh," she says, slouching with despair. "Last week in the middle of 'AppleGate' he definitely told me he liked me – he said it! But then I saw him at the tutorial and it was business as usual. No mention of liking me, nothing out of the ordinary. It was like it never happened!"

"He's a slow burner that one, for sure. Well, what about your Basingstoke conference plan?"

"Yeah, I'm still going to ask him about that. But maybe I'm just barking up the wrong tree. I mean if he can blow hot and cold like this..."

"Whoa, whoa whoa, don't give up at the first hurdle! Come on, you're a Dixbury Dancer, we don't give up!"

"Only when we can't do stuff."

"Fair point."

We laugh.

"So, how are things with you? Heard from Steve?" she asks.

"Yeah. Well, I met him, and Steve being Steve thinks he has to do exactly what his solicitor tells him – he doesn't get it that he employs them! Anyway – I'm thinking about agreeing to his petition, accusing me of unreasonable behaviour –"

"What?"

"Yeah, yeah, it doesn't make much difference to anything."

"But it's a lie."

"It depends how you look at things. I suppose he thinks I wasn't there for him, that I couldn't be bothered, and that, to him, is unreasonable."

"But he had the affair!" She forcibly returns the leotard she's been holding back on to the rail.

"I know." I shrug. "Anyway, I might just opt for a quiet life. The one thing we did agree on is to reduce the price on Rose Cottage, try and get it sold. I suppose once that's done we can really get on with our lives."

"Where will you go?"

I pause. Do I tell her the whole saga of Joshua and the withheld nest egg? Something stops me. Up to this point he's been painted the romantic hero and I don't want to tar his character in her eyes.

"I'll find a flat or house on the other side of town. If I can't afford to buy, I'll rent."

"Well, I hope you get a good price for Rose Cottage."

"Me too. Right," I sigh determinedly. "Let's concentrate on the important things - what do you think, pink or black flats?"

"Pink says 'I'm serious about this lark' and black says 'I'm serious about this lark, but I'm an adult and don't want to look like a three year old'," she says.

"And whatever you do, don't go for the nude colour, they look like you've vomited on your feet," chips in Lucia, en route to the changing room.

I pull a face. "Black it is."

Julay sashays down the shop, head to toe in the cerise that Josie had been admiring.

"Wow – that is…stunning!" Marion's eyes are wide.

“She looks like a flamingo,” Catherine says in a low voice and receives a dig in the ribs from her mother.

“It’s certainly eye-catching,” I say. “Leanne Cork will definitely be photographing you.” Julay smiles and lifts her chin with pride.

“What do you all think then?” We turn to see Lucia emerging, hands on hips, from the changing room, her voluptuous body covered in a purple unitard. Smuggling ferrets come to mind.

“Wow!” is all that will come out of Marion’s mouth.

“You’ll get photographed too.” I say.

Lucia turns this way and that, admiring herself in the mirror. “Yep, I think I’ll get it.”

“Do we all need striking colours?” Marion asks me, looking somewhat deflated.

“No, don’t worry, Marion, I’m sticking to black. Might race it up a bit with some grey leg warmers!”

“Oh thank goodness for that.”

“And anyway,” I say out of the corner of my mouth. “The photos might be in black and white.”

Marion giggles.

One by one we pay for our garb and whilst I’m waiting I grab a black one-size-fits-all shoulder shrug that I plan to give to Gloria. Not that I need an excuse to see her, but, judging from what Julay said, she might just be in need of cheering up.

“What now?” says Lucia, as we all crowd on the pavement, clutching our Chappelle embossed bags.

“Expresso High!” we chorus and head off down the street, crowing with laughter.

Chapter 18

After coffee and cake followed by more coffee and cake I make my excuses and jump on the bus to Gloria's house. I decide not to text first; if she's feeling down, a surprise visit from a gift-bearing friend might be just what she needs.

"Hello, dear," Gloria says, opening the door. She's not the wreck that Julay described but, with a hairband covering her usually sleek style and a lack of make-up, she certainly doesn't look herself. "To what do I owe this lovely unexpected pleasure?"

"Missed you today at the Get Kitted Out At Chappelle event."

"Oh!" she exclaims, her hand flying to her mouth. "Was that today? It completely slipped my mind."

I eye her curiously. "Tell me to mind my own business Glo, but is everything okay?"

"Come in, dear."

She ushers me into the kitchen and towards the large sofa at the far end whilst she puts on the kettle. We small talk waiting for it to boil and then she joins me with tea and biscuits. I refrain from telling her that I've just eaten my body weight in sugar and, purely to be sociable, reach for a Hobnob.

"Where do I begin?" she says, her eyes starting to water.

"Oh Gloria, what's happened?"

She sighs. "I told Brian we should see less of each other."

"Why?"

"I've rushed into it too quickly, I've disrespected Stanley's memory; he was everything to me and I can't just transfer my feelings to another man. It's not fair on Brian or…"

"Or?"

She smiles weakly. "Or to Fliss."

"Ah."

"She misses her father terribly and it hurts her to see me with another man – not that Brian and I are, I mean, were, at that stage." She gives me a knowing look.

"Gloria, you don't have to explain anything to me."

"We *were* very softly falling in love though. At least I know I was…and I'm pretty sure he was too."

She gazes out to the grey landscape, her face etched with unhappiness.

"Did Fliss ask you to stop seeing him?" I ask.

She nods slowly. "It makes sense really, I mean, if Brian and I put it on hold then, given time, we'll know if it's the right thing to do, rather than rushing in and maybe ending up with more heartache." Her voice peters out.

Does she even believe what she's saying? I dearly want to tell her that life is precious and short and if we don't follow our dreams we can end up lonely and bitter, but how can I do that? It would mean opposing Fliss and I'm not about to come between mother and daughter.

"What did Brian say?" I ask.

"He made a weak excuse about the wine affecting him and left the theatre. I had to let him go; I couldn't bear hurting him further. I really don't know how I'm going to face him again."

"Gloria, it's Brian, he's the gentlest, most understanding man in the world, I'm sure he'll wait for you."

"But I've chinked it, haven't I?"

"Chinked it?"

"You know when a relationship is new and shiny and everything is how it should be?" I nod. "Then one person does something – commits a 'love-sin', if you like; tells a lie, misses a date, makes a faux pas – it creates a chink, a crack in the perfection. It doesn't matter what you do, you can glue it back together but you're always going to see that crack." The thought of Joshua's guarded savings cross my mind. "I can't undo what I've done," she says, her tears brimming.

"Oh Gloria," I say, moving to put my arm around her. "It's called being human. No relationship is perfect – we make mistakes - that's what we do. It's how we deal with it and carry on that's important."

Her eyes travel to the garden. "I wish I could turn back time."

"If you could, would you not listen to Fliss?"

"Ah, well, there's more to it than that, I'm afraid. After the awful evening with Brian, I couldn't sleep so I came down here to read and Fliss got up, not realising I was here…she made a call to a clinic…"

"What are we thinking?" I can't read her expression. "What? Clap clinic?"

"Amy! No!"

"Sorry – it's the word 'clinic'..."

Gloria takes a deep breath. "Well, it's awfully sad, but between you and me, Fliss told me she can't have children and I wonder if it's something to do with that."

"Oh I'm sorry. What about her husband?"

"Hmm, I don't really know what's going on there either - they've fallen out over something."

"Gloria, there's so much you don't know; you need to talk with her."

"Ha! You don't know my daughter."

"No, I don't, but you're torturing yourself."

"I know, but she's a stubborn one. She won't talk about things unless she wants to. I've had all sorts of thoughts – supposing it's something really serious? I don't know whether I should just confront her or contact Tim -"

"Oooh that sounds a wee bit intrusive."

"You mean meddling?"

"Mmm. You kind of need to go under the radar. Did you redial to find out which clinic?"

"Dash it, why didn't I think of that?"

"Cos you're lovely and honest and not sneaky." I think for a second. "OK, so you know the date and time of the appointment?" She nods. "Why don't we follow her?" Gloria opens and closes her mouth. *Clearly stalking is a new concept for her.* "Just to see where she's going," I add. "Then you take it from there."

She thinks for a moment or two. "I would like to know what she's doing…" She looks up. "So you're with me on this?"

"I'm your wing man."

She thinks some more. "What if she sees us?"

"Then we just say we were heading to that side of town for 'fill in the blank'."

"Amy, all the years I've known you and all the years you've been coiffuring hair when you should've been a private detective!" Her face holds something like awe.

I lean back and pop the last of my biscuit in my mouth.

"I've just had a thought," she says, "When our legs give up and we can't dance anymore we could form the Private Dicks of Dixbury!" We both laugh. I'm dying to make an immature smutty joke but after the 'clap clinic' moment I elect not to shock her further. Instead I help myself to another biscuit.

"Oh, I forgot," I say. I rummage in my bag and pull out the shrug. "Just a little something."

"Oh my dear." She holds it up. "Thank you so much, it's lovely. That's so thoughtful." She kisses my cheek.

"You're welcome," I say. "Gloria, you *are* going to be there on Wednesday, aren't you? Leanne whatserface is going to be there. We need you, you add the touch of class to the group."

"Ha ha, you smooth talker. Yes, I'll be there."

"That's great." As I reach for my teacup I see her face has dropped. "Gloria?"

"I just wonder whether Brian will…"

Chapter 19

A flurry of Wednesday evening excitement fills the changing room.

"How do I look?" Marion asks me.

"Beautiful." The sombre black georgette skirt, navy leotard and pink tights transform her into a traditionally elegant ballerina. "Whatever it cost you, Marion, it was well worth it."

"Thank you dear." She beams with pride and my heart squeezes for her. I watch her in front of the mirror and think how she used to be a shadow of herself; living with her abusive husband took its toll on her both physically and emotionally. And now? She looks like a woman who no longer carries the world on her shoulders. With Jack in prison and her move into Julay's house, she has a new lease of life. None of her recovery was down to me, which makes my pride in her, although warranted, somewhat inexplicable.

My phone buzzes; it's Joshua.

Just realised I have a few jobs at the hall tonight – so how about meeting after for a date? x

Who is this?

Very funny! Meet me outside the changing room 9pm sharp. Dress casual with a slight whiff of B.O. x

I laugh and text back kisses.

Lucia runs in panting. "She's here!"

"What does she look like?" Marion asks.

"What does it matter?" says Julay.

"A bit skanky actually," Lucia elaborates. "Reckon she's a forty pack a day type who doesn't over trouble herself with shampoo."

"Delightful." Julay rolls her eyes.

"As long as she writes a good piece, I don't care," I say. "Are we ready?"

We all look to each other. The night we performed at Dixbury Does Talent we'd huddled together, united in our determination to put on the best show we could, and this moment feels the same; we want to show ourselves in the best possible light.

"Hang on, hang on, is there anything we *don't* want to say?" Sam asks.

"I suppose we don't have to be too up-front about our ages," Gloria says.

"And I don't want to say anything too personal," Marion understandably adds.

"I'm not going to shout about my dodgy pirouettes," Lucia says. "Or that little bit of wee that escapes in a grand jeté." We all stop and turn to her. "What!?" Her shoulders rise to her ears with indignation. "It's only natural!"

We all shake our heads and start making our way from the changing room.

Marion falls in step with Lucia. "Can I say something, Lucia?"

"Shoot."

"Tena Lady, dear, Tena Lady."

Lucia throws her head back in a raucous laugh. "Thanks Maz."

Entering the room I see that Lucia is right about Leanne Cork – with not a scrap of makeup and a dated outfit hanging on her small frame, she looks like someone more comfortable getting the scoop than tending to personal appearance.

"I told you he wouldn't be here," Gloria whispers to me at the barre.

"Well, - " Right on cue the door opens and Brian enters and judging by his drawn appearance I'm not sure if Gloria is relieved or distressed further. I squeeze her hand.

"Ladies and gent," Bendrick says. "I have the great pleasure of introducing you to The Tribune's finest, Miss Leanne Cork." We all smile and she raises her hand and nods. "Kind madam, please tell us how you would like to proceed."

"Right," she says, tugging a long lank piece of hair behind her slightly protruding ear. "I'd like is to get some photos and then do individual interviews. Okay?" Everyone nods and smiles. "Just pretend I'm not here and I'll try not to get in your way."

"Marvellous! Any questions?" Bendrick says, looking around at us shaking our heads. "Right, let's begin. Places at the barre please."

I take my usual spot and watch Gloria and Brian heading for theirs. I'm just thinking how I wouldn't want to be in such close proximity to a recent ex when they instinctively lower their heads and veer off in different directions. My heart pulls for them.

"Right," Bendrick says, making his way to the stereo. "Let's do plié, plié, grand plié with a high fifth arm. Dégagé à la seconde, repeat, dégagé derrière with an arabesque arm, repeat the pliés, dégagé à la seconde. So that's en croix. Finish with a beautiful balance in first with arms in bras bas, raising to fifth, OK?"

Lucia catches my eye and mouths, 'What The F…?'

I shrug and look around at the others. Everyone with the exception of Julay has a look of mild panic. Is Bendrick not going to demonstrate? Is anyone going to ask for clarification? It would appear not.

A plinky-plonky version of 'Somewhere Over The Rainbow' begins and the first pliés are done together, but that's as far as our synchronisation goes. I bend my knees to plié and see others rising; some arms are up and some are down. Usually I pick a dancer to follow – one I know has grasped it – but with so many differing variations and timings to choose from I'm floundering. To my credit I keep going, unlike poor Marion, who I see standing still, looking a little surprised at having finished two bars ahead of the rest of us.

Bendrick makes a small embarrassed cough. "Right, let's go straight away on the other side."

"Sorry, Bendrick," I speak up. "I haven't quite got it, could you go through it again please?"

I can feel the gratitude oozing all around me.

He verbally flies through the exercise again and we lurch back into action.

"Flippin' eck – he's gone mad!" Lucia says under her breath, trying to hold a balance for far longer than normally required.

"I thought this was going to be fun," Sam grimaces.

"Keep smiling," Gloria says through gritted teeth. "Look like you know what you're doing."

"I can't act that well," Sam replies.

Leanne watches deadpan as Bendrick wraps up the barre work and calls for everyone to move to the centre.

Goodness knows what we're in for now...

Leanne approaches the group.

"Right," she says, cuffing her nose. "I'd like to get some shots, if that's okay." She moves to the back of the room to pick up a second camera.

Oh great - photographs - just what we need...

"Right, my beautiful dancers, before we continue, I have some exciting news," Bendrick says, theatrically playing to the gallery.

"Oh blimey, is Carlos Acosta hiding in the broom cupboard?" Lucia says out of the corner of her mouth.

"Or has he got us all pink tutus?" Brian quips.

"Well," Bendrick starts. "I spoke with Helena yesterday and...you are officially entered in the Afton Village competition! She's registered you, paid the fee, checked out the competition and tells me that she thinks you have a very good chance of winning!"

Excited chatter breaks out.

"But what are we dancing?" Gloria asks.

"Well, after talking it over we think we should aim high – "

"- Ballet on trapezes?" Lucia interjects.

"Ha ha, no,no,no! Swan Lake!" His eyes shine with eager anticipation.

Swan Lake? As in what the professionals do?

"Erm, are we cygnets?" Marion asks.

"Yes, but the whole thing will be modified slightly to suit ability and to accommodate our fine male dancer," Bendrick says, smiling at Brian. "Let me teach you some of the basic steps. Shall we begin?"

Leanne starts snapping away and, luckily for us, for much of the time, Bendrick asks us to watch young Catherine as she demonstrates the new steps. This I can get on board with; photos of me standing and watching trump those of me dancing any day.

Leanne uses her bulky camera to take shots from all angles; she gets up close and personal – *not quite sure why she wants photos of our nasal cavities* - and then moves back for whole group shots.

"Bendrick, okay if I start the interviews?" she eventually asks.

"Certainly, who would you like first?"

Feeling like school children being picked for sports teams we stand expectantly.

With a blank expression she shrugs. "I'll get a couple of chairs. Just come over one after another. Only be a few minutes each." She drags two chairs and her feet to the corner.

"Who wants to go first then?" asks Bendrick.

"I don't mind," Julay says. We all nod agreement and she leaves to join Leanne.

"Whilst we're one dancer down, why not some good old fashioned pirouette practise?" Bendrick says.

Maybe one of the hardest ballet moves to perfect, but with group determination we all set about like spinning tops. Bendrick shouts encouragingly to 'get the knee higher', 'spot the corner', and 'spring into the turn', but after one particular landing that's more baboon than swan, I gratefully take my turn to slope off to Leanne.

"And you are?" she says, briefly looking up; the smell of stale cigarettes filling the air between us.

"Amy."

"Right, why d'you take up ballet?" she drawls, barely concealing a sigh.

"My husband left me and I needed a distraction. I'm a hairdresser and do Gloria's hair." I point in the direction of Gloria. "And she told me it'd be a good idea."

"Got it, thanks." She scores a line on her pad.

"That it?"

"Got any more you want to say? I kind of got everything I needed from Julie."

"Ju-lay," I correct her.

"Yeah, her."

"Right, well no then, that's fine. Nice to meet you," I say.

"Yup," she grunts.

Slightly dismayed, I return to my dizzy dancing friends and continue twirling until eventually Leanne wanders over and asks for a group photo.

"Can we bring in the pole? And you all stand either side of it and strike poses?"

We all look to Bendrick.

"Yes." He jumps into action. "Right Julay, you stand that side and rise in fifth, Amy, this side and give me arms in fourth. Now Marion and Josie, rise in first and Catherine, I'd like an arabesque. I love your high leg." He smiles. "And that leaves you two." He looks at Gloria and Brian.

Oh no...

"Brian, I would like you to support Gloria around the waist and Gloria," he says, positioning her arm towards Brian, "I would like you to look up at Brian with your arms in fourth."

I hold my breath, watching the awkwardness unfold.

Leanne adds to the tension. "You two lovebirds on the end, could you move in a bit?"

Gloria and Brian look to each other, their eyes barely able to meet, and inch closer. It reminds me of a past relationship where the fellow broke up with me on a night out but, trying to be civil, we travelled home together on the Tube. Unaware that an avalanche of people would descend at the next stop we then found ourselves squadged together with body parts touching that hadn't actually touched throughout the short lived relationship. It was one of the most uncomfortable ten minutes of my life and watching Gloria and Brian now, my heart hurts for them.

Leanne lifts her heavy lens camera. "OK everyone, smile!"

Trying not to wobble, up on tiptoes, and with fake smiles covering all manner of discomfiture, our image is captured.

Hmm, that'll be one for framing...

Chapter 20

"Let's hope she writes with a bit more passion than she seems to possess," Julay dryly notes whilst changing out of her leotard.

"Yeah, she didn't seem too enthused with us, did she?" Marion adds.

"Maybe it just wasn't her thing," Gloria says.

"Yes, I imagine she's more at home with local crime than a bunch of ballet dancers," Marion says.

"I think you might be right, Maz." Lucia says.

"Guess we'll find out next week. Did she say Monday or Tuesday's paper?" Josie asks.

Lucia impersonates Leanne's deadpan delivery, "Aiming for Monday, but depending on other news, it might be Tuesday."

Normally we'd be chuckling at that, in fact, normally we're a veritable gaggle of giggling ballerinas, laughing at our errors and baulking at the difficulties of ballet, but this evening just wasn't fun and for once we're quiet and downbeat.

The silence breaks with the buzzing of my phone. Ugh – it's Steve.

Just wanted to let you know the sad news that Daphne passed away last night. We were with her – peaceful end. Will let you know about funeral. S x

As I stare at the words my chest tightens and as the colour drains from my face, I look up to find all eyes on me.

"Amy?" Gloria moves next to me.

"Steve's mum's died."

"Oh I'm sorry. Were you close?"

I nod. "She was lovely, a very gentle soul. She had cancer for the last few years but seemed to be beating it." I swallow hard and Gloria touches my arm.

My fellow dancers murmur sympathies.

"You OK getting home?" Gloria asks.

"Oh yes! Oh Christ, Joshua is waiting for me. We're going on a date."

"Ah, that's nice – do you good." She smiles kindly.

"Yeah."

Slipping out of my ballet garb I wet wipe myself (more effective than a trot round the dilapidated changing room shower) and throw on my jeans and jumper. Crossing to the mirror I perform a make-do job on my makeup and re-tie my hair back. Well, I console myself, he did say casual dress with a whiff of B.O. - some folk really shouldn't wish too hard…

As I leave the changing room I see Joshua at the end of the corridor, leaning up against the wall, pushing his unruly curls out of his eyes, studying his phone.

"Hi there," I say.

"Hi." He looks up smiling. He wraps his arms around me and kisses me; a long, warm, soft pressing of his lips that I feel all the way to my tippy toes.

"Mmmm, I've missed you," I say, slightly breathlessly.

"Then quit your missing and let's keep kissing."

"You're a poet now?"

"A man of many talents."

"And master of none?"

"Ha ha. Oh, almost forgot, this came to the hall for Marion," he says, pulling a blue envelope from his pocket. "Can you just give it to her please?"

"Sure." I take the letter and return to the changing room. "Hey Marion, you've got a love letter," I giggle, passing her the envelope. "OK, I'm outta here!" They all chorus goodbye again.

As I approach Joshua, he takes my hand and leads me out to Sheila Skoda.

"Come on then, where are we going?" I ask, as he swings out of the car park.

"Ah-ha." He taps the side of his nose.

"Oh come on! Give me a clue, please?" I add, running my fingers up his thigh.

"Oh whoa whoa whoa, you want it to be to A&E?" We both laugh. He switches on the CD player and the opening bars of 'All You Need Is Love' sound out. Singing along (him, out of tune and me, not much better), we drive through the winding dark country lanes, leaving Dixbury behind us as we head out towards Bowden Lakes. I look out across the fields at the moon hanging heavy and low, casting a magical glow over the sparse scenery, and glancing up at the heavens, I'm reminded of Daphne.

"Steve's mum died," I say.

"Oh I'm sorry," Joshua says, looking across to me in the shadows. "Was it expected?"

"Yeah, she had cancer. But last I heard she was beating it," I say, hearing the small catch in my voice. "I tell you, I may not have fond feelings for her son, but she was a lovely lady; always sweet and welcoming and kind to me. I haven't seen her since we split…I imagine she would've been disappointed."

Joshua turns the sharp bend at the top of the hill and pulls the car onto a deserted plateau. Pulling on the handbrake he clicks his seatbelt free.

"Come here." He pulls me to him.

"I should've seen her. I knew she was ill; I should've visited her," I say to his chest.

He silently holds me, stroking my hair, and his steady heartbeat comforts and reminds me of how alive we are, and of how fleeting life is. If the death of my parents taught me nothing else, it was that death is a part of life and how all things come to pass; we really do only have these moments. And with that thought I pull away to take stock of my surroundings. We're on top of a hill under a swirling blue-purple sky that is lit by a thousand twinkling stars. If feels like we are perched at the edge of the world. Perfect.

"Lovely view," I say.

"Yes, you are."

I smile and lean back against him, and just as I am starting to lose myself in this exquisite moment I become aware of him sniffing in the manner akin to a bloodhound.

"You alright there?" I ask.

"Can you smell it?"

"Oh you haven't, have you?"

"No!" He sniffs again trying to trace the source. "Eurgh, that!"

I join in and a few seconds later the acrid unmistakeable odour of dog poo hits my nostrils. "Oh My God." I pinch my nose. "Where is it?"

"Hard to tell," he says, reaching up to flick on the light. Suspicious one of us has trodden in it, Joshua takes off his left shoe to find it caked in something some hound did earlier. He scrambles out of the car and I can't help but giggle as I watch him hop to a nearby stone to bash it clean.

"Dance, boy, dance!" I chant.

"Sod off," he says, losing balance and cursing as his socked foot hits the ground.

"Ha ha ha – just give up and go barefoot!"

He waves the offending shoe at me. "You do know I can bring this back in the car, don't you?"

"And you know I can lock the doors, don't you? Ha ha. Do you want a tissue?"

"Good idea!"

Ferreting in my bag I find an empty packet. "Sorry!" I say, holding it up.

"This might ruin the element of surprise but can you go into the holdall on the back seat and get me a napkin?"

I pull the bag over onto my lap and open it to find paper serviettes, a bottle of wine, two plastic glasses and a little wrapped square package.

"Aw, this looks lovely," I coo.

"Yeah, yeah, I'm hopping around here?"

I throw a napkin out of the window to him and after some dedicated wiping, deciding it's an impossible task, he tosses the shoe in the boot and returns to the front seat.

"Thank you," I say.

"For the smell?"

"For this," I say, gesturing to the bag.

"Know what this is?" He pulls out the waxed paper parcel. "Open it."

The folds of the paper fall open easily to reveal a chunk of pork pie with egg running through the middle.

I laugh. "A pork pie picnic – this *is* perfect!"

"You still love it?"

"I do."

"As much as you love me?"

I touch his cheek. "Let's eat and drink and then I'll show you."

His eyes twinkle as brightly as the stars as he sets about opening and pouring the wine.

Chapter 21

Taking the letter from Amy, Marion only has to give it the one cursory glance to know who it's from. And if she wasn't already sure, the HM Prison stamp on the back confirms it. Her eyes dart around the changing room, grateful that her friends are too busy to pay her attention. She quickly stuffs it in her jacket pocket, picks up the rest of her belongings and makes her excuses.

"Julay, I'll see you at home. I have a few things to do, OK?" she says.

"Yes dear, see you there," Julay responds absent-mindedly.

With her breath high in her chest Marion drives her clapped out car faster than she should until she finds herself in a dry dirt layby surrounded by fields. Pulling on the handbrake she fishes the letter out of her pocket and places it on the passenger seat. Too scared to open it but not brave enough to rip it up, she stares at the flimsy blue envelope. In a now or never moment she grabs it and slices it open with her finger.

The opening salutation of 'Dear Mari' immediately brings a lump to her throat – he is the only person to call her that – and by the time she reaches the sign off she is a mess of tears. '*Feeling remorse*', '*begging for forgiveness*' and '*finding peace*' feature highly on the five thin sheets that make up the longest letter, she presumes, that Jack has ever written. He alludes back to happier days; nights out in their favourite pub, evenings cuddled up in front of the telly and their annual jaunts to Wales.

Yes, she thinks, they were great times, wonderful, romantic, joyful days and nights. But what happened after then didn't have an ounce of wonder, romance or joy. Latterly days were filled with cruel words, controlling ways and, ultimately, physical violence. Can she blame it on the demon alcohol as Jack now seems to imply? Without its influence could he be a reformed character? Leopards and spots come to mind, but then she remembers that in the early days he *was* a kindly man…could he be that creature again? And if somehow he did rehabilitate, would she ever be able to trust him again? Not that his letter goes as far as to suggest a reconciliation.

As she re-reads his words it's his parting sentence of '..and, maybe I don't have the right to ask, and I understand if you refuse, but it would mean the world to me if you would visit me.' that weighs heavily on her mind.

She clutches the letter to her chest and sobs for what has been, what could have been and what on earth she should do next.

Chapter 22

I open one eye and take in the time – mmm, there's still time for a little snooze. As much as I love sharing a bed with Joshua - and I really do - I also enjoy him getting up for work and leaving me to splay my limbs and take up every inch of the bed. With the clock timed for a ten-minute snooze, I sink back into the bed and sigh. Ah, last night - what a magical night! How utterly romantic that he would take me to The Edge of The World, as we named it, (although by what we got up to 'The Edge of Heaven' might be more apt) and bring wine and a picnic. What a wonderful man, he is. So what if he's not ready to buy a house with me? I can live with that…at least I hope I can.

Barely closing my eyes again, the clock beeps its reminder that I need to get up and over to Gloria's house. Today is the day we don our deerstalkers to find out what Fliss is up to – and I'm praying that it's not something awful, for Gloria's sake.

I down a quick breakfast, shower and dress and then, after the obligatory fussing of Basil, I'm heading over to her house. As the bus meanders through the town I realise that I've never followed anyone in my life and have no idea if this crazy plan has legs – but there are some things you do for your pals without question.

Gloria, immaculately attired as ever in pale pink sweater and navy trousers, opens the door and ushers me in.

"Perfect timing," she whispers, kissing me on both cheeks. "Fliss is getting ready to leave. Maybe we can just stand here chatting for a bit."

"Excellent. How do you feel?"

"Incredibly nosey and slightly devious."

"Ha! Me too. Be good for you to put your mind at rest though."

"Mm hm. Oh, look sharp." Gloria clears her throat.

I look up to see Fliss gliding down the stairs. She is gorgeous with glossy golden hair that bounces gently on her shoulders and I honestly don't think I've ever seen such translucent skin. Your average woman on the street, she is not.

"Hello," she says.

"Hi, I'm Amy."

"Fliss." She says, smiling. "I've heard a lot about you. So nice to meet you."

"Yes, really good to meet you too."

"Mmm," Fliss says, glancing at her diamond-encrusted watch. "So sorry I have to run. I've got an appointment."

"Will you be home for dinner tonight?" Gloria asks.

"Yes, should be." She flashes me a brilliant smile. "Bye Amy, lovely to meet you."

"Same here. Bye," I say.

As the front door closes, Gloria and I first look to each other and then creep to the window to check Fliss' direction.

"OK, Operation Follow Fliss is a go." I say.

As Fliss' Audi disappears down the road we race out to Gloria's car and pull away quickly.

"Good grief, wheel-spinning – this is new," Gloria says.

"Needs must, Gloria."

Finding ourselves with two cars between us and our stalkee, we approach traffic lights.

I crane my neck to see her indicators. "Looks like she's going left."

"Excellent, thanks."

As we travel, cars turn off in different directions leaving us, at one point, directly behind her.

"I'm going to pull over, don't want our cover blown," Gloria says, tucking into a small layby. After a few cars pass she filters back into the traffic until eventually we find ourselves in the middle of town. Fliss turns into a large open car park and we follow suit, although we head to the far end. We remain in the car to watch Fliss pay for her ticket, return to her car and then stride off towards an alleyway.

Keeping in step, but far enough back not be noticed, we exit the alley to find a road of beautiful Victorian houses, most of which have been converted to businesses.

"We're doing well at this lark, aren't we?" Gloria says just at a moment when Fliss stops and turns around. We quickly duck into a doorway and feign interest in a window of properties for sale. "Oops, spoke too soon."

"I think we're okay," I say, peeping out to see Fliss continuing up the road. We leave the doorway to resume pursuit.

After a few minutes we see Fliss veer off up a wide driveway and disappear into a large detached property. We wait until she is clearly inside before we approach.

The sign on the wall simply reads, "The Belview."

"The Belview? That doesn't give us any clue about what goes on in there, does it?" Gloria says. "It could be anything!"

"Yeah, you're right. But there's one way to find out." I reach for my phone and type 'Belview' into Google.

As the page loads Gloria clocks my face. "Oh no, dear, what is it?"

I turn the phone for her to read.

"Oh my!" she gasps.

"Coffee, Gloria?"

"Yes dear. Expresso High, and I think I need a double shot."

Chapter 23

I take the seat opposite Gloria and put the two-shot espresso in front of her. In her current state I thought it was prudent to bypass waitress service and just order at the counter – sometimes you just need a quick hit. Gloria gulps back the drink and shakes her head, wincing.

"OK, show it to me again please," she says.

I get out my phone and pull up the Belview website. She scans through the drop down menus.

"Right," she sighs heavily. "So, we have breast enlargement, breast reduction, breast uplift, nipple correction, nose surgery, eye bag removal, facelift, ear correction, liposuction, cheek implant, chin implant, arm lift, thigh lift…dear Lord if they can lift it or shift it, it seems they will! But why? What does Fliss dislike so much about herself that she would resort to this?"

"No idea, she looks stunning to me. Great figure, lovely looks. I have no idea. But there again I don't get the whole plastic surgery movement. If it meant you lived longer then I could kind of get my head around it – but for fewer wrinkles or propping up a part of you that's drooped, I just don't get it."

"Yes, I agree." Gloria's brow knits. "You know, sometimes I just don't understand that daughter of mine."

"Are you disappointed that it isn't to do with getting pregnant?"

"Mmm a little."

I stir my coffee. "So what're you going to do?"

"Do about what?" Sam says, appearing at our table.

"Oh hi there," I say, looking up. "What are you doing here?"

"I need coffee," she says, shrugging her bag from her shoulder and sitting.

Gloria grabs the attention of the waitress.

"Aren't you supposed to be studying?"

"I am, I just can't hack the rancid coffee I've got at home."

"Very wise, dear," Gloria says.

We place our orders – I strongly advise Gloria not to opt for another double shot, but she tells me that she'd heard 'wired is wicked'. *She's so gangsta...*

"So, what are you going to do about what?" Sam reiterates to Gloria.

"Ha. Well, long story short, my daughter, Fliss, is home for a while, been having a few marital problems from what I can gather, and today...well, today I found out she's planning to have some kind of cosmetic surgery."

"What's she having done?"

Gloria looks blank. "I don't actually know."

Sam shrugs lightly. "Well, it doesn't have to be the full nip and tuck – could be something as innocuous as a chemical peel."

Gloria' eyes light up. "Hadn't thought of that. Thank you Samantha, maybe it's not as dire as I'm imagining."

The waitress brings our drinks.

"And how are things with you?" I ask, turning to Sam.

"Confused. I've been emailing with Jason this morning and I suggested we go to Basingstoke together for the conference and HE suggested sharing a room! All this time I've not been able to read him. Do you think he's just thinking about saving money? Or is he making a pass? One minute I feel sure he likes me, and the next, I just don't know."

"Hmm," I say, pondering the male species in general.

"It's so confusing." She slumps with a heavy sigh.

As we continue to knock about likely reasons for Fliss's makeover and Jason's likely motives, I realise how much I love the female bonding ritual of thrashing out problems – it may not lead to solutions but it certainly makes us feel better.

"So Amy," Sam says. "In the competition of 'who's got the most to moan about' what about you? And you're not allowed that miserable husband of yours."

"Ha! Well, if I have to have something…" *Do I come clean?* I sigh. "I mentioned to Joshua about buying Rose Cottage with me. You see, he has money saved for a rainy day, but it seems he's not ready to invest it in us."

Their slightly stunned faces indicate they didn't expect anything like this from Happy-In-Love Amy.

"Don't read too much into it, dear," Gloria rushes.

"Yes, I know. I'm probably just being silly." I look down and play with my teaspoon.

"It's the beginning of a romance," she continues. "You're still learning about each other. You both seem so well suited and so happy. Take baby steps and you'll get there."

"From little acorns great forests are made," Sam says.

"Don't think that's quite right." I frown.

"No, it's not," says Gloria. "But you get the gist."

"I do. To be honest, it's given me the jitters a little, and it's a bit ridiculous, as I don't even know if I'M ready to buy a house together. It's just that I want to believe that we're perfect and always on the same page – I don't want to think I'm ahead of him in the love stakes."

"Nonsense, dear. The man came back from New Zealand for you not knowing where you were in 'the love stakes' – that's quite bold, isn't it? You could've shot him down in flames!"

"Yes I know," I say.

The chatter continues and I think how I do know that – well certainly my head does. Much like Gloria's head knows that calling time with Brian is the right thing to do and Sam knows that she needs to play the long game with Jason. But once again I'm reminded of that vast difference between what goes on in our heads and what we feel in our hearts…

Chapter 24

'My dearest Dixbury Dancers, I have heard from Leanne Cork and she has assured me that your glorious piece will be in Tuesday's edition of The Tribune. I suggest you all buy as many copies as possible and revel in your celebrity. See you all Wednesday evening, usual time for competition rehearsals! I very much look forward to seeing you all then. Yours Bendrick'.

My heart races a little at the anticipation of the article. Who would've thought that me, Amy Gathergood, hairdresser to the residents of Dixbury, would be in the local rag for ballet dancing? This time last year it would have been unthinkable. Mind you, this time last year I was happily married, or so I thought, and had my life all mapped out. Just shows how life can flip on a coin and you can find yourself going in a whole new direction.

I relax back on the sofa and cast my eyes back over Bendrick's text. I smile at the use of the Queen's English with proper punctuation and salutations; there's not a 'LOL' or a 'PMSL' in sight - he really does belong to a bygone age. As a teacher, he frustrates me with his demands – we are not Royal Ballet dancers as we keep telling him – but he's sweet and his heart's most definitely in the right place.

Just as I go to put my phone back down, it rings.

Ah - Steve.

I draw in breath before pushing the button to answer. "Hello?"

"Hi Amy."

"Steve, how are you doing?"

"S'not easy," he says, his voice low and shaky.

"No, I'm sure it's not," I softly say. "She was a lovely lady."

"Yes she was. Judith and Mike are here and we're working through all we have to do."

"Ah, it's good you've got their support."

"Yeah, it's quite nice spending time with them, actually. We haven't done it since we were kids."

"Please give them my love."

"You can do it yourself…I mean...if you're coming to the funeral?"

"Oh yes, of course, I'd like to. When is it?"

"Eleven, Friday after next at St Mary's on Church Road."

"OK. Yeah, I'll be there. Is there a dress code?"

"Um, I don't know, I'll talk to Judith, she'll know. I do know it's only flowers from family."

"Right."

"So you can chip in with the ones I'm sending, if you like?"

"D'you think that's appropriate?"

He expels a long tired sigh. "OK, OK, fine, don't then. I was just trying to be nice."

"Look Steve, I –"

"No, it's fine, Amy." He pauses. "Erm, actually…" *Here we go.* "There is something I need to talk to you about. We went through Mum's papers and we've read the will and it turns out I'll have enough money to buy Rose Cottage." I hold my breath. "Amy?"

"Mmm?"

"Did you hear me? I can buy you out of Rose Cottage." Every fibre in my body wants to scream and shout and hang up on him. "You still there?" he asks.

"Yep."

"I'm sorry, Amy, but you're going to have to sell it anyway, so why not to me?"

"Because," I start, trying to keep the quiver out of my voice. "It was our home. Our marital home and I love it."

"But if you could afford it you'd stay there with Lover Boy, right?"

He has a point. "Yes Steve, you're right, I would. But the difference is that I wasn't carrying on with him behind your back. It's the thought of you with Justine and the baby here. Why can't you start afresh and buy somewhere else?"

"I would, but it's Justine – she loves it -"

"When has Justine been in my house?" He goes quiet as the temperature of my blood steadily rises. "Steve? When did Justine come here?"

"She came in once for a cup of tea and –"

"You brought her into our home? Oh My God, Steve – did you bring her into our bed?"

"It wasn't like that –"

"Really? So what *was* it like?"

"Like I said, she came in for a cup of tea."

"And where was I?"

"I don't know. It's not important."

"Not to you maybe, but it is to me!"

Blood thumps in my ears. I'm furious and wounded and heartbroken all over again. How could he do this? Bringing her into my home and more than likely into our bed? Does he have no morals? How many more times is it going to hit me that he is not the person I used to love? He's now nothing more than a deceitful liar and a shadow of that man. Damn him for still being able to cause me pain.

The constriction in my throat turns my voice to a squeak. "Steve, I can't do this. I'm going to hang up now."

"Look, wait, before you go, there's just one more thing..." I fear how he could possibly add to my pain. "…It's going to take a while for Daphne's money to come through, which means I'm not in a position to buy you out right now. So can we take it off the market until we're ready, please?

Oh I see – he's that man who wants his cake AND eat it!

I take a deep steadying breath. "Let me be clear. If I take that For Sale sign down, there's only one place I'll be sticking it…"

"Got it, got it."

"You've got such a cheek, Steve."

"OK, have it your way, Amy. I'll be talking to my solicitor."

"Yeah, good idea. Just be careful you don't shag her too."

"Talk to you later."

"Not if I have anything to do with it," I say, to the click of him hanging up.

As I lower the phone I catch sight of my face in the lounge mirror and realise that stress is not a good look. Amid the pronounced wrinkles there's thread veins, near-to-bursting vessels and jowls that hang almost to my shoulders. Damn him.

Basil, always so finely in tune with my emotions, moves to my feet and I kneel to stroke his silky ears.

"So that's it now then, Bas? Solicitors at dawn? Well, bring it on! And you know all that stuff I told you about how it's not you, and how it's Mummy and Daddy who've fallen out of love, and how Daddy still loves you and it shouldn't change how you feel about him? Yeah, forget it – go ahead and despise him."

Basil looks up at me with those almost black eyes and I'm pretty sure he nods.

Chapter 25

The texting frenzy went on for ages. Should we all meet up and read the newspaper article together? Where should we meet? As some of us work, what time suits everyone? No, we can't do it if one person can't. Yes, early morning would be good. What time does Expresso High open? What time will the newspaper be on the newsagent's shelf? Right, Tuesday morning, eight o'clock, Expresso High it is.

I arrive to find Julay and Marion seated with coffees, having already pushed two tables together to accommodate us all. Gradually the rest of The Dixbury Dancers file in and the last to arrive is Gloria who awkwardly takes the last seat left that's next to Brian. The waitress takes our order.

"Right, has everyone got a copy?" I ask. They all nod. "Shall we?"

The pages rustle as we frantically flick through.

"Got it! Page seventeen!" Josie announces.

More rustling and then we fall silent.

Before me is a full-page feature with four colour photographs in amongst plenty of writing and I settle back excitedly to read. *Oh, this looks good...very good...hmm, hmm...'Dixbury's own dancers'...blah blah 'practise at the village hall' hmm hmm...blah blah...oh wait a moment...no, no no* - "GERIATRIC BALLET! WHAT?"

Shocked and horrified faces briefly look up before returning to devour the article.

"Delusional?" Julay shrieks. "She's calling us delusional?"

"Where?" I ask.

Julay thrusts her copy under my nose, stabbing the offending text with her finger.

"Oh no," I say, reading how the delightful Ms Cork believes that ballet should only be for small children who grow up to be prima ballerinas, and that we are merely kidding ourselves that we can achieve anything of worth.

'...an assorted gaggle of swans of varying ages and abilities who are yet to grasp the art of grace, but who put their hearts and souls into it nevertheless... ' Marion reads.

"Who does she think she is?" Lucia says. "Patronising cow!"

"Indeed, and one who doesn't know that the collective noun for swans is a bevy, herd or flock, but never a gaggle! What kind of journalist is she?" Julay harrumphs.

"A bad one." Marion says.

"What does she mean, we don't have grace?" Catherine, our youngest, most shining protégé says, on the brink of tears.

"Darling." Her mother puts a protective arm around her. "This is the way of some of the press, unfortunately." She lowers her voice slightly. "And anyway, I don't think she's talking about you."

We pretend not to hear – it's true, Catherine is bathed in grace - the comment is clearly not aimed at her.

"Oh this sucks!" I say, reading more. "And look what she says about Bendrick! Third paragraph from the bottom."

All heads bob back down to read. One by one grimacing faces look back up.

"Flamboyant in dress and over optimistic in choreography," Brian says.

"The Pied Piper of ageing amateurs?" Lucia says. "Ageing amateurs?"

"Well that's kind of true, except for Catherine." I offer.

Lucia says "Well if it is then what's wrong with that anyway? Does she think we all wanna be Darcey bloody Bussell?"

"This is disgusting," Gloria says, tossing her paper to the table. "And those photographs don't do us justice either."

We all take another look. Catching the absolute right moment to photograph ballet is tricky – really tricky – an un-pointed toe, a spaghetti arm or Lego fingers become the focal point of the shot, and the inimitable Ms Cork has managed to capture all of those exactly. We look like idiot would-be ballerinas, and it seems that through our serious desire to dance ballet, we have left ourselves wide open to ridicule. We deserve better than this.

I was so grateful to lose myself in dancing; ballet was my salvation. If I hadn't started these classes my lardy derriere would be glued to my sofa and I'd be twenty pounds heavier from Chardonnay and Dairy Milk. Plus, I've met you guys – it really has been a win win." I choke back a tear, unlike Marion who has one rolling down her face. "Oh Marion, don't, sorry, are you okay?" I say, squeezing her arm gently.

"Yes dear, I'm fine," she sniffs. "You're right. I went through so much with Jack and I don't know how I would've coped without you all. It's what we do, isn't it, us lot? We stick together." She searches our eyes. "We're family."

"Oh blimey, don't Maz, you'll get us all going!" Lucia says.

"To hell with Leanne Cork – what does she know about doing something good?" Sam says. "She writes her gripey little piece, putting us down, making herself feel better, no doubt. I think it's her who has issues!"

"Yeah, but she's the one with the microphone, so to speak," Brian adds.

We slump in our seats, slightly dazed but indignant; this wasn't supposed to happen.

"Right," Gloria straightens up and takes charge. "It's done, we can't change it and it's upsetting, but there's always a silver lining."

"And that is?" I ask hopefully.

"I don't know, give me a moment…"

"Shall we re-read it and see if we can find some positives?" Josie asks.

"Yes, top idea," Brian agrees.

We scour the article trying to find something, anything, that's not damning or patronising. It's not easy.

"She does encourage people to support us in the Afton competition…" Josie says.

"And she does say that we've got all the gear," Marion says.

"Not sure that's a compliment, Maz," Lucia adds.

"Mmm, there's not much there then, is there?" I say.

"How about we buy up every copy?" Most of us nod slowly, considering Sam's suggestion.

"Yeah, cos that's not gonna cost much, is it?" Lucia says cynically. "And we'd have to cover the whole flippin' county."

"So, what do you suggest?" huffs Julay.

Lucia has no answer.

We all sit staring at the walls or the floor – anywhere except at the newspapers discarded on the table - wondering what the come back from this is. This was supposed to be our moment of notoriety – and now it's nothing more than a big fat embarrassment. How can something that started with such good intentions turn into something so ugly? I'm belittled and humiliated and looking at my friends I'd say they feel the same.

"More coffee?" Julay suggests.

"Make mine with cake," I say to a low rumble of agreement.

"Oh I almost forgot." Julay raises her hand. "I do have a crumb of good news. Bendrick told me that Helena's had her pot off and is now just using a stick. She's going to pop in to see us."

Small noises of approval ring around the table as we try to lift our sagging spirits, but I wonder if even Helena, our champion of inspiration, can turn this disaster around.

Chapter 26

"I like the way we deal with big-scale disappointment - two coffees and a giant slab of carrot cake for breakfast." I say, rubbing my stomach that's spasming from early morning sugar overload.

"Cake's always the answer," Josie smiles. "Oooh crikey," she says, looking at her watch. "Better get you to school, young lady." Both mother and daughter rise and put on their coats. "See you all tomorrow."

"I'd better get going too," I say, thinking how, after the two caffeine shots, I'll be speeding through the cut and blow-drys today.

One by one the dancers rise. Only Brian remains seated.

"Gloria has popped to the powder room." He gestures to her coat hanging on the back of her chair. "I'll just wait until she returns."

Lucia gives him a 'nudge nudge wink wink' look and we all bid our farewells and leave for our daily routines.

I head straight to Hip Snips and find Karen setting up whilst Gina is behind the reception desk, eyes down reading whilst filing her nails. When she sees me she quickly hides something under the desk.

"Mornin' Boss!"

"Morning Gina. What you got there?"

"Eh?" Gina couldn't lie if the world depended on it. "Nuffin'"

"G, you wouldn't happen to have a copy of The Dixbury Tribune under there, would you?" Her big Bambi eyes fill with sympathy as she nods. "Don't worry," I say. "I've seen it. We all met this morning at Expresso High and consoled ourselves with cake and coffee."

"It ain't all bad," she says to which I raise my eyebrows. "Oh alrigh' – it's bleedin' awful. Didn't she like you or summat?"

"I don't know. I thought it was going to be a gentle article, you know, encouraging people to join a community activity, that sort of thing. I certainly wasn't ready for the patronising and downright humiliating piece she's written. I feel like the laughing stock."

"Nah, nah, don't say that. You know wot they say abou' newspapers?" I look to her expectantly. "Today's news is tomorra's fish and chips, innit."

"Thanks, but I don't even want people seeing it around their cod."

"Ha! That'd make it a cod piece!" Gina howls at her own joke.

"Right. Okaaaay."

"Aw mate, wanna coffee? Cheer you up?"

"Coffee, no. Valium, yes please."

The door opens and the first customers of the day enter. One is carrying a shopping basket and sticking out of it is The Dixbury Tribune and I have a sinking feeling that this day is only going to get worse before it gets better…

***

"Erm, erm, I didn't want to leave without making sure you have your coat. Can't trust folk these days," Brian fumbles his words.

"Ah," Gloria says. "That's most considerate." She smiles gently at him and is once again struck with the realisation of how much she's hurt him. "Did the others leave then?"

"Yes, they all said goodbye. Jobs to go to and school for young Catherine."

"Ah, lovely girl."

"Yes, she is. I think she'll be the legacy of The Dixbury Dancers. I hope she mentions us in interviews when she's famous."

"Not sure I want to be in print again," Gloria says, eyeing the abandoned newspapers on the table.

"In the grand scheme of things this matters not one iota," he says, lifting one of the newspapers with a finger and letting it drop.

And there it is again, that grounding quality he possesses that draws her to him. The world could be crumbling around them and his would be the voice of reason. He's right, of course, one newspaper article doesn't matter – it'll all be forgotten in a week or two. Holding onto the important things in life is what counts, and sadly she knows that, one of those important things, for her, is him.

"Yes, you're right," she says, without meeting his eyes.

Brian exhales and Gloria shuffles in her seat.

"How are you?" he asks in a low voice.

She raises her eyes to his. "So-so." She sees his hand twitching and wants nothing more than to cover it with her own. "And how about you?"

He smiles weakly. "So-so."

She should leave, get up and walk away right now; break this bittersweet tension between them - but she can't. She likes sitting here with him; she's used to looking into his gentle eyes, laughing at his easy humour and enjoying…well, him! She mentally bargains to stay for ten minutes, reasoning that it can't do any harm.

"How are you liking our new dance?" she asks.

"Oh, very much. I do like it when we're practising for something specific – makes all that time at the barre worthwhile," he says, lightening a little.

"I especially like the rond de jambes – if we can all get in time!" Gloria gives a small chuckle.

"Out of all the things we have to remember, timing is most definitely my weakness,' he agrees.

"Oh I wouldn't say that - you never miss a beat."

"Ha ha – now that is funny! I am constantly trying to catch up with you ballerinas. Have you not seen me lolloping?"

"I have not." She shakes her head.

"Do you need spectacles, my dear?"

"How rude, sir!" she giggles.

Brian laughs and shakes his head gently. "Never miss a beat, ha!...I tell you what I do miss though..." He shifts awkwardly as Gloria feels the heat creep across her neck. "OK, look, I'd better get going," he says softly and with a sigh he gets up and puts his wallet in his back pocket.

"Of course."

"See you at rehearsals, my dear?"

"Absolutely."

He bows slightly before leaving. As Gloria watches him go she thinks that if this really is the right thing to do, if they are truly meant to be apart, why does she feel in such a tizzy when he's near? And why is her heart racing? And why is there a light sweat on her brow? And, moreover, why are her fingernails digging into her palm and causing her such pain?

Chapter 27

The morning light had flooded in through the voile curtains and, as usual, I felt a little ripple of happiness seeing Joshua lying next to me. I softly reached out to stroke his hair but my fingers got stuck in his matted corkscrew curls and I inadvertently woke him up.

"Ow!" he groaned.

"Sorry, sorry, sorry!"

He rolled over, squinted at the light and raised a hand to his head. "It is attached, you know." He gave me a half-asleep smile.

I moved closer and ruffled his hair.

"I know and I love it," I kissed his nose. "Although you might think about accompanying Basil to the groomer next time."

"Hey!" He'd started the tickle-torture of breathing down my neck.

"Aaaargh aaargh, get off me, get off me!" I squealed.

Lightly pinning me down, he raised his head. "You know, it's just occurred to me - I sleep with a hairdresser - why aren't you sorting out my hair?"

"I don't have industrial strength equipment?" He went to resume the tickling. "No, no no! I surrender, I surrender!" I held my hands up and he smiled.

"OK. Come here then." He pulled me to him and we laid entwined under the puffy duvet, warm and happy and slightly out of breath.

"I don't seem to be getting any fitter through all this ballet," I'd said.

"You will. Takes time, that's all."

"I know it's wrong, but with the newspaper piece and everything, I feel like my motivation has got up and gone."

"Aw, don't say that! You love dancing! You're good at it. Plus you're all mates now. This'll pass, you'll see. You've got the competition coming up and you'll all be back up there. Small minded journalism, that's all it is."

"What if we *are* just making fools out of ourselves?"

Joshua had raised himself up onto one elbow. "What? One lousy piece of writing and you think she's right? Who's to say whether you guys should be dancing ballet or not? Who makes the rules, eh? You all enjoy it, it *is* getting you fit." I raised my eyebrows. "Come on, where's Fighting Amy that I've come to know and love?"

"She's taking a rest." I scoffed. "Oh I dunno, I guess it's all this stuff with Steve…"

"Oh." He put his hand to his forehead. "I forgot, you're seeing that solicitor this morning, aren't you?" I nodded solemnly. "Are you sure you don't want me to come with you?"

"No, I'll be fine. But thanks for asking."

"I want to be there for you."

"And you are, Josh, you are."

And with that we'd kissed and disappeared back under the duvet. Which is why I now find myself sitting in Simone Bletchley's waiting room, sweaty, slightly out of breath, and precisely fifteen minutes late for my oh-so-expensive appointment. So much for creating the right impression.

The receptionist's buzzer sounds and with monotone flatness and dead eyes, she tells me, "Ms Bletchley will see you now."

I nod contritely and walk down the oak panelled corridor, through an oak panelled door to a room replete in oak panelling; definitely a gentleman's club vibe. Simone is sitting behind a large leather topped desk but stands to shake my hand. The height of the ceiling dwarfs this thirty-something petite blonde who is wearing a sharp tailored suit and the kind of square dark-framed glasses that are seen on pretty models in opticians' windows.

"I'm Simone. Nice to meet you." She flashes perfect white teeth.

"Hi, I'm Amy, so sorry I'm late," I say, offering my clammy hand and wishing I hadn't. To her credit she doesn't wipe hers down her suit.

"No problem. It just means we have slightly less time." She smiles kindly. "So, I understand you've received a divorce petition?"

From out of nowhere tears spring to my eyes. She perfunctorily plucks a tissue from the box on her desk and passes it to me.

"I don't know why I'm crying," I say.

"It's okay, it's okay. We'll take things slowly."

"I'm not that unhappy about it. I mean, I was, it was terrible and I was heartbroken when he left. He was unfaithful to me and then she was pregnant and then there was the awful Jeremy Kyle thing and then, to make things worse, he decides that he wants to buy me out of the cottage." *I can't seem to stop talking.* "But really I'd like to stay there with Joshua – he's gorgeous – he was supposed to move to New Zealand but he came back for me and we haven't been together for that long but you just know when it's the right one, don't you?" *Someone shoot me now.* "We get on so well and have a great time together and in fact he's the reason that I'm late and..." I abruptly stop to see her with one eyebrow perfectly arched, staring at me.

"Right," she says. "I'm glad we've cleared that up."

"Oh God, sorry." I can feel my cheeks burning beetroot. "Can we start again?"

"Why don't I ask you the questions and we'll take it from there?"

I nod gratefully and she then methodically goes through a list of questions that she must ask every sad prospective divorcée who comes through her door.

"OK. This petition he's filed, do you agree with it?"

I shake my head. "No, I don't. He had the affair but wants me to agree to unreasonable behaviour."

"To be honest, Amy, it's immaterial. You could issue your own petition stating adultery, but if he contests it, you could have a fight even before the main event begins. It doesn't affect the division of assets."

"That's what he said."

"So for ease and to let him 'win this battle', you could agree."

"Seems wrong."

"Yes, it does. But believe me, it won't go against you. In fact if you were to end up before a judge she or he would look favourably on your amiability."

I sigh. "Okay then."

"So, what about the property?"

"Right. His circumstances have changed, his mother died, and he can now afford to buy me out. But I really don't want that either. I love my home and hate the thought of him and his 'new family' in there. Because his mother's estate won't be sorted for a few months he wants me to take Rose Cottage off the market until he's in a position to buy it. I would rather it was sold to someone else. Is there anything I can do about that?"

She touches her glasses. "Hmm, it doesn't work quite like that. As you're still legally married to him you're entitled to half of his inheritance."

"Oh no," I shake my head. "I couldn't do that."

"I'm only telling you what's legally yours and what your rights are."

"Right." It wouldn't be right though, would it? I don't feel that connection of being married to him any longer – the man I married has gone and has been replaced by a two-timing philanderer who goes on Jeremy Kyle. "No, I can't go after his mother's money."

"OK then. What we could do, and it's a bit unusual, but we could offer him a deal; basically I write a letter stating how you won't pursue a claim on his inheritance if he will reconsider his decision to buy you out of the property. How does that sound?"

"Worth a try, I suppose."

"Yes it is. OK, leave that with me and I'll get a letter sent off today." Just then her phone rings. "OK, Madeleine. Hold on a moment." She looks up at me, cupping her hand over the receiver. "Sorry I have to take this call. I can either email you or you can make an appointment with my secretary for the end of next week. OK?"

"OK. Thanks."

She half smiles over the rim of her glasses. "And in the interests of punctuality, try to resist the charms of John."

"Joshua."

"Right." She nods and returns to her call.

I get up and shrug on my jacket with half an ear on Simone and her unintelligible legal speak. Solicitors eh? Guess *they* must understand each other. I head for the door passing framed certificates and photographs on a display table. Catching my eye is a photograph of Simone, in graduation robes, entwined in the arms of a man. Mmm, there's something familiar about him. Where do I know him from? I shrug, figuring he must just have one of those faces. Suddenly becoming acutely aware that I could be perceived as eavesdropping, I quietly leave and present myself to Monotone Madeleine.

"I'd like another appointment for next week."

"Right."

Keeping her eyes on her computer screen she drones, "Next Thursday, same time?"

"That would be perfect, thank you."

She writes an appointment card and hands it to me with barely a smile.

Someone likes her job…

Stepping out, I check my watch and calculate that I can take a leisurely stroll as my first cut and blow-dry isn't until ten thirty. I wander past the shops, stopping to browse here and there, thinking back through the appointment with Simone and wondering just how this divorce will pan out. The man in the photograph flashes through my mind; I'm on the brink of recognising him before it slips away again. Aargh, where have I seen him before? Work? One of Steve's friends? Does he work in a shop or a café? Or restaurant? Who is he?

Slowly realisation dawns on me. Oh no - I know who he is. I may have only met him once, but I'm pretty sure it's him….

And my next thought is how on earth I'm going to tell Samantha.

Chapter 28

With hardly any chatter in the changing room we file into the hall to find Bendrick and Helena with their heads together in the corner.

"Hello, you lot!" Helena looks up, beaming.

"How are you?" Marion asks.

Helena puts forward her plaster-less leg. "Getting there. And I'm feeling all the better for seeing you lot."

A general happy chorus goes up of welcoming her back.

As the chatter dies down, Lucia asks, "So, have you seen it then?"

Bendrick plasters on a fake smile. "Helena and I have just been discussing your moment in the spotlight."

"Would've preferred to stay in the darkness," Lucia quips.

"Tsk tsk, Lucia, you know the old adage; any publicity is good publicity. It's getting you known!"

"As ridiculous old biddies who are crap at dancing," she retorts.

"Now now, come come, let's be positive."

"Helena," Sam intervenes. "What did you think of it?"

She looks to Bendrick and then back to us and opts for shaking her head softly and lowering her eyes.

"Anyway, we have bigger fish to fry," he continues with aplomb. "The Afton competition is only weeks away and we have work to do to get us stage-ready! What we need is practise, practise and more practise!"

I scan the room to see Bendrick's words falling on deaf ears attached to heads hanging low; no one looks like they have the desire to walk let alone dance.

"Come on everyone, to the barre," Helena says, chivvying us along.

Bendrick drills us in our usual succession of tendus, pliés, fondu, developpés, frappés and grands battements until our bodies are warm. The phrase 'going through the motions' has never been more applicable – our bodies are moving, but our hearts aren't engaged.

As we conclude our session at the barre Helena walks with the aid of her stick to the middle of the room. "OK, I'm taking centre today. Bendrick, would you be so kind to demonstrate please?"

"Certainly madam."

"Right, before we get into the piece for the competition, let's really get moving. Who remembers being in the playground in infant school?"

"I don't think I can remember that far back," Marion mumbles.

"Did you play horses and gallop around?" Helena continues.

"Ha, yeah I did," I say.

"Me too," Sam agrees.

"Nah, more Postman's Knock for me," Lucia smirks.

"At infant school?" Gloria asks.

Lucia winks lasciviously. "Started young Glo, what can I say?"

"Well," Helena continues. "I remember holding the belt of my best friend's coat and the pair of us galloping around. And that's precisely what I want you to do now!"

"Hold a belt?" Josie queries.

"No – gallop!"

"Why?" Lucia asks.

Helena gives an exasperated sigh. "Because when a dancer wants to reach the heights she or he will gallop. Bendrick, please demonstrate."

Bendrick moves to a back corner of the room. He begins with one leg behind, his foot perfectly pointed. He prepares his arms outstretched and then moving forward, he leaps and his feet gather together in the air as he raises his arms overhead in a perfect oval. With his eye-line raised and soaring skywards he looks every inch the ballet dancer. He lands and then repeats.

"Gosh, that was magnificent!" says Marion, her eyes wide like saucers.

I suddenly realise that, with the exception of his minimal demonstrations, we have never seen Bendrick dance. From this exuberant display I'm guessing he was quite a big deal in his day.

"See?" Helena says, "The joy, the life, the energy, and the exhilaration?" Helena and Bendrick exchange smiles. "Thank you Bendrick, that was beautiful. Right, Dixbury Dancers, are you ready to try?" We all nod. "I'll put some music on for you to practise to, and Bendrick and I are here for help if you need it."

And so our galloping begins. I watch Catherine traverse the room effortlessly and then finish with perfect poise; poor Marion falling over her feet repeatedly, and Lucia propelling herself with such gusto that people have to flee from her line of travel. Gloria looks sleek and graceful and I think how, if she were an animal, she would make a fine horse. (I think better of sharing this – the comparison might not be perceived as a compliment.)

Sam joins me in a gallop and we both giggle that my posture is wrong - at least I don't think my bottom should be sticking out so much – balletic, it isn't. As we stop momentarily to grab some water *that photo* comes back to mind. Could there be another explanation? Simone's brother? A youthful looking uncle? A cousin? Hmm, relatives don't usually look that intimate. Whatever the connection, I think, the middle of a ballet class isn't the right place to bring it up.

"You enjoying this, Amy?" she asks.

"Mmm, not easy being a horse."

"Aw, Neddy, why the long face? Race you to the wall!" I laugh and then, tucking in my derriere, I join in pursuit.

From galloping we then spend the best part of an hour rehearsing our competition piece before Helena calls for cooling down. We all amble into our own individual space and begin the gentle stretches that finish class. We started this evening with low morale and now, as we come down from our endorphin rush, a cloud of gloom descends once again.

"And that's it for tonight, folks," Helena says, closing the class.

We all meekly clap, offer our thanks and turn to leave. There's no chatter, no giggling, no post mortem over what we found tricky or what we've managed to achieve. We are disparate and lost in thought – that newspaper article has a lot to answer for.

"Hold on please," Helena calls after us. We all turn back to face her. Leaning on her stick she takes a deep breath. "You asked me earlier what I thought about the article. Well I think it could have been kinder." She eyes Bendrick who nods his assent. "I think you're all doing marvellously. Are you all destined to dance at Covent Garden? No. But that doesn't detract from the fact that incrementally, in every class, you're all making improvements. They may not be huge, but a deeper stretch here, a stronger relevé there, a landed pirouette, a more pointed toe, a sharper frappe, a higher eye-line, a longer held balance – they are all improvements! Are you sitting at home on your sofas watching mind-numbing television programmes? Are you out in the pub drinking all evening? Do you choose to be here or do you choose to be there?" Lucia opens her mouth to answer as Helena continues, "That's right, you choose here! And you are all beautiful committed dancers who deserve to be here. You've earned your places in this corps de ballet. When that limousine broke down and we couldn't compete in the competition, did you give up? No! You all performed beautifully from your hearts! You did something of majestic greatness. Don't let the words of a burnt out hack take that away from you. That *article*," she spits the word, "wasn't flattering for anyone; it was a sloppy piece – anyone can mock, anyone can be sneering, that's easy! But if she had genuinely been interested in what you all do and had wanted to put her paper in a better light she would have portrayed you all as the gracious, hard-working dancers that you are. Any shame lies firmly on the shoulders of that bent-out-of-shape, past-her-sell-by-date journo and not on yours!" She smooths down her top, nods defiantly, taps her walking stick on the floor and turns to leave.

Lucia leans into me. "And *that* is what you call a pep talk."

Chapter 29

Gloria places her keys on the side table and kicking off her shoes, heaves a sigh. When did things become so distorted? What with Fliss and the mystery clinic appointment, the palpable tension with Brian and now the Dixbury Dancers feeling lack lustre and in disarray, life seems out of kilter and laden with stress.

"Mum? Is that you?" comes Fliss's voice from the lounge.

"Yes darling." Gloria enters the room to see Fliss sprawled on the sofa, glass of wine in one hand and a bar of dark chocolate beside her. "My, someone's having a good evening!"

"Ha! Yip!" Fliss raises her glass. "Just thought I'd have a pick-me-up."

"From what?"

"Life in general."

"Tell me about it." Gloria says, flopping down on to the large floral armchair.

"You okay?"

"Just a few things on my mind."

"Wanna share them?" Fliss asks. "Fancy one of these?" She holds up the half empty bottle of wine.

"Do you know, I think I just might." Gloria heaves herself up and crosses to the large wall cabinet and picks a crystal glass. "Make mine a large," she says, holding it out to be filled.

"Gosh Mum, it's not like you." Fliss pours the wine.

"That article in the paper – it's upset us all. I just don't understand why that journalist had to be so mean."

"Oh Mum, forget it – I have already."

"Well that's nice for you, darling, but it wasn't written about you."

"What I mean is it was so inconsequential that I've forgotten it. What was it you used to say? Fluff and nonsense?"

Gloria smiles. "I did use to say that, didn't I?"

"Many many times though my childhood…usually when some friend had fallen out with me."

Exchanging warm smiles Gloria asks, "Fliss, is everything alright with you?"

"Yeah, why shouldn't it be?"

Gloria takes a deep breath. "Dare I ask about Tim?"

"Ah, well, you know he bought those tickets for that ball? I've decided to go – it's the week after next. He's going to pick me up here and we'll travel to London together. Think 'date'."

"Oh darling, that's wonderful news."

"It is if it all goes according to plan."

"Which is?"

"Ah." Fliss taps the side of her nose.

"What are you up to?"

Fliss winds a silky lock of hair around her finger. "Let's just say I've seen a man about a dog."

Gloria spots an opportunistic wine-loosening-the-tongue moment. "Was the man in question in a large building on Bramley Road by any chance?"

"What?"

"I saw you coming out of one of those beautiful old buildings the other day."

The colour rises in Fliss' cheeks. "Did you?"

"Mmm."

"Okaaaaay. In that case, I might as well tell you," Fliss says, her eyes avoiding her mother's. "I saw a cosmetic consultant. I'm having some slight adjustments. You know, Botox, fillers, that sort of thing."

"I see. What are you having Botoxed and filled?" asks Gloria.

Fliss pouts her lips. "This."

"Your lips? Fliss! What's wrong with them?"

"Oh Mother, calm down. I knew you'd react like this – that's why I didn't tell you."

"Well pardon me for liking your face the way it is!"

"It's my cupids bow – this here." Fliss points to the middle part of her top lip. "It's been shown that this is the part of a woman that a man can't resist." She smiles suggestively. And then this," she scrapes back her hair to show her forehead. "These lines – they'll be zapped with Botox."

"Darling you have very few wrinkles!"

"And after next week I'll have none."

"You're getting it done next week?"

"Yes. Before the ball. I want to look my very best, you know, turn Tim's head."

Ah, that was the time limit...

"Fliss, darling, Tim loves you just as you are. I doubt he would approve of you doing this to yourself. Beauty is in the eye of the beholder."

"Yes Mum," Fliss snaps. "But the beholder isn't here, is he? The beholder is off playing golf and gawping at Lexy. I need to get us back on track and to do that I need to look my best."

"But I'm sure he'd want you looking as natural..."

"Mum! You don't know him. You don't know what he wants! I'm trying to save my marriage and the least you could do is support me."

"What? To mess up your beautiful face?"

"Who said I was messing it up?"

"Have you seen those women who are Botoxed and filled? They look poker faced – they can't smile for goodness sake!"

"Some of them look amazing and anyway I'm only having my forehead and Cupid's bow done."

"And you really think this'll get Tim running back into your arms?"

"I DON'T KNOW!" Fliss shouts, her fists clenched.

"Look," she takes a deep breath. "I'm really worried, Mum. He wants children and I can't give him them, so I have to make the best of me; make him want to stay for me. If that means a couple of minor procedures then..."

Gloria's heart wrenches for her child. Will Tim really be satisfied not having children as long as his wife is plumped and taut? Does it really work that way? "Why not talk with him, darling?" Gloria asks gently.

"I will. And with my face done I'll feel more...it'll give me a boost."

Gloria bites her tongue. Yes, cosmetic procedures will give a boost, but as she learnt from Stanley a long time ago, marital woes can only be truly resolved by communication. Stanley would say, "If it's left to stew it becomes soggy and if you store it up it'll go stale. If you've got something to say, just say it!' Gloria's heart pulls at how his method served them well throughout their marriage. She misses his no-nonsense love.

Fliss' phone buzzes. "Excuse me," she says, attending to a text, leaving Gloria staring at the cream and turquoise fleur de lis wallpaper. Are nips, tucks, injections and tweaks, she wonders, just the 'modern way' along with online dating, YouTubers and text speak? Or were her mothering skills somehow lacking to end up with a daughter whose self worth is so reliant upon her appearance?

Putting her phone to one side Fliss looks back at her mother. "Look, I know you don't understand, but I need to do this, Mummy. You may not understand it, but please just support me."

Gloria sadly nods and thinks how acquiescing to Fliss' demands is becoming disconcertingly too often and wonders whether, despite her daughter's troubles, at some point she might have to stay true to herself and not oblige. She sighs, knowing that time is not right now. "Of course, darling, of course."

Chapter 30

Group text: Julay, Samantha, Gloria, Marion, Josie, Catherine, Helena, Bendrick, Lucia, Brian.
Hi, this is Joshua from Amy's phone. This is TOP SECRET – Amy has her (trumpet fanfare) thirty-second birthday coming up and I have booked the room above The Swan on Saturday 28th April for a little surprise party. Would love you to be there! Please bring a song, joke, dance, story – or anything to entertain! Be there at 7pm and the birthday girl will arrive at 7.30pm. My no. to confirm is 07778 310999. Joshua.

Joshua hits send and, hearing footsteps approaching, throws Amy's phone on her bedside table, dives back under the covers and closes his eyes. He hears her heels on the floorboards circumnavigating the bed and then the sound of her phone and keys being picked up. Her hair tickles his face as she lightly kisses his forehead, and then her footsteps leave the room. Phew! Nice timing, he thinks, opening his eyes as the front door shuts.

He drifts in and out of sleep, thinking about how he's going to fill his Saturday. The garden could do with some work, the bathroom tap needs fixing and Sheila Skoda needs a bit of a clean. Slowly he gets out of bed and heads for the shower before sitting down to breakfast. Basil is happy as usual to have some company and sits at Joshua's feet, awaiting any crumbs that fall or opportunistic crusts that may come his way.

"Lovely here, isn't it, Bas?" Joshua says, looking around, stroking Basil's silky ears. "I know why your mum wants to stay."

He looks out at the garden that has, only this week, become peppered with sunlight yellow daffodils that are doing a great job of brightening the otherwise tired lawn and beds. He'll get the mower out, plus do some weeding and generally spur the garden into life ready for summer. With Amy not being particularly green-fingered he is perfectly happy to garden alone – just as he used to when he was with Sophia.

Hmm Sophia – he seems to be thinking a lot about her at the moment…

Amy's suggestion that he should share his nest egg to invest in Rose Cottage had arrived a bit out of the blue and had, quite frankly, knocked him a little. The last thing he wanted to do was upset her, but why did the thought of putting his savings into the pot make his gut wriggle? It's true they haven't been together for long, but that's not the reason. Is it because of what happened with Sophia? How he'd thought *she* was his life person, the one he'd grow old with, 'til death do they part and all that. He grimaces remembering what happened there; one minute they were on the road to happily ever after and the next she'd replaced him. Just like that. The heartbreak had taken what had seemed like an age to heal. Days and weeks of missing her blurred into months of painting on a false smile and telling everyone he was 'doing okay'. How he hated that façade and the sympathetic eyes of well-intentioned people.

It's always money, isn't it, he thinks. When Sophia sauntered off to her new life with her 'colleague', she took half the CD collection, half the chattels, and half the value of the flat. (Not forgetting, of course, the whole of his heart.) Yes, he'd invested in their relationship every way he could, financially, physically and emotionally – he'd been that sure. And is this why he's uncertain now? He's pretty sure that Amy *is* the one he's going to live out his days with – but a voice keeps nagging, 'if I was wrong then, I could be wrong now'.

But it's different with Amy, isn't it?

He smiles remembering the first time in the village hall when he'd looked through the glass and watched her in class. She was chewing her lip with concentration and laughing when she'd danced the wrong steps. Right at that moment his damaged heart was jump-started back to life. He's not sure about God but he sends out a silent 'thank you' to whatever or whoever brought her into his life.

He looks down at Basil again.

"What about you, Bas? Ever been in love?" Perfectly round dark eyes lovingly look up at him. "Hmm, you quite like that pretty Collie in the park, don't you? You old rascal." He ruffles the fur on his head. "Just going to wait and see how it pans out, eh, Bas?"

He rests his elbow on the table. Mmm, maybe that's the answer for him too? Just give it time? Time for insecurities and broken trust to be past problems and time to feel certain that he can give his heart completely again.

Drinking the remains of his tea, he sends out another silent prayer that whatever he's capable of giving right now is enough for Amy.

Chapter 31

Sam sits in the big-enough-for-two nook at the back of the library. The baby pink of her sweatshirt brings out the blue in her eyes but the sexy-sliding-off-the-shoulder style is now making her fidget; it may give off an air of casualness but does she really want to greet him baring this much skin? Yanking it up again for the umpteenth time she spots him making his way over.

"Hello there," Jason says, plonking his briefcase on the desk.

"Hi, how are you?" she asks, looking up at his neat attire, clean shaven handsome face and cropped ginger hair.

"All good, thanks. How about you?"

"Not bad at all, thanks." Sam watches as he sits and takes a notepad out of his briefcase. "Right," she continues. "I've got on with the corrections you gave me for the essay," She passes him the paper.

He starts reading and Sam studies his knitted dark eyebrows and rose coloured lips that purse in concentration. Resting her chin in her hand she admires his gorgeous-ness.

He looks up, beaming, breaking Sam's stare. "This is very good, I'd say it's a definite pass."

"Really?"

"Yes! You need to have more confidence in yourself, Samantha. You're doing great."

Sam blushes. "Thank you."

"I think this essay calls for a celebration."

"It's that good?"

"Yes! And as it's Saturday, once we've finished here why don't we head to The Joiner Arms for a drink?"

Sam gulps. "Sounds great."

The tutorial continues with Jason proffering praise and furtive glances and Sam reciprocating with blushes and giggles. Hands brush, warm smiles are swapped and at times he leans in far closer than necessary. Throughout the whole flirtatious tutorial their eyes keep meeting and messages are exchanged without being said. This is it, Sam thinks, everything I've been wishing for is finally happening…

•

With the early evening crowd out in force it is sheer luck that the small round table at the back of The Joiner's Arms is vacant. With two large glasses of red wine and a bowl of nuts, Jason and Sam have to lean in to hear each other above the pounding bass of something vaguely musical coming from the speakers above.

"So how's business?" Sam half-shouts in his ear.

"Good. Good. It helps that there aren't many physios in Dixbury."

"Yeah. You must be worried about when I qualify," she teases.

"No! Not at all. In fact I hope there'll be an opening at our place; my dad is always looking for physios with potential."

"Oooh, is that what I am? A physio with potential?" Sam grins.

"Plenty of potential," Jason replies, and with absolute solemnity adds, "I'd love to have you around."

"Really?"

He locks his eyes onto hers and touches her arm. "Yes, really." Bolts of electricity fire through her and her cheeks flush. In lieu of fanning herself (as she desperately wants to) she reaches for a handful of pistachios. The music comes to an abrupt end and, releasing his touch, he rests back in his chair and adjusts his glasses.

"So, Basingstoke?" Sam asks, fuelled with confidence.

"Ah yes. Have you seen the conference timetable? Really interesting seminars on neural stem cell research in spinal cord injuries, tendonopathy and the latest diagnostic technology - fascinating stuff."

Not quite what was meant... "Yes, it looks really interesting." Sam takes a sip of her drink.

"And what you said," he says, leaning in again, their noses almost touching. "About going together? I think that's a great idea." He lightly brushes her arm. "In fact I think it could be the best conference since twenty thirteen –"

"-What happened then?" she asks breathlessly, her lips almost touching his.

"Top seminars, interesting speakers, really futuristic metho -" Sam leans in the few centimetres needed to press her lips to his. After a moment he responds by cupping her face and kissing her firmly. Her whole body tingles in response and she only pulls away at the loud burst of the band plugging in their amplifiers.

Grinning, Jason says, "Why don't we get out of here?"

"I couldn't agree more."

They knock back their wine and head out into the street. Once outside he pulls her to face him and with his eyes glinting, he manoeuvres her against a wall, "You are gorgeous."

"You too."

Their breath is heavy as they lock together and ardently kiss in the street like a couple of teenagers who have no available bed.

"Yours or mine?" Jason asks, pulling back.

Sam thinks of her semi-damp cold little flat. "Yours?"

He smiles and moving towards her again but then steps back. "Aargh I forgot, I'm in the middle of decorating – can we go to yours?"

"If you don't mind a bit of a draught?"

He smiles. "I don't think we have to worry about heat." And with that he presses his body against her and kisses her like his life depends on it.

•

Sam wakes to see the morning light shining through her tangled hair that covers her face. Oh my, what a night, she thinks, puffing a lock of hair that rises and falls. She looks to where Jason had been sleeping – or rather, resting between bouts of wild sex – to find only crumpled sheets. Where is he? She hears the running water from her tiny bathroom. Ah - the shower. She sits and pulls the sheet up to cover herself, quickly tries to fix her hair and pinches her cheeks for a burst of healthy pinkness. Catching sight of herself in the dressing table mirror she realises the cheek pinching was needless – she post-coitally glows. She puts her head back on the pillow, fans out her hair, and dreamily smiles. *Oh. What. A. Night!*

"Morning," Jason says, entering the room, fully dressed.

"Oh," she says, pulling herself up on her elbows. "Do you have to go?"

"Sorry," he says, sitting on the bed and leaning over to kiss her.

"You don't have time to stay…for anything?" she says, pulling him down and pressing her body against him.

He puts his hands on her shoulders and gently pushes her back against the pillow. "Sorry Sam, I have to be somewhere else."

"On a Sunday?" Sam pouts.

"Yep. Thanks for a lovely night." He leans forward and pecks her on the lips and before she has time to say, 'see you at tutorial', he is gone. Sam frowns and sits up to hear the front door's bang leave an all-consuming silence. What? What happened there? A night of all nights followed by the dampest squib of a morning.

She quickly jumps out of bed wrapping the sheet around her and scampers to the lounge window. There she sees her knight in not-so-shining armour hot-footing it up the road like his feet are on fire.

What on earth did she say or do to make his exit so hasty? Sniffing her armpits and cupping her breath she accepts that she doesn't smell of roses – but who does after they've been swinging by the chandeliers all night? Eurgh! What should she do? She flops into a chair, digs out her phone and starts to text.

Amy! Huge SOS. Are you free please? Your house? Expresso High? Mine? ANYWHERE – I NEED TO TALK! S x

•

Dragging Basil along, not allowing him to stop for his usual every-other-bush wee, I race to find Sam perched on a bench at our agreed meeting place, near the boating lake in St Thomas's Park.

My heart sinks to my boots as she relays the whole story of her night with the apparent love-god, Jason. *Why didn't I tell her about my suspicions?*

"Oh Amy," she says, picking at a nail. "It was an amazing night, but…I woke up and he was in the shower, and then next thing I know, he's dressed and ready to run. And, oh boy, did he run! Left a Jason shaped hole in the front door where he bolted."

I listen to the age-old tale of lust and leaving and all I can think is 'bloody men'. Even though I have a fairly useful and good one, this kind of behaviour makes me cross. Is it always about sex for the man? And once he's filled his boots he can run away in them as fast as he can?

I can't help but wonder if this is how Steve started with Justine? A night together? Did he run away from her the next morning? Only to run back again, and again? Is Sam unwittingly 'the other woman'? I shudder. Guilt stabs me. I need to do something. But what? March into Simone Bletchley's office and demand to know her connection to the ginger fella in the photo? I can't see me doing that. But looking at Sam with her sad confused eyes and hunched shoulders, checking her phone for the umpteenth time, I know that I have to do something.

Chapter 32

Marion drives past the curled barbwire topped fences and up the sweeping drive to the visitors' parking area. She's never been to a prison before; even when her drunken brawling uncle was put away her mother had not let the young Marion accompany her to visit. Approaching the imposing cold stone structure, and then having the heavy iron gates lock behind her, she shudders with the thought of losing her liberty and, more pressingly, one of those riots happening today.

After security checks, a portly warden leads the mishmash of visitors down a corridor and into a bare stone-walled room lined with tables and inmates sitting behind them, waiting. Marion gives the guard her visiting pass and is directed to a table to the side of the room. She can hear her heart beating as she walks the distance to Jack who is smoothing his hair and shuffling his feet under the table. He looks up and smiles.

"Mari, you came."

"I did," she says hesitantly.

"Sit, please."

Marion perches on the chair and fans her skirt neatly. Raising her eyes she's struck by his prison look of pallid complexion, shorn hair and the cuts on his face that reveal the use of a half-blunt razor.

"How are you?" she asks.

Jack looks calmly around the room. "I'm okay, considering." He smiles sweetly, revealing teeth that have worn and yellowed.

"Thank you for your letter," she says with a small tremor in her voice.

"I've done a lot of thinking, Mari. I hope I explained it well."

"It was very clear."

He takes a breath. "How are you?"

"Er," Marion falters to think. "Happy, I suppose."

"Good. I'm glad to hear that," he says, although a flash of disappointment crosses his face. He leans across the table but the warden shoots him a glare so he quickly settles back. "How's that dancing coming on?"

Marion relaxes a little. "I'm still loving it. We're about to enter another competition – the one in Afton." He nods encouragingly. "And we have this new teacher who is pushing us on – really believing in us."

"Why would anyone not believe in you?"

Hmm, the journalist from the paper for one... "Indeed. We're quite a troupe."

"It's good you've got friends, Mari."

"Yes, good friends."

"Well, I'm sure you'll do great at the competition."

Marion fiddles with her cheap beaded necklace and looks down.

They embark on further small talk until eventually, except for the muted conversations of others, silence falls between them. Jack coughs lightly and his expression turns earnest.

"You know Mari, I am a changed man. I don't expect you to believe me, but I have sorted myself. I can't believe the way I treated you. You were the most important person to me and I let you down."

"Yes Jack, you did," she says, the tremble in her voice returning.

"But God has forgiven me. I'm on the right path and I'm never going to stray again, and I hope *you'll* find it in your heart to forgive me."

"A lot happened, Jack. It's not easy to snap my fingers and forgive you."

"I know that." He reaches for her hand on the table, but as she automatically recoils his expression pains. "I know I've hurt you, Mari. Too many times. But I honestly believe that I've been given a chance to put things right. I want to make amends. I will do whatever you want. You can walk out of here today and never see me again, if that's what you want." He runs his fingers through his hair more out of habit than necessity. "Argh, I was a selfish bugger – didn't give much thought to you."

"Jack," she says, tears pricking the back of her eyes. "That last night, you nearly killed me."

"But I wouldn't have, Mari. You have to believe that! It was the booze acting, the booze talking – it was all booze. But I'm clean and I'm not going back to it either." He looks deep into her eyes. "You know, the nights in here are difficult, but with my bible by my side and you in my heart, I get by." He twitches with a thought. "That was quite romantic for me, wasn't it?"

She gives a little sigh. "You used to be quite the romantic. You used to write me poems."

He looks down at his hands and gently laughs. "I still do, love."

A bell rings and groans fill the room before people start to hug or, in some cases, passionately kiss their inmate. Marion stands and a moment passes when she's not sure how to say goodbye; shaking hands seems too formal and yet a light kiss or a hug, inappropriate. Jack makes it easy for her as he leans over and rubs her arm.

"Bye Mari. Hope you come again."

And with that he turns, leaving her standing, watching as he follows the line of grey-clothed men back to their prison cells.

Chapter 33

Fliss pulls her coat on. "OK Mum, I'm ready."

Gloria looks at her daughter. "It's not too late to back out, you know. I really don't want to say, 'are you sure?' but are you sure?"

Fliss rolls her eyes. "Yes! I am! Thanks for offering to take me, but I wish you were more on board with this."

"Darling, I'm happy to take you and wait."

"Thanks." Fliss kisses her mother before they pick up handbags and keys and head out. Once in the car Fliss pulls down the sunscreen mirror and checks her appearance.

"Taking a last look?" Gloria asks mischievously.

"Ha! Yes, these wrinkles," she says, pinching her forehead skin, "will be no more."

"Wrinkles are the marks of a life well lived," Gloria says cheerfully.

"And all that old tosh." Fliss laughs. She looks at the radio that's playing Gloria's beloved classical music. "Does this radio only have one station?"

"Yes, and you can get your hand off that dial!" Gloria playfully raps her daughter's knuckles.

They drive the rest of the way with Fliss gazing out of the window and Gloria silently worrying that today's procedures will be the catalyst for Fliss to explore the world of cosmetic surgery further. The alarming images of those taut feline faced people rise up before her again.

Pulling up in the private parking area behind the clinic the two women get out of the car. Fliss takes a deep breath. "You do think it'll be ok, don't you, Mummy?"

"Darling, I'm sure it'll be fine. Come now." She takes hold of Fliss' hand. "Best foot forward."

Fliss links her mother's arm and as they make their way around the building a black BMW screeches past them into a space and a figure leaps out.

"Has it been done yet?" His eyes are wild as he grabs Fliss' shoulders.

"No, Tim, does it look like it?"

"Don't do it, Fliss! Just don't!"

"Hmph, like you care."

"I care that my wife wants to change her face; that she's about to take the risks of an operation and go under the surgeon's knife." Gloria raises her eyebrows and turns to Fliss. Tim looks from one woman to the other. "You *are* about to go under the surgeon's knife, aren't you?"

"Well," Fliss squirms. "The *doctor's needle* might be more precise."

"Huh?"

"I'm having some Botox and lip filler…"

"You're not having the whole works? Bandages and bruising and a face that won't smile again?"

Fliss shakes her head. "A few pin pricks and slightly tighter skin."

Tim takes a step back with his mouth slightly open. "So I rushed all the way here, to save you from a couple of injections?" Fliss warily nods.

He puffs a sigh of relief and shakes his head grimly. "Felicity Arnold, what am I going to do with you?"

"Divorce me?"

He shakes his head and then looks up at her. "So is this what it's all been about? You and your looks?"

"Sort of," Fliss pouts. "You hardly notice me anymore."

"I've told you a thousand times, I'm busy building a future - for us!"

"But you're never home…and I miss you."

He lets out a small exasperated sigh. "And I've missed you."

"Then why didn't you call me?"

"You told me you needed space!" He bats back.

Gloria rolls her eyes, checks her watch and coughs lightly.

Tim turns to give his mother-in-law a hug. “Hi Gloria, sorry, how are you?”

“Fine thanks, and I don’t want to break this up but it’s nearly time.”

“Stay with me, Timmy?” Fliss holds out her hand to him.

“Of course.” Just then his mobile rings. “Sorry, excuse me one mo,” he says, holding up one finger.

Fliss’s hand falls back to her side as she turns back to Gloria. “Thanks for coming with me, Mum, but I’ll be okay now; Tim can take it from here.”

Gloria nods and tugs Fliss’ arm. “But Fliss,” she half whispers. “How did he know?”

“Ah.” Fliss’ cheeks fill with colour. “That’s social media for you – I honestly didn’t think he checked his Twitter that often…”

“Ha! Well at least he got the message.”

“Yeah,” Fliss looks over to him as he winds up his phone call. “Don’t know what’ll happen from here on in, but at least he’s here.”

“It’s a step in the right direction.”

“Right, let’s get this done then.” Tim says, putting his phone back in his pocket. Fliss nods and takes his hand.

“Thanks again, Mum. See you later,” Fliss says.

“Thank you, Gloria,” Tim adds.

Gloria smiles and shoos them away. “Off you go, you’ll be late.” Watching them head to the door and seeing Fliss slip her hand inside his, Gloria suddenly has an urge to shout, ‘So, you don’t need me now, eh? I’ll go then, shall I? All the support I’ve given you, all the bending I’ve done, putting your needs before mine. Yes, fine, don’t worry about me now!’

She reaches her car just as bitter tears start streaming. Climbing into the driver's seat she bows her head to the wheel and giant sobs wrack her body. Reaching for a tissue from the glove compartment she blows her nose and catches her reflection in the rear-view mirror. 'So, Gloria,' she says quietly. 'Your spare room will be vacant again, ballet classes and lunch-dates with friends will continue and life will resume its normalcy.' She wipes away a line of mascara. 'But life hasn't been 'normal' for a long time, has it?'

She blows her nose with a resolute feeling that she can't abide by Fliss' requests any longer…but how? Her daughter is juggling a precarious marriage, the blow of not being able to have children and the misbelief that cosmetic surgery is, in some part, the answer to her problems. No, even though it feels like pandering to a spoilt child, she can't be the one to add to her daughter's misery.

Reaching for another tissue, she starts the car and the familiar feeling of guilt wraps around her. As she pulls away she thinks how the tears that are clouding her eyes should be for Stanley – but they're not – they are tears of frustration for not being able to 'fix' Fliss's life. And, if she is completely truthful, they are the tears of longing for a certain man who's still very much alive.

Chapter 34

"Gather round, gather round," Bendrick calls. "Right, this is it – your final rehearsal before the big day! How are we all feeling?" Most of us look to our feet. "Dahlings, come come, let's dance the piece all the way through and we can pinpoint any glitches and then put them right. By the time the big hand is on the twelve and the little hand is on the ten," he says, flicking his wrist over to look at his watch. "You will be performance ready!"

"In the A.M. maybe," Lucia mumbles.

"As we run through it," he continues, "I want you to believe you're on that stage. *Feel* like it's the night of the competition. All eyes are on you. You can smell the atmosphere."

"I hope that's all we can smell," Lucia quips.

"Thank you, Lucia," he says. "Actually, before we begin, I'd like to try a little experiment. I'd like you to stand in a line, arms length apart from each other." We shuffle into a row. "Now, dancing isn't just about the body;" he says. "It's everything within you and the space around you. So I want you to breathe the space!" He gesticulates grandly, appearing ever so slightly more eccentric than usual.

"Breathe the space?" Josie asks.

"Yes! With vocals."

"Are you asking us to sing?" Josie looks aghast.

"I'll show you." He raises his arms out to the sides and then begins what can only be described as the noise of a cow giving birth. He then starts to twist his body, his arms flying back and forth, exhaling the noises louder and louder.

Marion's eyes are on stalks, Julay's mouth falls open, Gloria bites her lip, Lucia stifles a giggle, Brian is doing his best poker face, Sam, Josie, Catherine just stare and I quietly smile at this heart-warmingly ridiculous man.

Finishing his demonstration, Bendrick looks at us innocently. “Ready to give it a go?”

“Why not!” I say and lift my arms.

As we slowly begin, it hits me that it is preposterously absurd but, at the same time, wonderfully liberating. We swing from our waists, let our arms fly, empty our lungs of stale air and inhale deeply, all in a great cacophony of farmyard noises.

“That’s it! Wonderful! Superb!” Bendrick shouts above the din.

We build quite a rhythm and somehow synchronise our sound and movement. We catch each other’s eyes and smile with the pure idiocy of it all.

“OK, that’s enough now, please,” Bendrick calls after a few minutes. We all wind down until we are left motionless with only our heaving chests panting. I, for one, am tingling all over. “Marvellous!” he continues. “Did you see that? Did you feel that? It was magic! You performed as a group, perfectly in time.”

“Shame that’s not our performance piece,” Gloria jokes.

“Swinging cows – who’d’ve thought!” Marion says in wonder.

Bendrick smiles. “Never underestimate the momentum, the energy and the power!” He walks to the stereo leaving us all wondering if that sentence was supposed to have an ending. Exchanging shrugs and smiles we move to our starting positions.

As we try to perform his challenging choreography I suddenly want to be a swinging cow again. I look around at my fellow dancers’ faces, taut with concentration, and I realise how we use all our might to please this teacher who wholly believes in us. At one point, using every ounce of strength to hold a tricky balance on demi pointe, Bendrick calls, “Smile and breathe, Amy, smile and breathe!”

SMILE? AND BREATHE? I have to balance my weight on one leg, the toes on the foot positioned at my knee have to be pointed, both legs have to be turned out, I have to engage my core, arms must be controlled by my back muscles, my fingers have to be soft, tailbone has to be down, my hips square and even, I have to lift out of my waist but keep shoulders down, my breastbone must be open, but my ribs mustn't flare – and on top of all that he wants me to SMILE AND BREATHE?!?

Purely out of respect I try, but in truth I'm grimacing like a rabid dog. "Lovely," he says and quickly moves on.

At the end of the first run-through he has notes for each of us. Marion needs to raise her eye-line, Brian must be mindful of his sickling foot, Julay needs to hold the arabesque until the end of one particular musical bar and so on. We stand around, slightly out of breath, with our hands on our hips taking in his every word.

"So, the coupé into the chassé," Gloria asks. "Where do I look?"

"Up, dear lady, always up. Let the audience follow your eyes to a mythical invisible point far in the distance – let your gaze take them there."

"What are the arms in the pas de bourée?" Josie asks.

"This and this." He demonstrates unfolding one arm then the other.

"How many counts for the port de bras?" Marion asks.

"Four."

"If I land on my jacksie in the pirouette, what do I do?" Lucia asks.

We all laugh. "There will be no falling on anything." He smiles. "Any errors will be in the blink of an eye. Let's run it again – I want you to remember your corrections and, this time, I'm not going to say a word."

"Reckon you can manage that, Benny?" Lucia says.

He smiles curtly and crosses to the stereo. "Right, I'm going to turn the music up loud and I would like you to make your entrance and then perform for me."

We all congregate at the back wall. We are about to do the same dance, in the same hall, with the same one-man audience, and yet knowing that this is the last rehearsal before the actual competition I suddenly have a massive dose of the jitters.

"I need the loo," I say, crossing my legs.

"Me too,' says Sam.

Josie exhales nervously. "This is it, then."

"Well, until the night." Marion says practically.

"Let's show him we can do it," Catherine says.

"Even if we can't," Lucia chips in.

"OK ladies, positive feet forwards," says Brian, and with that, the musical introduction of strings and piano blasts out and we take to the middle of the floor.

Chapter 35

I open the door to Wood and McMillan's, check the wall clock and inwardly high five myself for my punctuality. As Monotone Madeleine raises one syllable above the rest in her welcome, I'd say she's glad to see me. I take a seat on one of the leather chairs in the waiting area and try, once again, to form a plan. Hmmmm. Now, my mother, God rest her soul, always told me to tell the truth. 'It doesn't matter what kind of fix you're in, Amy, always tell the truth," she'd say. "Lies lead to lies.' I think she was right…for most situations, but do you think telling my solicitor that her boyfriend/partner/husband (God forbid!) has enjoyed a night of carnal activity with my friend might be a little too much?

Madeleine's intercom buzzes and her dead eyes look up. "You can go in now." I smile politely, thinking how intonation really is overrated, and head into the office.

"Amy, come in." Simone waves me over.

"Hi, nice to see you again," I say.

"How are you?"

"On time."

"Ha! Duly noted. Right, let's get down to it. I contacted Mr Gathergood's solicitor and received a reply only yesterday. I do hate it when they delay like that – a bit of game playing," she says conspiratorially. "Right, they have come back saying…" she looks to her screen and reads, "because you have agreed to the terms of the divorce, and you aren't seeking a claim on his inheritance, he is willing to agree to leave the house on the market and if a buyer does come along before he receives his inheritance then it can be sold."

My nose wrinkles. "That's big of him."

"Well, at least there's a chance it won't be him buying it."

"True. Although judging by the little interest we've had so far he probably thinks he's on to a safe bet."

"Yes, probably. But you can chalk this up as a little win." She smiles kindly.

"OK. What happens now?"

"Division of assets."

"Right."

"If I can give you this," she says, passing a thick white form across the desk. "His solicitor will give him one. You have to put down all your assets, your income, pension funds etc, and Mr Gathergood will do the same. Then we exchange forms and start the financial settlement."

"Ah, the 'who get's what' part."

"Yes – as there are no children involved it should be quite straightforward. Were your incomes comparable?"

"Yeah, not too dissimilar."

"I only ask because if he earned a lot more than you we could make a request for maintenance. Oh no, you have the fellow who waylays you living with you, don't you?" she says with a glint in her eye. "That's out of the question then."

"Ha. Joshua, right."

"Yes. Right. So it should be a straight fifty-fifty division of assets. For this part of the process the more that you and your ex can agree between you then the easiest, and, I have to say, cheapest it'll be in terms of solicitor fees. If you can't agree we can arrange mediation..."

Then it happens again, out of nowhere, my throat constricts and tears force their way out of my eyes. Hard as I try, I just can't seem to shake the notion that getting a divorce is just another way of saying that my marriage failed; I failed. "I'm so sorry," I sob.

"No, no that's fine. It's perfectly natural," she says soothingly, passing me the obligatory tissue.

I fight to regain self-control. "It's just painful."

"Hmm, I know."

"You've been divorced?"

"Me? No."

"Lucky you." I sniff into my tissue.

"I'm not even married," she says. "Well not yet anyway," she adds, just loudly enough for me to hear.

Quickly wiping my nose I take my moment, "Are you getting married?"

"Yes I am, actually. It's all choosing flowers and favours and learning how to waltz at the moment." Her face turns a pretty pink.

"Ah, it's soon then?"

"Yes, August." She allows herself a wide smile before checking herself back to professional mode. "Sorry, the last thing you want is your divorce lawyer cooing about her forthcoming nuptials."

"No, really, it's fine. It gives me, er, renewed hope. Who's the lucky man? Is he a solicitor too?"

"No. He's a physiotherapist."

Oh.

All the hopes that the man in the photo could be an overly friendly brother/cousin crash around my ears. My heart plummets as I damn my suspicions for being right. Finding myself in the unusual situation of having strong feelings of disgust towards a man I haven't even properly met, I can only think to say, "Oh how nice."

"Anyway, sorry, back to you." She puts her glasses back on. "When you've completed the form, return it to me. I would also recommend talking with Mr Gathergood about dividing the chattels etc."

"We have kind of discussed it; he doesn't want much but I'll check with him again. Thanks."

"Great." She leans forward over the desk. "And I have to say you're doing really well. It's not an easy process but you're getting through it like a trooper. OK?" I nod, feeling the recipient of teacher's praise. "Now, I won't need to see you again unless there are any hitches which hopefully there won't be. So I'll stay in email touch, OK?"

I nod, thank her and we bid our farewells.

As I step out into the crisp daylight I think how I like her; she's gentle and kind…and judging by her doe eyes, very happily in love. She seems like the sort who, unlikely as it seems for a divorce lawyer, wouldn't hurt a soul and yet she's about to hitch her wagon to Jason's. Philandering Jason. Wham-bam-don't-give-a-damn Jason. Why do good women choose wrong men? So, he's already betrothed - no wonder he sprinted from Sam's bed.

Passing the row of shops raising their shutters for the day ahead I wonder what on earth to do with this minefield of information? Do I have a moral obligation to tell Sam? Yes, of course, I do. But supposing I tell her and in her blind infatuation or for whatever reason she doesn't believe me? I wouldn't be the first messenger in affairs of the heart to be shot. I've seen it happen before and I can't do it to her – or to me.

So that only leaves me with one option.

And tomorrow, after Daphne's funeral, I know just where to find him.

Chapter 36

I arrive at the draughty church early, as the last thing I want is to get caught up in the funeral party. I'm here to pay my respects to Daphne, a lovely lady, who was always kind to me, and for that I can squeeze in the back pew and keep a low profile.

The church gradually fills up with a few faces I know, but none that I know well enough to sit with. I wave at one old man I recognise as Daphne's neighbour but he looks straight through me. I lower my hand awkwardly and bury my head in the order of service - he clearly needs to go to the opticians.

Eventually the vicar asks us to stand and Daphne's coffin is brought in, carried by Steve, his brother, Mike, and four pallbearers. Justine and baby Beyoncé follow behind as does Steve's sister and respective family members. I idly view them taking their seats in the front rows and consider how, even as little as a year ago, I would have been down the front too. Do I wish I were still part of this family? I was always very fond of his relatives - I've known them for years - but the link to them is broken, and my place is now here at the back. Beyoncé lets out a little cry and my heart jolts. When am I going to get over him being a father?

'All Things Bright And Beautiful', a touching tribute from Mike and a rousing 'Jerusalem', and we are heading out into the drizzly day. With burials I have a theory that when we open the ground, something triggers in the universe to start the rain – I have yet been to an interment where it's stayed dry. Mind you, it does feel appropriate. I stand at the back of the group amongst the black umbrellas (and the flowery one from someone who obviously didn't think they'd be using it today) thinking how, when it's my turn, I want mourners in black clothing, wailing and crying loudly enough to drown out The Last Post. Oh - and with Joshua supine over my coffin. *Dramatic – moi?*

As soon as the vicar has finished, people rush back to their cars to escape the downpour.

"Are you coming to the wake?" Steve's sister, Judith, asks as she rushes by, her umbrella flapping in the wind.

"Er, I wasn't going to."

"Please come, Amy. Would love to catch up."

I really don't want to go... "Okay. See you in there."

•

Entering the Tudor beamed pub I throw my umbrella onto the pile of equally battered umbrellas and, shaking the rain from my hair, I grab a sherry from a standing waitress. *I'm going to need this.* I look about for somewhere likely to sit – I really don't want to be near the main family. *I wish I knew someone else here...anyone!* After a couple of sips of the copper coloured firewater masquerading as sherry, I see Judith making a beeline for me.

"Come on Amy, come and sit with us," she says, squeezing my arm and engineering me over to her family table. I start to relax and apart from when one of her boys calls me 'aunty' and then pulls himself up short and says, 'do I still call you that?' I have to say I enjoy seeing them all again. I pride myself that Steve's family always liked me...even if it turns out that Steve ultimately didn't. And just as I'm thinking of the devil himself, he sidles over.

"Thanks for coming, Amy," he says, standing awkwardly behind an empty chair at the table.

"Of course. I loved Daphne very much."

"I know," he says.

Looking crumpled around the edges and with red-rimmed eyes I can't help but feel sorry for him. "You doing OK?"

"Not bad. Look, I know this probably isn't the time but can we have a quick chat?"

I look to Judith who nods encouragingly at me. "Well, I was going to be off soon, but yeah, I've got a minute."

I get up and bid my goodbyes to Judith and her family. Cries of 'keep in touch' are appreciated but, in my heart, I know they are just cries – it's too difficult. Steve leads the way to the front of the pub and out into a small grey-stone lobby.

"So," he says, taking a deep breath. "You've seen your solicitor, right? You know that I've agreed to keep Rose Cottage on the market and if someone comes along I'll agree to sell it. I'm leaving it in the lap of the Gods!"

"Very admirable and spiritual."

"No need for sarcasm."

"Sorry."

"I thought it'd make you happy?"

"It does. Thanks." *Why am I thanking him for just being decent?! Is he thanking me for foregoing Daphne's money?*

"My solicitor mentioned about dividing things up. I already told you what I'd like, didn't I? Apart from that there's nothing else. But my solicitor says there's value on household goods so we need to work that out and split it."

"How much exactly do you think we'll get for a slightly melted plastic spatula?" He gives me an exasperated look. "Well, seriously!"

"Yes seriously, half of that house is mine!"

"Nice how you remember that now. Shame you didn't when you were waltzing out of it to Justine!"

"You're never going to get past this, are you?"

"Oooh, let me think, you go behind my back with another woman, have a baby with her and expect me to be 'over it' in a few months?"

"Look, I came back, I wanted to make another go of it – it was you who called it quits."

I sigh, softening to his truth. "Doesn't stop what you did from hurting." He looks down. "Okay, fine. I'll draw up a list and write estimated worth – don't expect to get rich on your half though, okay."

"Okay. And I do want shared ownership of Basil."

I exhale. "Hmm, as I said, we'll talk more about that when you're not living in a flat." He nods. "Right, if that's all, I'd better be off."

"Sure. Thanks for coming." He looks up at me through his dark lashed eyes. "It means a lot to me."

"I didn't do it for you, Steve," I say softly. "I did it for Daphne."

I put my shoulders back and exit the pub with as much dignity as I can muster. And it's only when I'm half way up the road and the heavens open once again that I remember my battered brolly.

Chapter 37

Afton Village Hall houses a creaky brown parquet flooring that's seen better days and a stage that looks capable of collapsing at any given moment. But credit where credit's due and that's to the organisers, who have packed the place to the rafters, although, as we put our heads around the door, the ratio of competitors to spectators isn't clear.

"Blimey, thought this was a minor competition," Lucia says, staring around at the crowded hall.

"Big fish, small pond," Julay says. "Easier to win a small competition and then you're more confident to try the bigger ones like Dixbury Does Talent."

"Mmm, you could be right," Sam says.

"Are you looking for registration?" a woman sporting a sharp haircut, glitzy cardigan, clipboard and a name badge, asks.

"Yes please, dear lady," Bendrick answers.

"This way then. Please follow me."

We fall in line to a tiny room off the main hall where we check in, pick up our competitor ribbons and are then told that we are the fifth act to perform. In the meantime we are advised to 'sit in the audience and enjoy the show'. We take seats at the end of two rows and browse the printed programme.

"OK, dancers," Bendrick says, getting our attention. "I suggest that when..." he looks at the programme, "one, two, three, four, 'Jenny's JamJar Jingles' are on, we go out for a quick warm up and then wait around the back until it's our turn." We all nod. "Until then, let's, er..." he looks dubiously at the programme again, "enjoy the show."

Turning back to face front, Sam whispers, "If this show is as dire as it looks on paper d'you think we're in with a chance?"

"Ha, could be!" I laugh.

Just then a man wearing a tux and a frilly shirt circa nineteen seventy-two appears from the wings.

"Good evening ladies and gentlemen, boys and girls, and welcome to The Afton Village competition." The audience applauds. "Thank you. We're honoured to have an array of acts to entertain you here tonight, but before that, let's meet the judges." Familiar music rings out.

Oh no, they're not doing X Factor…

Four people who look just shy of collecting their pensions appear holding hands. The two women in the middle appear to have been dipped in sequins and one of the men is wearing a box jacket suit. The other chap has his trousers pulled up high around his middle and is sporting a V-neck white t-shirt that accentuates his fine moobs perfectly.

Good Lord, they are.

Whoops and cheers go up as the compere introduces Arthur, Deidre, Pat and John who, after being helped down the stage steps, are eventually put in their seats. The first act of the night, optimistically called 'The Comedian' opens with some slightly off colour observational humour. Sam and I exchange looks.

"Guess what?" she whispers out of the corner of her mouth. "I heard from him."

I look at her. "Who?"

"Jason. He texted me last night."

"What did he say?"

"Sorry about running off in a hurry, said he had things to do and has a lot on his plate at the moment."

Hmm, yes he does.

"I see. Are you seeing him again?"

"Got a tutorial next week. It's cool, you know, even though we haven't planned a date, I know we'll be together again – I can just feel it."

"Right."

I curse my lack of action. The day of the funeral I had planned to go to his physio practice, but after crossing swords with Steve I just wasn't ready for another awkward conversation. And now I feel really bad. The longer he messes around (literally) with Sam, the more it's going to hurt her. I mentally vow to confront him first thing Monday morning; he has to sort this out – both Sam and his fiancée deserve better.

The Comedian, who needs to be sued under the Trades Description Act, shuffles off to make way for Beth Underwood who gives a blinding rendition of O Sole Mio.

"How was Daphne's funeral?" Sam asks, as we applaud the mighty opera singer.

"It was okay. Nice to see some of Steve's relatives again – not so nice to see Steve. You know, even though I ended it the last time, it still hurts. I think if he didn't have a child it wouldn't be so bad."

"Amy, give yourself time. It's not been that long."

"But I have Joshua and I'm happy with him – why am I still getting upset about Steve?"

"It was a long relationship – one you invested your all in. Of course it's going to hurt. My friend whose husband left her said it took a good two years to feel okay about it."

"Two years? Urgh!"

"I know. Mmm. Now, who's this?" Sam asks, looking down at her programme. "Ah, Girls Alive."

We sit, mouths slightly open, watching five girls, no more than twelve years old, writhe around in little more than crop tops and loin cloths, holding their microphones suggestively and pouting through red lips.

Oh my.

"Their mothers should lock them up," Julay hisses from the row behind.

"What? They're the best so far!" Lucia says, jiggling in her seat in time to the thumping beat.

"Are you blind as well as deaf?" Julay retorts, to which Lucia pulls a face.

"OK dancers," Bendrick says, leaning forward. "Time to get round the back."

"Oh," says Marion in earnest disappointment. "Aren't we going to see any of Jenny's JamJar Jingles?"

"'Fraid not, Maz." Lucia grins. "Not unless she wins and gets to do an encore."

"And we certainly don't want that," Bendrick says under his breath.

We convene to the small backstage area and Bendrick takes us through our drills. To warm our bodies we jog on the spot, bounce up and down and do some basic barre exercises. We remove leg warmers and wraps to reveal our all black tights, leotards and, with the exception of Brian in shorts, georgette skirts. Black costumes for Swan Lake didn't sit quite right with Julay who, when questioned it, was told by Bendrick that 'the audience will expect white, sequins and feathers and so we're going to shock and awe them from the start.' Julay hadn't looked in the least convinced.

"Right then, danseurs, it's nearly show time!" he says, with impromptu jazz hands. "You're all wonderful students and now is the time to show your grace, your poise and your elegance to the audience. Keep your eyes up and the smiles on your faces. Go and show the good people of Afton just what The Dixbury Dancers can do!"

We hear the applause for Jenny.

"Gotcha Benny," says Lucia.

As Lucia signs herself with the cross Bendrick looks slightly aghast but then gathers his all to give one last rally cry, "Do. Me. Proud!"

We hear our introduction and begin moving on to the stage to take our positions. I'm poised stage left when Marion flies past my eyes having tripped over something en route. She stumbles into place and out of the corner of my eye I see Bendrick in the wings lowering his head into his hands.

Standing in the darkness, waiting for our cue, I hear Lucia whisper, "Whoever stuffs this up the most has to buy the first round after."

And with that the music begins…

Chapter 38

Swan Lake we're supposed to be doing, right? Not a comedy sketch, not a parody, the absolute straightforward, modified-to-suit-our-abilities, Swan Lake.

Mmm – I wonder if the audience realise that.

Judging from their laughter I don't think they do.

OK, so I miss a step and land in the style of that baboon that I'm so good at impersonating; Marion trips again and head butts Julay's stomach and Catherine almost falls off the stage by misjudging a jump, but, and I can't stress this enough, we are not doing this for laughs! Even the relatively simple steps go awry, and as for our nemesis of pirouettes, we don't manage to land even one elegantly between us. But it is only after Lucia's multiple leaps across the stage (a little heavy footed maybe) that the first giggles begin. As our tour de force continues the giggles turn to chuckles, and then morph into laughter and, for a section of the audience, some belly laughter breaks out.

'Keep smiling', Bendrick had said and so we do. Our achingly fixed smiles reveal teeth gritted in determination. Each error increases the volume of their laughter and the intensity of our smiles. If I felt that we weren't the laughing stock after the newspaper article – we are now.

Giving silent thanks to God/The Universe/Time Itself that our dance has reached its conclusion, we stand in our finishing poses as the crowd applauds, albeit with a large section of them shaking their heads in disbelief. I'm grateful that Joshua isn't here due to a friend's emergency plumbing situation, but, as I scour the room, I'm utterly crestfallen to see Helena at the back. I can see the disappointment in a smile that stops short of her eyes.

We bow quickly and exit the stage.

"Well, well, a brave effort," Bendrick says, greeting us, his smile also not reflected in his eyes.

We turn to him slowly.

"Bendrick, that was the cock-up of all cock-ups!" I say.

"A comedy of errors," Gloria chimes in.

"Sadly lacking," adds Marion.

"A right load of old boll…"

"Thank you, Lucia," he cuts in. "Come, come danseurs, don't lose heart! The judges haven't made their decision yet and if you win you'll get that encore opportunity to have another go."

"I don't think I want one," Catherine says softly.

My heart goes out to her. She's the one here who will have a future in dance; she doesn't need a knock-back like this. Josie puts her arm around her daughter. "This is a one-off darling, you'll see."

Bendrick coughs and as I turn back to him I think I catch a look of genuine sorrow. He has taught us so much and I'm torn between feeling disappointed that we've let him down and a little angry that he set the bar too high. "Come on then," he says. "Shall we go and watch the rest of the show?"

Just as we're gathering up our belongings, Helena appears.

"Hello, you lovely lot," she says, as we all turn to greet her.

"You're here!" Marion says.

"Yeah, sorry I missed the beginning of the show, but I got here just before you came on." An embarrassed silence falls. "Look, I know how you're feeling, believe me. I did a show once where we were doing a character dance in a line – similar to the cygnets in Swan Lake – and I was in the centre and completely messed up. I trampled on my fellow dancers' feet and said, 'aw balls!' very loudly." The tension eases as we laugh. "The conductor looked up, unable to believe what he'd heard. And do you know what made it worse?"

"It got worse?" Josie asks.

"There were scouts in from a few ballet companies. It was supposed to be the night I was spotted; all my dreams were resting on that performance. I imagined finishing the night with a newly signed contract in my pocket and instead I ended it drunk and throwing up in a cab."

"Well, I guess the night's still young for us then," Lucia jokes.

"What I'm saying is, this is part of dance, part of being on stage, everyone has a bad night where nothing goes right. But we can't let it play on our minds. Whatever the outcome of the competition tonight, tomorrow morning you will get up and go on. Tomorrow you'll remember all your work and effort and the possibilities of what you can achieve. You'll focus on how you *usually* dance and the grace you bring to the stage." We all nod meekly. "Come on, let's go and watch the rest of this show." She smiles encouragingly and we follow her out.

After the interval we endure four more acts, (although following our atrocious performance I'm less critical,) before Mr Nineteen Seventy-Two reappears clutching an envelope.

"OK, ladies and gentlemen, boys and girls, I have in my hand the names of the winners." Lots of 'woos' and cheers go up. "So without further ado." He opens the envelope and squints at the page. "In third place is..." Drumroll. "Blazes." The ensemble of, now very happy, fire breathers make their way to the stage to collect their prize. We applaud. "In second place and runner up is…" Drumroll. "Jenny's JamJar Jingles!" Jenny looks close to tears as she makes her way to the stage and then tries to take the microphone to make a speech. Clearly not keen on that idea Mr Nineteen Seventy Two steadfastly grips it and only lets her utter a brief 'thank you'.

"And finally, the moment you've all been waiting for…the winning act of The Afton Village competition…" We look to each other, knowing that it is the longest shot possible that he'll call our name. "Beth Underwood!"

We clap with as much gusto as we have – which isn't much.

"Tonight sucks," Lucia moans.

I nod. “You can certainly say that again.”

Chapter 39

"Come on Mrs Mope, let's go," my beloved says, the evening after the competition.

"You've got to admit I've good reason – you didn't see the performance but my God, it was humiliating," I say, grabbing my handbag and following him out to the car.

"A couple of wines and a bite to eat'll make you forget your troubles."

"That's your answer to everything."

"Damn right – it works!"

He pulls away and Aretha Franklin comes on the stereo.

"Aw, I love this," I say, starting to sing along quietly.

"Me too, so would you mind?"

I smack his arm. "Oi!"

"Amy, blessed with the gift of dance, you may be, but singing?" I poke my tongue out at him and sing louder. "Woman, you're hurting my ears!"

Still giggling we make our way into the quaint beamed pub: the site of our very first date. Momentarily disappointed that 'our' table is occupied, we take another near the large leaded light windows at the back.

"Your usual, madam?" he asks as we browse the menu.

"Ham and cheese platter to share and a large white, yep, wouldn't have it any other way!"

"At your service." He half bows and grins and heads off to the bar.

I look around at the sepia framed photos hanging on the walls and the flock wallpaper and think how this place will always hold a special place in my heart – it was the start of our love story. I'm looking around and haplessly smiling to myself when my eyes land on a couple at the bar.

You have got to be kidding me!

"Here you go," Joshua says, placing my drink down. "Hey, what's up?"

"Look!"

"At what?"

"There," I gesture to the bar. "The fella with that girl. Do you know who that is?"

He follows my hand. "Not a scooby."

"Jason! As in Sam's Jason. My God, why do I keep finding out things about that man that I don't want to know?"

Joshua gives him the once over. "I presume that's his bride to be then?"

"No, it's bloody not. Oooh I tell you, I was planning to go by his work tomorrow morning but I might just have a word now." I start to get up.

"Whoa, whoa, easy there tiger." Joshua grabs my arm to pull me back to my seat. "You don't want to be causing a scene in a pub, do you?"

"Ah no, maybe not." I think for a second. "D'you think I should wait for him in the car park?"

"Amy, no! Look, it's great that you want to support your pal – but you don't have to sort this out. You don't even know who she is – she could be his sister!" I look at him quizzically and he sighs. "I'm no psychologist, and shoot me down if I'm wrong, but do you think you're getting upset about this idiot's infidelities 'cos of Steve?"

There's a reason they call it a light bulb moment. I sigh heavily. "You'll never cheat on me, will you?"

"Why on earth would I want to do that? Why go out for a frankfurter when you have a sausage at home?"

I laugh. "Joshua Milne, you KNOW that's not the phrase."

"Aargh, sausages, burgers, steak – it's all meat to me." We both laugh. "So, what you gonna do?" He nods towards the couple.

"You know, I thought it would be best to confront him and give him the chance to sort it out, but now I think he's forfeited that chance. I don't want him to be able to redeem himself; the two timer."

"Or technically," he nods to the bar, "three timer?"

I purse my lips at him. "I'm going to tell Sam that she's found herself a right player. I'll tell her everything, and to be honest, I think I'll feel better for it."

He raises his glass to clink mine. "I think you will too." As the platter piled high with bread, pickles, olives, hams and cheeses arrives he says, "So, what's happening with the house?"

Eugh, do we have to talk about this? "Didn't I tell you? Steve has agreed that if a serious buyer comes along before he gets his inheritance then he'll agree to sell."

"Just gotta hope for a buyer then."

"Yep, or a Lottery win."

"That'd help if you played."

I laugh. "I know."

Smiling, he leans back in his seat. "Ten to or twenty past?"

"Eh?"

"We just had a silence and my dear mum says that when that happens it's either ten to or twenty past."

I check my watch. "Your dear mum is wrong, it's twenty-five to."

"Dammit, what else has my mum lied to me about?" he mock frowns.

"Mine used to tell me that when the ice cream van had its music playing it meant that they'd sold out."

"Oooh brutal! One Christmas Eve my dad was getting the ache that me and my brother wouldn't sleep so he banged a door shut and told us that he'd just shot Santa."

"Ha ha ha, my God, what kind of a family do you come from?"

"Ha ha. I'd like you to meet them – seems only right as we've been co-habiting for weeks!"

"I'd like to meet them too."

"I'll arrange something after…" He stops.

"After?"

"Well, we've got your birthday coming up this weekend – so after that. I hope you haven't booked anything."

"Nope, nada. Why? What you got planned?"

"You and me, food and drink."

"Perfect."

"Yes you are." He looks down at the platter. "When we've licked the plate clean how about I take you up to our little spot?"

"What? The Place In The Clouds?"

"That's not what we called it!" He laughs.

"No, it's not. But what *did* we call it?"

We both sit and ponder and then shake our heads.

"Blimey Amy Ballerina, if we both can't remember something like this, how're we gonna cope when we're old and grey?"

"Hair dye and post-it notes."

"Ha! I like a woman with a plan. Come on, eat up before I forget what I've offered."

Chapter 40

Julay peers out of her diamond leaded window at a decidedly dull April day. It looks like someone has swept a misty grey paintbrush across the sky and, even before setting a foot outside, she can tell that the air is hanging low and damp.

"I'm just popping into town," she says, zipping up her navy quilted jacket. "Is there anything you need, dear?"

"No thanks. I'm going to get some washing done this morning and then I thought I'd vac round," Marion says.

"OK, well I shouldn't be long…" The house phone ringing interrupts.

"You get off, Julay, I'll get it." Marion gets up.

"Thanks."

Julay is gathering her belongings and checking herself in the hall mirror as Marion picks up the phone.

"Hello."

"Hello, could I speak to Marion Travis please?" a voice says.

"Speaking."

"Hello Mrs Travis, this is Joan Smithfield from the Eastern Region Victim Liaison Service. I'm calling in connection with your husband, Jack. Is it a good time to talk?"

Looking up to Julay, Marion fakes a smile, points a finger to herself and mouths, 'it's for me'. Julay nods and smiles and, with a quick wave, leaves the house.

Marion clears her throat and returns to the call. "Yes, it's fine. How can I help?"

"Jack has a parole hearing coming up and I've been asked to compile a report for the board. I met with him last week to discuss his case and he happened to mention that you've been in contact with him and that things are affable between the pair of you."

"Well, I only visited him once at the prison." Marion stutters her words defensively.

"It's okay, Mrs Travis, I'm not saying you shouldn't have. It's not that unusual for the victim and perpetrator, especially if it is a marriage, to re-engage. I just wanted to explore the status of your relationship. And get your opinions of him."

"I see. Can I ask why?"

"Well, the parole board will look at Mr Travis' crime, his behaviour since being incarcerated and his future prospects. I just need to get a full picture."

Marion sighs. "Well, Jack wrote to me. A long letter full of begging for forgiveness and telling me that he is at one with God. I didn't plan to visit, but I suppose I went looking for closure."

"And did you find it?"

"I don't know, really. It was reassuring to hear that he wants my forgiveness."

"It's an important part of rehabilitation," Joan says.

"I was surprised actually. He's not the old Jack that I knew thirty years ago, but he's not the violent drunken Jack either. I think he's quite a new man."

"Thank you, Mrs Travis. I shall include that in my report. You know, the board will certainly look favourably upon the prisoner making amends for his actions. And even better if the victim is seen to be amenable. It goes part way to indicate a reformed character."

Ping! The light bulb flashes on. Marion feels her heart pick up a pace.

"Could I ask how long Jack has known about this parole hearing?" she carefully asks.

"Oh, erm, let me just check my notes." Marion clutches the phone wire as she hears the rustle of papers. "He's known a couple of months."

Marion's mind gallops back through the timescale of events and, sinking into the hall chair, she's consumed by deep suspicion. *All about forgiveness, eh? Or all about just getting out of prison?* A shiver runs down her spine. "Right, if there's nothing more?" Joan goes on.

"Er," Marion says. "There is something else. What if it's an act?"

"Hmm?"

"You know, surely people would do or say anything to get out of prison?"

"Yes, that's why there are reports from various professionals who are involved with him; to make sure we get the full picture. It's a multi-disciplinary process."

The gnawing in Marion's gut won't stop. "I see."

After the obligatory end of conversation etiquette, Marion replaces the phone, slumps in the chair and views her shaking hands. What has she done? How has she let him back in her life only to fool her once again? 'God' and 'forgiveness' are powerful crowd pleasers, but, in themselves, might not have been enough to secure him an early release. Now with the victim's testimony, *her testimony,* surely they will throw open the wrought iron gates and celebrate his freedom with him?

And what then? When he's got his liberty? Will New Jack persist or will he disappear at the first sight of a whisky bottle? Leopards and spots, leopards and spots.

Choosing to calm her dizzying mind with the washing, she goes to the basket and picks out a bundle of dark colours. Heading for the machine, and hearing a loud thud from outside, she jolts and finds herself on the floor. Sitting amongst the dirty items strewn around her she realises that it was only the bin men, but she also realises that she hasn't jumped like that, like a petrified squirrel, for a long time. Gathering up the clothes she curses her gullible nature that seems to have transported her right back to where she started – and that was never a good place to be.

Chapter 41

Gloria glances at the clock on her dining room wall. Hmmm, I should be in ballet, she thinks guiltily, but Fliss had wanted a last evening, just the two of them, and it would've been churlish to refuse.

"Hope you like it," Fliss says, placing a large casserole dish onto the gold trivet. She lifts the lid, "Ta da! Chicken cacciatore à la Felicity!"

"Oooh marvellous - it smells divine. Thank you."

"No, Mum, *thank you*, for everything." Fliss serves both plates whilst Gloria tops up their wine.

"So, what time are you off tomorrow?" Gloria asks.

"First thing. I want to get home and see what kind of a mess Tim's left it in." She softly laughs to herself.

"It's good seeing you happy again, Fliss."

"You can tell, eh?"

"Now that the Botox has calmed down I can."

"Mum!"

Gloria giggles. "I hate to admit it, but you do look fantastic."

Fliss grins widely. "See I told you!"

"Yes, yes," Gloria concedes, laughing. "Right," she says, raising her glass. "Here's to a fresh start!"

"And facing it all with a new face!" Fliss laughs.

Pushing aside her reservations of plastic surgery solving marital woes, Gloria sips her wine and smiles for her daughter's renewed happiness.

•••

"Can we pause it for a moment, I need a wee," Marion says.

"Of course," Julay says, reaching for the remote control as her housemate dashes out of the room. She stares at the freeze framed figure of Sergei Polunin in full grand jeté flight and feels a stab of guilt that they're not in class tonight. Ugh – that god-awful newspaper article followed closely by their scrappy performance in that stupid competition – it's all too much humiliation. And, despite the affection she holds for him, she wasn't even able to bring herself to notify Bendrick that she wasn't going to be there tonight.

"This is nice for a change, isn't it?" Marion says, scampering back into the room, and grabbing the vodka bottle to top up her glass.

Julay nods. "Yes, it is." She carefully eyes her friend. "Did you want to go tonight, Marion?"

"No dear, I told you, I'm quite happy here," she says. "The dancing hasn't exactly been going well, has it?"

"No." Julay sighs wearily.

"That's a big sigh, dear. You okay?"

"Not really, no. In fact, Marion, I've been thinking…I'm not sure if I want to dance anymore."

•••

Lucia lifts one leg out of the duvet and raises it up.

"Great pins you have Luchi," Geoff says, as he lifts one of his legs to copy.

"You too, Geoffois – what mine have in shape, yours make up for in hair."

"You cheeky mare." He laughs. "So, remind me, why don't we do this every Wednesday?"

She turns her head on the pillow to him. "Well, I'm usually in ballet class."

"And why are we playing hooky?"

"Everyone is on such a downer – it's just not fun at the moment."

"Oh dear." His smile fades from his handsome face. "I feel partly responsible; it was me that started that whole newspaper thing."

"Aw, Geoffy, it's not your fault," she says, stroking his chest hair. "You didn't know the skank would slag us off. And anyway, you certainly didn't have a hand in our slapstick dance routine. The girls've taken it really hard."

"Isn't there a fella in there too?"

"Yeah – Brian – one of the girls." She shrugs.

Geoff smiles and runs his finger down her cheek. "Don't you worry about it, Luchi, they'll all bounce back."

"I hope so." She looks up at him suggestively. "Talking of bouncing back – you ready for another go, big boy?"

A lascivious smile crosses his face. "Come here, you little minx."

Squeaking mattress springs topped with squeals of joy fill the room.

•••

Sam switches off the television and heads to the bedroom to change into her running gear. 'If I'm not dancing I need to be doing something,' she thinks, as she pulls on her trainers. Grabbing her door key and water bottle she heads out to pound the pavement.

It's a warm spring evening with the scent of cherry blossom filling the air and she easily gets into her stride even without her usual motivating music. Tonight she needs silence and time to get her mind straight about Jason, although she seriously wonders if she can be objective about matters of her own heart.

When she is a few streets along her mind wanders back to *that night.* She may have had other lovers but no way has she experienced the passion, desire, and sheer delight – the hat trick of pleasure - that she shared with him. Although, now thinking about it, it may have lacked tenderness and it wasn't particularly romantic, but maybe that will come later. Hot fiery sex is usually the way these things start, isn't it?

She stops momentarily to retie her laces and then takes the dirt path up by the cemetery. So, she thinks, since their night of thrills he has loosely explained why he ran off and they've arranged another tutorial for Friday, so what's the next move? He's not exactly bombarding her with messages or flowers, but his texts are flirty and keen. Hmmm. Surely he would've dropped off the radar completely by now if he weren't interested? Maybe that geeky side of him is just a little shy and maybe she has to be the one to instigate things?

Right, that's it, at the tutorial she'll ask him if he wants to accompany her to Amy's surprise party – she'll lay her cards on the table and show him she's interested - then the ball will be firmly in his court.

•••

"Arms in fifth and balance," the ageing ballerina calls to the young girls. Josie surveys the room filled with slender young bodies clad in black leotards and pink tights. Is it just her or does Catherine really stand out?

Josie wriggles on the hard bench and takes another sip of coffee. She watches her daughter pay close attention to instruction and then elegantly execute the required steps. Josie feels the tension in her own belly – if Catherine passes she'll be accepted into one of the best ballet schools around and will have the greatest chance of a successful career. But does her daughter realise the sacrifices that have to be made? When her friends are out partying or just hanging out together she will be rehearsing; when she forms an interest in anything outside of dancing it will be denied to her – such is the enormity of this commitment. It really is all or nothing.

"Mum, it's all I've ever wanted," her daughter had said on the drive over.

"I know, darling, but it's such a commit…"

"…Commitment and you won't be able to have a boyfriend, and your life won't be your own and you'll get bunions, blah blah blah. Yes I know, you've told me a hundred times, Mum."

"As long as you're sure."

"I am."

Josie chuckles to herself, 'my little headstrong girl.'

"You!" Josie looks up to see the teacher pointing to Catherine. "You've got it, could you please demonstrate to the others."

Josie gulps as Catherine, blushing deeply, steps forward into the middle of the room.

•••

Brian picks up his ballet shoes bag but stops as he reaches his front door. He sighs. How did ballet class go from being the highlight of his week to something to be endured? It's not just the disastrous newspaper article or the shambolic performance – it's seeing Gloria... how his heart aches.

He thought he'd be able to handle just going back to being two people in a ballet class – but were they ever just that? Wasn't there always a spark between them? Having lived most of his sixty some years as a single man, her emergence into his life has given him the greatest joy – and now the greatest sorrow. They were so happy in each other's company, enjoying meals, theatre trips and other such outings. He'd confided his feelings to his niece and she'd told him it's called 'friends with potential'. He'd liked that very much.

He walks slowly back to the lounge and, still clutching his ballet shoe bag, sinks into the armchair. He can't face class tonight. His old heart is too bruised and he needs to start building a wall to protect his feelings. He must learn to treasure the memories he has of times spent with Gloria and, at the same time, learn how to let her go.

•••

'Oh My God, am I late?' I think as I quickly throw on my leotard and tights in the empty changing room. A quick check on my phone says I'm not, but I rush into the hall anyway.

"Amy! Good evening," Bendrick says.

"Hi, am I the only one?"

"So far, yes," says Helena. "Let's give them a few minutes."

So we do. We wait. And we wait. And the polite conversation dries up pretty quickly – it seems that avoiding the group's recent failings is tricky for all of us.

Five minutes turn to ten and then to fifteen.

"Private lesson?" Helena asks me cheerfully. *Crikey, we always are a small group but at least usually there's the notion of hiding at the back.* "I'm happy to help if there's something in particular you'd like to work on?"

"I really don't mind," I say. *Please, please make one of them cancel the class*. "But if you both have other things to do?"

"Nope, nothing," she says brightly. We both turn to Bendrick to find him looking dejectedly at the floor. "Are you okay, Bendrick?"

"Amy." He turns to face me. "Where is everyone?"

"Bendrick, I really don't know."

He swallows hard and tears line his eyes. "Oh, this is all my fault. I've pushed them away, scared them off, gave them too high a mountain to climb."

"Bendrick…" Helena begins in protest.

"You entrusted me with these fine dancers," he says, turning to Helena. "And I've let you down. I wanted to stretch them, for you to return to the helm to improved, blossomed dancers. I wanted them to explore their limits and surpass them, but I fear I've done the opposite."

I want to tell him that he has hit the nail squarely on the head. His goals for us were insurmountable and now we have not only lost our way but also our confidence. Helena wouldn't have put us up there, attempting steps that were beyond us; she designs dances we can execute with ease to highlight our strengths. I want to tell him all of this, I really do – but I don't. He may still be wearing the bold frills and colourful necktie but his crumpled face, quivering lips and toupée sitting slightly off kilter today, make my heart soften.

"Bendrick, I'm sure them not being here is nothing to do with you, honestly," I say, looking him squarely and kindly in the eyes. "It must just be one of those things."

He nods his head. "It's irrelevant anyway, as now you're back," he says to Helena. "I won't be needed any longer. I shall gracefully bow out."

"Oh Bendrick," she says softly. "There's always a place for you here if you want it."

"You're too kind. But I think my work here is done." His eyes are downcast.

"If you want to leave, that's fine," Helena continues. "But please don't go with a cloud over your head. Come next Wednesday when, I'm sure, all the dancers will be here and we can give you a proper send off. Mmm?"

"Very well, madam."

They hug and he bids his farewells and crosses the hall. As we hear the main door close, Helena turns to me.

"Right Amy, we need to do some texting and calling and get our disheartened troupe back together again – and whatever happens, we need them here next Wednesday!"

Chapter 42

"OK, Gina, I won't be long," I say, sweeping out of Hip Snips for my lunch hour.

"You jammy cow – you know Rep-tile Dave is due in, don'tcha?" she calls after me.

I laugh over my shoulder and disappear out of the door and up the street. I literally have one hour to break it to Sam, in the gentlest, kindest way, that the fella she shared *the* night of her life with, is nothing more than a low down dirty bottom-dwelling rat. *Hmm, this is not going to be fun.*

Sam is already waiting in Expresso High.

"This is a welcome break!" she says, closing her lever arch file.

"Been hard at it?"

"Yep, trying to impress my mentor." She grins.

Oh, she looks so happy…

"Yeah, how is that 'mentor' of yours?" I ask, sitting down.

"Well, I've had some texts – all good – and I've decided that I need to make the next move. I'm going to ask him out." *Oh crikey.* "You're always telling me life is too short and you have to go after what you want, so I'm going for it!" *Oh God, I do always say that, don't I…*

"But Sam…" The sound of my phone buzzing madly in my bag interrupts me.

"Sorry," I say to Sam, fishing it out of my bag and hitting the answer button. "Hello."

"Mrs Gathergood?"

"Speaking."

"Mikey from Johnson's Estate Agents here. How are you?"

"Fine thanks."

"Good, good. We've got someone who wants to view your property."

"Oh great."

"Yeah, only prob is the lady can only make tomorrow mid morning. Is that okay?"

"Er, I'm working, sorry, there'll be no one there." *Hells bells, get the house 'viewer ready' by tomorrow? Not a chance.*

"Well, if you can drop in a key here, we can show the viewer around?"

Darn it. What excuse do I give now? "Er. Well, erm, okay, I suppose so. Look, I'm in town at the moment so I'll drop it in on my way back to work."

"Sound. See you then. Thanks, bye."

I hang up and turn to face Sam.

"You were saying?" she says.

Grrrrr, I really don't have time for this now. In fact why did I think I could do this in an hour? This kind of news needs extensive hand holding and stoic, friendly shoulders for crying on – I can't just tell her and walk away.

"Nothing that can't wait. Do you mind if we grab something and run? Wanna walk with me to Johnson's? It seems I have a viewer tomorrow and they want the key to show the person around."

"That's great news. Yeah, suits me fine, I need to go that way to the stationers anyway."

We purchase a couple of 'yuppie sandwiches' as Sam calls them, and saunter along the high street, chatting between bites.

"Oh yeah," I say. "I need to talk to you. I was the only one in class last night."

"Oh no!" Her eyes widen in horror. "Oh how awful – what happened?"

"Well, Bendrick got really upset, he's blaming himself for pushing us all too hard."

"He's got a point."

"I know, but I felt so sorry for him - he's only been trying his best, don't you think?" She nods. "So he's convinced that everyone didn't show up 'cos of him. He's handing the reins back to Helena and sloping away!"

"Blimey, he did take it badly," she says, taking a mouthful of pulled pork and pesto.

"Yeah. When he'd left, Helena and I divvied up dancers and I have you, Julay and Marion to contact, to ask, nay, BEG you to come on Wednesday. If he *is* going, we have to give him a send off. What's happened has happened and we just need to give him a positive note to leave on."

"Yep, course I'll be there. I'm quite fond of him, you know."

I nod in agreement. "Me too."

We turn the corner and file into the ultra modern estate agents. The woman at a glass desk directs us to Mikey who is seated near the back. The grey with splashes of orange décor generates a youthful vibe and Mikey, who at first glance looks about twelve, fits his surroundings perfectly.

"Hi," he says, jumping up like an eager puppy and thrusting out his hand.

"Hi, I'm Amy Gathergood, we talked on the phone."

"Ah yes, Amy, take a seat." He gestures to the gunmetal low stools and looks to Sam.

"Oh, this is my friend, Sam." They nod and smile.

"Right," he says, dragging his fingers through his long fringe. "Let me give you the lowdown on your viewer, s'cool?"

"Thanks," I say, starting to disentangle my front door keys from my overloaded key ring in a Rubik's Cube style.

He pulls the information up on his screen. "Right, so, first time buyer, no property to sell. The lady's renting – so could happen pretty quick. All looks pretty sick, eh?"

"Er, absolutely sick."

"And dope," Sam adds and I kick her.

"Anything specific you'd like the lady to know about your house?"

"Er, no, not really. Had a new shower fitted recently."

He jots it down on a piece of paper. "Got it. It's me doing the viewing."

"Great," I say as I pass the keys to him. "That one is the top and bottom Chubb and that's the main one."

"Dead good. Thanks. Keys: check," he says, jangling them. "All sorted. So, Rose Cottage, tomorrow at ten thirty and I'll be meeting the viewer there, a Ms," he looks back at his screen, "Leanne Cork."

"LEANNE CORK?!"

He looks up quickly. "Is that a problem?"

"Er, er, no, not at all." I give Sam a half exasperated questioning look and she shrugs in return. I clear my throat. "Well, if that's everything, Mikey, thanks for your help."

"No probs. I'll be in touch." He does the universal hand sign for phone. I smile, rise, shake his hand. As we retrace our steps I link Sam's arm.

"Oh My God, Sam, do you think it's her?"

"I dunno."

"Thank God he's doing the viewing, eh? Can you imagine her turning up on my doorstep and me having to show her round? You know, I thought it was bad enough when Steve and Justine wanted to buy the cottage – I feel between the devil and the deep blue now!"

"Aw, Amy, you'll be moving on, let that useless hack have the house if she wants it."

"Oh but the thought of her in my pretty cottage…" I whinge.

"She might not even want to buy it."

"True, true. But if she does I'm gonna leave a whole load of bad juju in there!"

"Amen sista!"

We are laughing when my phone buzzes again. I mouth 'sorry' to Sam before answering. "Hello?"

"Mrs Gathergood, Mikey here again."

"Hi, long time no see."

"Ha ha yeah. Anyways, just as you left your viewer called. She wants to rearrange, she'd like to see it on Sunday around three if that's okay?"

Oh Lord give me strength.

I sigh. *Urgh, I'd rather not. But I do need to sell...* "That's fine, Mikey. Sunday at three. Thanks."

"No probs. I'll let her know. Sound."

"Sound indeed."

As I'm replacing my phone in my bag I catch sight of the time.

"Aw dammit, sorry Sammie, I've gotta run."

"No problem," she says. "Hang on, was there something specific you wanted to talk to me about?"

"No," I lie. "Nothing that can't wait." I kiss her cheek cursing to myself that I haven't managed to tell her and vowing that the very next opportunity I get, I certainly will.

Chapter 43

"Hey G, do me a massive favour, will you, please?"

She mock rolled her eyes and sighed. "What is it? Whaddya need?"

"As it's my birthday..."

"Is it? Ain't noticed," she said, looking around at the banner, balloons and left over cake that she and Karen had kindly organised.

"Very funny. Seriously, would you do my last client, please? Just give me a little extra time to prepare myself for tonight. Please? It's a new client and she didn't specifically ask for me."

"What is it?"

"Cut and blow – and I'm sure it's short hair."

She gave me a disbelieving look. "Where's lover boy takin' ya then?"

"I don't know. All he'll say is there'll be food and drink. And then he keeps giving me 'that look', you know what I mean?"

"Ha! Yeah, I know *that look* - my Barry uses a lot!"

"Will you do it then?"

"Wot? Wiv me Barry?"

"No! My last client."

"Yeah babe," she laughed. "Course I will."

And true to her word, Gina is curling my last client's unfortunately not-so-short hair as I fly out of the shop, hop on the bus and head for home. There follows a full routine of shaving, plucking, exfoliating and all round pampering, with hair being left only on head and nether regions – just as God intended. I browse the cherry red strappy dress I bought specifically for the evening and, as I have no idea where he's taking me, I decide that it's better to be overdressed than under and stick with it.

As I'm sitting in my undies, applying the finishing touches to my make up, I hear the front door.

"Honey, I'm ho-ome," he calls.

"In the bedroom."

"Better be alone!" He appears at the door laughing. "Oooh someone's looking fancy!"

I look down at myself. "Ha, you men are so easily pleased!"

"Too right. Anyway, you look ready to me." He walks towards me with a glint in his eye.

"No no no, mister. I got off work early today to primp and preen and you are not going to mess it up…no matter how enjoyable that might be."

He laughs and takes a step back, holding up his hands. "I'm heading for the shower then."

"Good man."

I go back to applying eye makeup as I hear the shower start and Joshua belting out Stevie Wonder's 'Happy Birthday'. Tuneful, it's not, but it makes me giggle, which then makes it harder to apply eyeliner - thick wonky eyeliner is all the rage, right?

At six-thirty we're both ready. We make quite a dapper couple with my figure hugging calf length dress and his smart shirt and jeans matching in formality. My stomach is awash with giddy butterflies.

"Are we off then?" I ask.

"Thought we might have a drink here first?" he says, checking his watch for the hundredth time.

Whilst I carefully perch on the sofa he puts soft music on and then disappears only to return with a bottle of champagne and two glasses. Placing them on the coffee table he leaves again to reappear with his arms full of presents, each individually wrapped in silver shiny paper. I'm so impressed with all the attention to detail - bows, ribbons and glitter - that I wonder (unfairly) if he's employed someone else to wrap them.

"Wow! Josh, these look fantastic!"

"You're worth it," he says.

He pops the corks and pours the fizz and we clink glasses.

"Right, I'm going in," I say, pretending to roll up my sleeves. Each present is thoughtful and needed; he has literally spoiled me rotten. After the fifth present: two theatre tickets to West Side Story, thank you very much, he goes behind the sofa and pushes an identically wrapped, big, square gift into the middle of the room. Taking another swig of my fizz I'd hazard a guess at Ikea flat packed furniture, but, ripping at the paper, I see exactly what it is – a portable barre!

"So you can stop practising with that old dining room chair," he says with a winning smile.

"I love you."

"Come here," he says, pulling me up and pressing his lips to mine. Cocooned in each other's arms we sway to the music.

"Mmmm, I could quite happily stay here," I say with my head resting against him. He subtly tries to see his watch over my shoulder.

"Ah, sorry Amy Ballerina, that's not possible." And with that I am left dancing alone as he charges out of the room, calling over his shoulder, "Just getting my wallet. Drink up and then get your coat – phase two is about to begin…"

The taxi driver texts his arrival and, feeling nicely tipsy, we wobble out of the door and into the awaiting cab. Before long we pull up outside what I presume is our first destination: The Swan. (At least I hope it's our first destination as, although it's nice enough, it can't really top the presents, champagne and smoochy dancing that I've enjoyed so far.)

"Ah, good evening, sir," the barman says to Joshua. "Please go on up." Turning to me, Joshua smiles and takes my hand.

Up? Maybe they have private dining rooms I don't know about.

We climb the doglegged stairs and emerge into a dimly lit open space.

Ah - no private dining room.

'SURPRISE!'

The lights flicker on and my hand flies to my mouth as I see the faces of so many people I love, all cheering, clapping and laughing. I turn to Joshua who takes a step back, giving me a 'there you go' look.

"Did you do this?" I ask. He nods smiling with raised thumbs.

'Thank you,' I mouth and he blows me a kiss.

People surge forward and I'm lost in a whirl of accepting drinks, compliments and best wishes - boy, I should have a birthday everyday!

I commit myself to doing a lap of the room to meet and greet all my wonderful guests. (Memories of a birthday party where some guests left bitching because I favoured drinking with close pals over hostess duties still haunt me.) Here I have the hairdressing crowd, school friends, a few friends I made through Steve who 'chose me', a handful of elderly relatives and, of course, The Dixbury Dancers. As I approach their table I see Helena (dancer physique gorgeous in a silk two piece) but sadly no Bendrick. *Darn it.*

"Hello, hello, hello," I say, kissing and hugging them all. "So good of you all to come."

"Wouldn't've mished it for the world!" Lucia says, clearly taking advantage of the free bar. "It's not everyday you're forty!" she cackles.

"Oi! Watch it! Thirty-two as well you know." I laugh. "Did Joshua contact you all?"

"Yes dear. He texted us all from your phone, all very clandestine," Marion giggles.

"He's a good 'un," I say, looking over to him listening intently to my Great Aunt Ruby. Bless him. She didn't make a lot of sense when she had all her faculties so goodness knows what kind of yarn she's spinning him now.

"Hiya," a voice from behind me makes me swing round.

"Sam, you're here." I hug her warmly.

"I am indeed. And I even got me a date!" She is beaming.

Oh please no.

I follow her eyes to the bar and although it's three deep there's no mistaking her carrot topped, geeky spec-wearing date.

"D'you want a drink while he's there?" she asks.

"Yeah please," I say, not taking my eyes off him. "Better make it a double."

She flashes me an odd look and then looks at my drink. "Okay, double vodka tonic coming right up." Heading off to the bar Joshua instantly appears in her place.

"How's it going?" He smiles broadly.

"It *was* going great."

"You okay?" He tilts his head.

"It's him," I hiss. "I haven't had the chance to talk to Sam yet. Look."

Joshua follows my eye line to the bar where Sam is on tiptoes talking into Jason's ear and in return he is smiling and running his hand up and down her arm.

Joshua takes my shoulders to face him. "Amy, listen to me. You are not going to do anything about this tonight, okay? You know that dealing with stuff like this when you've been drinking isn't a good idea, don't you?"

"Yes Dad." I pout.

"Amy!"

"OK,OK."

"That's my girl." He jokingly pats my bottom. "Now, come on, party face back on."

I smile and he pecks me on the lips.

"Oi, you two, get a room." Sam laughs as she returns. "Guys, this is Jason." He grins and nods. "And this," she points to us, "is Joshua and the birthday girl, Amy." Joshua shakes his hand whilst I try not to bare my teeth. Jason hands me my drink.

"Thanks." I say, feeling Sam's eyes on me again. *Behave Amy, Josh is right, it's not the time or the place.*

"So, I hear you're a physio?" Joshua says.

"Yep, guilty as charged."

What an apt phrase.

"How's business?" Joshua asks.

"It's good. In this day and age of people hunching over laptops and smart phones there's a real need for physios. Upper back, neck and shoulder troubles are the biggest causes of seeking professional help."

"It's where we hold our tension, isn't it?" Sam says, looking up adoringly at him. "It makes me laugh in ballet, we're always being told to relax but when we're concentrating and trying to do it right, I totally tense up,"

"That's the beauty of regular massage – gets rid of the knots," Jason says.

"Whenever I'm feeling tight, I get me a lovely Swedish one," Lucia joins the conversation.

"Yoga and massage helped me through my divorce," Josie chips in.

We all turn to her. "You've been divorced, dear?" Marion asks.

"Oh, yeah, married when I was far too young. It didn't last long. I met Ed after that. But yeah, I had a friend who was training in yoga and massage while I was divorcing and I was her guinea pig – really helped me through."

"Hmm, maybe I should think about that," I say under my breath as people break off into smaller conversations.

Marion turns to me. "How is your divorce going, dear? If you don't mind me asking."

"No, I don't mind. It's going okay, I suppose. It's never easy, but I'm just so grateful that Gloria recommended a wonderful solicitor to me…" I look across to Jason. "…Simone Bletchley." I immediately clock the recognition and fear in his face. "She's really good – worth her weight in gold. Nice person to boot." He remains focussed on Sam, maintaining an expression of listening, but that minor twitch in his lip tells me I've hit the target.

"Ah, that's good," Marion continues. "Nice to have someone you can trust on your side."

"Exactly, trust is such an important thing, isn't it?"

Jason gulps a mouthful of his drink and then, like a magnet, his guilt ridden eyes meet mine.

Chapter 44

The essentially background music that's been playing so far stops and DJ Slam waves Joshua over and passes him the mic.

"Ladies and Gentlemen," Joshua starts. "First of all could we get a chair for my beloved please?" An old school friend hastily places a chair in the centre of the room and, feeling quite grateful to get the weight off my drunken legs, I sit. "Right, thanks. OK," he continues. "Before we go any further I'd like to thank you all for coming tonight. I think it's safe to say that we totally surprised the birthday girl, didn't we?" He looks to me and I nod, laughing with my thumbs aloft. "But the night isn't over yet…and neither have the surprises. Some of your friends here have organised a little show – so, Amy, please sit back and enjoy."

I smile in a fuzzy alcoholic haze as I am treated to a magic trick, a poem, a few songs, some jokes and a handful of heartfelt speeches. Even Great Aunt Ruby gets up and does the Charleston's 'Bees Knees' move to raucous applause. My cheeks remain puce throughout that all the turns are in my honour, but I thoroughly enjoy every single moment.

"And now," Joshua says, taking the mic again. "To finish this evening's performance please give it up for The Dixbury Dancers!"

Applause fills the room as my lovely dancing friends appear in ballet class apparel. The Nutcracker's 'March' starts and the act begins with everyone in the centre following Helena's mimed instructions. From the side Lucia appears, holding a blow dryer and sporting a t-shirt with 'AMY' on, and proceeds to create slapstick mayhem. When the dancers step one way, 'Amy' goes the other, crashing into them and getting fingers wagged at her. When she launches herself onto Brian in what looks likely to be a swan dive she ends up with her legs around his waist. In the pirouettes she is the sole dancer to end up with her back to the audience, and with the final curtsey she exuberantly opens her arms and smacks Julay in the face. Tears of laughter roll down my face as the house erupts into applause. I love my Dixbury Dancers – friends, dancers, comedians and all round good eggs - so much so that I jump up and grab the mic.

"Aw, I am having the best night ever! Thank you all so much. I am so grateful. I'm so blessed. You've all been there for me, and I don't know what I'd do without you. You're all so wonderful - " Stopping me from giving either the 'I've only known you for X amount of years but you're the best friend/relative/stranger I've ever met' speech, or from spiralling into a soggy maudlin mess, Joshua steps up.

"You're worth it, Amy Ballerina, we love you." He deftly steals the microphone from me. "And now, the buffet is open and the music will play on! Thanks again for coming and have a great night." He takes my elbow and steers me away from centre stage. "Let's get you some food, my love."

"Sounds great." I hang around his neck. "I flippin' love you."

"You too, my little drunkard."

"Ha! I feel great!" I laugh, throwing my head back. "Ooh, and in need of a pee."

"I'll get the food and meet you back here."

I seal the agreement with a smacker on his lips and then totter off to the toilets. I smile and nod at folk on my wavy lined way to the long corridor that leads to the loos. I'm double-checking the gender signs on the doors (men at urinals is never a pretty sight) when Jason appears from the gents.

"Oh hi," he says. "Great party."

"Uh-huh."

"I think you want this one," he says, pointing to the 'ladies'.

"Yep," I say, trying not to slur. "I want the ladies, just like you seem to too."

He bristles and the fear returns to his eyes. "Look, I don't know what you think…"

"Don't you? Well let me tell you. I think you're a two-timing rat who has no right to do that to my friend, a lovely young woman…that's what I think." *Oh hell, Josh told me not to do this tonight…*

"Look, I don't expect you to understand, I just need to sort out a few things."

"Really? A few things? You mean like your fiancée and the other 'other woman' I saw you with?"

A voice from behind us says, "What?" We turn to see Sam standing frozen, her face contorted in confusion and pain. "What fiancée?"

I lower my head and Jason rushes forward to take her hands. She steps back.

"Look Sam," he says. "I can explain. I am breaking it off – I want you."

"You have a fiancée?"

"I would've told you, but then we had that night together and it just felt too late. So I thought it'd be better if I just broke it off with her first."

"And have you? Have you broken it off?" He looks down and shakes his head. I walk over and put my arm around Sam but she recoils. "And you! You knew? And you didn't tell me?"

"Sam, I tried, I wanted to the other day when we met for lunch, but then it didn't seem like the right time."

"And when would it've been the right time?"

"I know. I'm sorry. I should've told you."

"You know, I can't decide which of you is worst. You," she looks at Jason, "are an idiot. And as for you," she turns to me with tears brimming, "I've never been so disappointed."

She turns and walks away with Jason scampering after her, protesting his true intentions. Standing statue-like outside the toilets, with the full weight of guilt sobering me up, I'm sickened by my own inaction – I should've tried harder to tell her. What have I done? Or rather what haven't I done!

Slowly opening the door to the loo I consider staying in there until everyone has gone home. With both my heart and conscience weighing heavily, going back to my own party is the very last thing I feel like doing now.

Chapter 45

My cheek is wet on the pillow and, as my mouth is wide open, I can only deduce that it's from drunken dribble. As my eyes peel open, the deep feeling of dread spreads through me. *Oh God, what happened last night?* Recalling each piece of the evening makes me incrementally nauseous. So, Sam found out about Jason and left, and on the way home in the cab I told Joshua what I'd done and he wasn't happy either.

"Amy, I told you not to do it when you've been drinking!" he'd said, with annoyance burning through his voice.

"I couldn't help it! He was just standing there and it just came out. I didn't know she was standing behind us." I'd put my head in my hands.

"Can you remember exactly what you said?"

I'd shaken my head and the rapid motion was too much. "Can you stop please?" I'd asked the cab driver. He'd abruptly braked and the force of it made me vomit all over his floor.

The driver was cross. Joshua was silent. I was pitiful.

As we pulled up, Joshua helped to clear up my mess, paid the driver handsomely and then half carried me in and put me to bed. I remember him fetching a glass of water and a bowl, but then I don't recall him joining me. And now as I look across at his side of the bed, it's empty.

I gently turn over and wonder what all my other guests were doing whilst I was heavy-handedly dealing with Sam's love life. Do The Dixbury Dancers all know what I did? My skin crawls with the 'what else did I do?' feeling that inevitably follows inebriation. As a teenager, my friend, Sue, had an empty house for a night so we all bundled round there for a party, bringing with us any half empty bottles of booze we could snaffle from our parents' drinks cabinets. All the said booze was placed on, in my defence, a slightly rickety table in the lounge. Whilst enthusiastically recreating the lift from Dirty Dancing with some spotty youth I managed to career into the table and smash every single bottle. In groans and curses the party pretty much ended right there. I'm no stranger to being sent to Coventry.

I hear the lawnmower's thrum – ah, that's where he is. Getting up slowly in an effort not to shake my dehydrated brain I grab my dressing gown and head to the kitchen. Thankfully there's a pot of coffee on the go and I pour one, not even contemplating adding milk, and slump at the table. Out of the French windows I see Joshua, handsome as ever, in a light blue checked shirt and ripped jeans, striding across the lawn with Basil jumping at his feet. Insecurities crowd my mind as I try to catch his eye, desperate for a wave or a smile. Nothing. He's far too involved with neatly mowing tramlines. I tap on the window and Basil bounds towards me, and only then does Joshua look up and, thankfully, crack a smile.

"Soooooo," he says, entering the dining room. "How are we feeling this morning?"

Regret and shame fill my eyes. "Dreadful. I'm so sorry."

"Oh dearie me," he says, pushing my hair from my face. "You don't have to be sorry to me, and in fact you don't even have to apologise to the taxi driver– you did that about a million times."

"Did I?"

He nods and grins. "Quite a party, huh?"

"Akin to nightmares of being naked in public."

"Ah, now you mention that…" he says, sitting down.

My eyes widen as I try to recall any further indiscretions, but then catch the teasing in his eyes. "Joshua!"

"OK, there was no nakedness."

"Well, at least that's something." I reach for his hand. "Thank you so much for organising it. It was all such a lovely surprise and I'm so sorry I was an arse."

He places his hand on top of mine and looks me in the eyes. "You keep saying sorry but you're saying it to the wrong person."

"Yes." I look down. "I know. Sam. But I don't know how I'm going to start with that."

"Start by calling her, ask her to meet. Then talk her through it all – be honest."

"You make it sound so easy." I stroke his fingers. "Thank you for not being cross with me."

"Amy." He leans forward to brush my cheek but instead picks off some dried mascara. "Huh," he says, screwing up his nose and brushing it from his finger. "As I was going to say, we all make mistakes. No one's perfect."

My heart swells. "You still love me then?"

"Vomit and all. And anyway, most people seemed to have a good time. The free bar was certainly a hit."

"A bit too much for some." I point to myself. "I'm going to blame you – it was that champagne rendering me half cut before we even left home."

"You're welcome."

We laugh. "Seriously though," I say. "Apart from upsetting my best pal, spilling that drink on Great Aunt Ruby and throwing up in the taxi, it was the best night." He smiles and leans over to kiss my cheek.

"So," he says, brightly, tapping my hand. "What's the hangover cure plan for the day?"

"Oh crap! I'd forgotten, Leanne Cork is coming to view the house at three. Urgh! My life just gets better and better."

"Better get a move on then." He gets up. "Oh, thinking about it," he turns back, "there might be someone else you need to apologise to…"

I look up at him through my fingers. "Oh no, who?"

"Gina's Barry."

"Oh Christ, what did I do to him?"

"Let's just say the Dirty Dancing lift didn't go quite as planned."

Chapter 46

Preferring a gentle ease into the day rather than an energising shower, Gloria runs the bath and adds her favourite rose scented bubbles. Sinking into it and feeling the warmth on her bones, she thinks about the night before.

The Dixbury Dancers had bagged a corner table and enjoyed their usual repartee, or 'banter' as Lucia likes to call it, with animated conversations and in-jokes flying. Brian had arrived late and edged himself to the other end of the table, which, in some ways, had only made it worse as they had a birds-eye view of each other.

Towards the end of the evening, when the DJ had announced it was 'that time of the night to slow things down,' Brian had looked directly at Gloria and made her heart jump. He'd raised his eyebrows and she'd nodded. He'd walked over, taken her hand and without a word led her around the floor in a social foxtrot. At the end of the dance he'd nodded a small bow, walked her back to the group and left for the night. It felt dangerously like it was his final parting shot – some kind of closure – and this was something she definitely didn't want.

Nonchalantly, with her index finger she makes a heart shape in the bubbles around her and writes his name, and then swiftly rebukes herself for behaving like a fourteen year old. She sighs and turns her head to one side, resting her cheek on the bath's cold enamel.

I miss him.

Defiantly she stands up, swaddles herself in a white fluffy towel and heads downstairs to the hall where she picks up the phone and dials his number. With her heart thumping in her chest she listens to the rings. What is she going to say? Ask him out? What if he is past that point? Doesn't see her in that way now? Or even worse if he views her as cold hearted for dropping him and then attempting to pick him up again when it suits her. Can she bear his rejection? Was that dance their swansong?

Very softly she replaces the phone back in its cradle.

•••

Julay is getting used to Sunday mornings alone. It hasn't failed to escape her notice that Marion seems to be drinking more and last night at the party was no exception. There's nothing wrong with pushing the boat out at a celebration, Julay thinks, but it's the weekday evenings at home with the vodka bottle that's registering alarm. The general pattern these days seems to be Marion appearing bleary-eyed in the morning, nursing her hangover 'til noon and only then does normal service resume.

Julay hadn't given it too much thought until last night at the party when a man crossing the dance floor had sparked a reaction in Marion.

"Dear," Julay had said. "Is everything alright?"

Marion stared at the man and when she saw his face clearly, she'd let out a little sigh of relief. "Yes, I'm fine. He just looked like…" She'd lost her words.

"Jack?"

"Yes."

"Old wounds, eh Marion," Julay said, rubbing her friend's arm conciliatorily.

At the end of the evening Julay had had to help, a by then legless, Marion into the car and later into bed. She thought of the metaphorical earthquakes Marion suffered at the hands of Jack, and how that lookalike man tonight had unwittingly created an aftershock. Poor Marion – would she ever escape the memories?

Suddenly remembering Bendrick's absence last night, Julay goes to the hall and dials his number.

"Hello?" his voice booms after a few rings.

"It's Julay."

A short pause follows. "Hello there! For what do I owe this pleasure?"

Never one for beating around the bush, she says, "Rumour has it you're leaving us, Bendrick."

"Ah." He pauses. "Yes. Helena's appendage is healed, so my services are no longer required."

"Bendrick?" she says sternly. "Are you blaming yourself for our haphazard performance and that dreadful journalist."

"Well, I did have a hand in it all."

"Maybe, but you're not to blame! You didn't do the dance and you didn't write the article!"

"That's as maybe." He sighs deeply down the line. "I suppose the life of a dancer is the pursuit of perfection. We train everyday, trying to be better than we were the day before. We want our legs higher, our spins faster, our jumps more buoyant – and when we retire and teach, we want those things for our students. That's what I wanted for you all. I wanted to develop you all as dancers, for you all to blossom and I pushed too hard. If I had choreographed sympathetically you might have stood a chance. Instead I feel like I've hung you all out to dry."

"Bendrick, dear man," she says, twirling the phone wire around her finger. "None of us feel you've let us down."

"That's very kind of you to say."

"It's the truth." She pauses. "Right, I won't be beaten, see you Wednesday for a proper farewell?"

He half chuckles down the phone. "Very well." The line goes quiet before he says, "Hmm, talking of being beaten…"

"What was that?"

"Never you mind, my dear lady. I shall be there and I might just have a plan to right a few wrongs."

"OK. I won't pretend to understand that. See you Wednesday, bye bye."

"Bye."

She is just hanging up when a dishevelled Marion appears at the foot of the stairs.

"Oh dearie me, coffee?" Julay asks, pulling a sympathetic face.

Marion puts her hand to her head. "Yes please."

As she's boiling the kettle, Julay recalls how Marion used to drink quite heavily, but then when Jack disappeared from her life, she'd become virtually teetotal. Taking stock of her sickly hung-over friend across the kitchen table it troubles her that Marion appears to be returning to old ways.

"Marion dear, tell me to mind my own business, but is something troubling you?"

Just being asked the question, Marion feels the floodgates open. In a rather nonsensical, random way she spews forth all that that's been happening. She tells of Iain, the patronising vicar, Jack's letter, the prison visit and the call from the victim liaison officer – but not necessarily in that order. Julay's jaw hits the floor at not knowing what her housemate has been going through. Gulping hard she splutters, "Marion, why didn't you talk to me?"

Resembling a beaten, caged animal, Marion lowers her eyes. "I knew you wouldn't approve. You'd think I was silly for believing him. And you've been nothing but kind to me…"

Julay places her hand on Marion's. "Oh Marion, I wouldn't have told you off! I would've helped you, supported you through it."

"Sorry."

"And don't apologise for that!"

Marion half smiles and then, pulling her dressing gown around her body, says, "I received the parole officer's report yesterday."

"Right. Why don't we have some coffee and then we'll take a look at it together. And if needs be, when the parole hearing comes around I'd be honoured to accompany you." Marion chokes back a tear. "Come on, dear, we don't give up," she says, rubbing her friend's hand.

As Julay rises to pour the coffee, Marion shifts in her seat and turns to her friend. "No, we don't give up, do we?"

"Hmm?" Julay looks over her shoulder.

"Dancing, Julay, we don't give up, do we?"

"Totally different subject."

"True. But I'm not going to tell you off, and I'd like to help you, support you through it…" Marion risks a smile.

Holding the mugs of coffee, Julay sits back in her chair and laughs. "Touché, Marion, touché."

Chapter 47

It's ten to three and the house is pristine. Lights are on, cushions are plumped and my three copies of Homes and Garden (dated 2009 if anyone looks closely) are fanned out on the coffee table. I have even taken the coffee pot on a tour of the place, wafting the aroma into every room. (It suddenly occurs to me that if you're not a coffee lover the smell might put you off buying a house, but in this instance I'm going to assume that Ms Cork is a rabid coffee drinker.)

Sitting with one buttock on the sofa trying not to leave a dent, I call Sam for the third time and for the third time it goes straight to voicemail. Hmm, either she doesn't want to speak to me, she's still asleep, or her phone is switched off. Bottom line is, for whatever reason, she's just not picking up.

Just then Basil harks the arrival of my viewer.

"Shh, shh, okay Bas, in your bed."

Clearly not understanding spoken English, he fusses at my feet as I swing open the door to find Leanne Cork dressed in saggy jeans and a washed out hoodie, her hair just as lank as I remember, extinguishing her cigarette underfoot.

"Hi, I'm Leanne Cork, come to see the house," she says, looking up.

"Certainly. Please come in."

"Thanks," she says, stepping in.

"We might as well start here," I say, taking her through to the lounge.

She wanders around the downstairs, asking questions without any flicker of acknowledgment that we've met before. Isn't that typical? I have been rattled by her demeanour, offended by her written words and in dread of her imminent visit here and she is totally oblivious! She doesn't know me from Adam. I follow her around the house, wondering how she can create such havoc and then have no memory of the people she's hurt. I want to say something – to see her take responsibility for that scathing article, but then the image of Steve, Justine and Beyoncé living here spurs me on to sell my beautiful home to this sloppy journo.

"Would you like to see the garden?" I ask brightly.

"Thanks, yes please."

We exit out of the French doors to find Joshua on his hands and knees assembling the birthday gift barre.

"Hi there," he says, looking up, squinting in the light.

"Hi. You look busy," she says.

"A ballerina has to have her barre." He nods in my direction.

Leanne looks momentarily confused. "Oh, is this the pole that ballet dancers use?"

"Uh-huh," he answers.

And there it is. A flash of recall and recognition. She slowly turns to me. "Have we met before?"

I nod. "The Dixbury Dancers."

"Ah, yes, I thought you were familiar. Annie, right?"

"Amy."

"Of course. Sorry – hazard of the job, I meet so many people. Nice to see you again." She nods, giving the garden the once over and then says, "Right, I think I've seen all I want to see. Thank you."

"If you're sure?" I say.

"Yep, thanks"

After further standard compliments about the house; 'beautiful spot, lovely lawn, good sized rooms etc.' she heads for the passage along the side to leave. Joshua and I exchange a look.

"You gonna say something?" he asks.

"Oooh I really want to!" I say, chewing my lip.

"What you waiting for then?"

I smile and turn on my heels. "Leanne, sorry, Leanne," I call, chasing her up the path. "Before you go, could I ask you something please?" She turns slowly, tilting her head back with a look of knowing. "You know the article you wrote?"

"Mmm." She clicks her tongue.

"Why?"

"Why what?"

"Why write something hurtful?"

"I kinda told it like it was."

"But you didn't! You didn't bother to find out what it was! You talked to each of us for under a minute and then just wrote humiliating stuff about us being too old, too amateur and very daft to be dancing ballet."

"Amy, love, it's the press. No one wants to read the banal stuff – people want to be entertained."

"Even if it's at the expense of others."

"Especially if it's at the expense of others. National papers trade on shock, horror and outrage, the local rags have to rely on making fun of what's on their own doorstep. I'm just a cog in that machine. Look, if it helps – it's not personal."

"Not personal? You ruined our confidence. You made what we do seem trite and ridiculous. You could've written something inspiring and uplifting, something encouraging for anyone who's ever dreamed of dancing ballet. I know you think it's silly what we do – but you had no right to attack our dreams." From studying her shoes she looks up at me with a world-weary expression. "Look," I continue. "You have no idea what you've done with your spiteful words – just remember these are real people with feelings!" She breaks our stare and fiddles with her keys.

"Look, I'm sorry – it's the job." She shrugs.

I nod and stand awkwardly not really knowing what to say next. I guess this is an apology – albeit an unsatisfactory one. But what did I expect? That she would immediately offer to print a retraction? That she would march back to her office, write a glowing piece about us and immediately submit it to her editor? No – I guess in situations like this all we usually want is for our hurt to be acknowledged; that the perpetrator understands the consequences of their actions. And I suppose that is done.

I eye her carefully and sigh. "Anyway. Hope you liked it?" I gesture to the house.

She splutters a small laugh. “Yeah, I like it. I’ll contact the agent.”

“OK. I’ll wait to hear.”

“OK, thanks. Bye.”

She turns, reaching in her pocket for her cigarettes, and leaves.

“Blimey Amy, you tell it as it is, don’t you?” Joshua says, appearing at my side.

“I know. I never used to be able to say the right thing at the right time.”

“Still not sure you’re quite there,” he quips.

“Ha. No, maybe not. But I did today.”

He takes me in his arms. “Yep, I heard you. Very nicely said.”

“Wish it had gone that well last night; I’ve called Sam three times and no luck.”

“Maybe she needs time.”

“Yeah. I think I’ll leave it for now. I’ll see her at class – maybe I can sort it out then.”

“I think I like this new ‘Expressing Amy’! Nothing you want to say to me is there?”

Yeah there is actually. Why can’t you ‘invest’ in us and plan a future of blissful cohabiting...“No. Nothing.”

“Thank goodness for that.” He kisses me on the forehead. “Come on, your barre awaits you.”

“Oh great. I’ll teach you how to plié.”

“You’ll make a Yehudi Menuhin out of me yet.”

“I think you mean Rudolf Nureyev, my love. Yehudi was a violinist.”

“Violin, ballet, it’s all rock ‘n’ roll to me.”

“Clearly.”

Chapter 48

"I've brought sausage rolls," Marion says, wriggling into her black leotard.

"Aw Maz, I brought sausage rolls too!" Lucia complains.

"Me too!" wails Josie.

"No worries – everyone likes a sausage roll," I placate. Julay walks in and places two large bags crammed full of all sorts of tidbits on the changing room bench. "He deserves a good send off, doesn't he?" she says, looking at the bags.

"Yep. I've brought the cake," I say.

"I've also got soft drinks, mini scotch eggs and some homemade hummus." Josie adds.

"French stick and butter," Gloria raises her arm.

"And I have the contents of Marks and Spencer's Food Hall! Including a little bit of fizz," Julay says.

"Just Brian and Sam then," Marion says. "Hope they got the message."

So do I. Despite constant efforts to contact Sam regarding buffet food and the need to explain myself, I've heard nothing. And the longer she fails to respond to me, the harder my heart thumps with worry that she's not going to give me the chance to make amends.

Helena sticks her head around the door. "Hiya. It's good to see you all!" People mumble apologies for missing class last week. "That's okay. Just glad you're here now." She eyes all the plastic bags bulging with food. "Glad to see you're all ready to party too. Class as normal with me and then Bendrick should turn up and we'll have a do."

"Is he definitely coming?" Marion asks.

"Yes, he contacted me," Helena says. "OK, see you in there in a mo." A moment later she pops her head back around the door. "Oh, I forgot, Sam sent me her apologies - she can't make it."

Whilst the others commiserate her absence, I'm left rooted to the spot, pierced with sadness. She really doesn't want to see me, does she? I've royally messed things up and now have no idea how to put things right. A wave of resentment towards Jason surfaces – if it wasn't for him and his shenanigans I wouldn't be in this position. But then again if only I'd talked to her…

"Right," says Helena, as we stand around in the hall. "Let's do Prayers and Pains. Who wants to go first?"

Josie raises a finger. "I'd like to concentrate on my balance again. And just to say my lower back is giving me some gip."

"Be careful with the forward port de bras and don't try to lift your legs too high in grand battement." Helena turns to the next dancer.

"I'm still wanting that elusive triple pirouette," Catherine says.

"I've got a sore toe," Marion offers.

"How did that happen?"

"Er, my toe got in the way of Amy's enthusiastic dancing the other night."

Another apology to make… "Sorry Marion," I say and she shakes her head as if to say it's not a problem. "Er, I have no pains," I continue. "But I would really like to think about spotting in pirouettes."

"Good, good. And you, Brian?"

"No pains as such. And I'm not sure what I want to achieve."

"Me neither," says Lucia.

"I'm feeling a little stiff," Gloria says. "And I would just like to dance again."

"Right, fine. Let's get to the barre."

We begin as usual, the same pliés, the same tendus, frappés, fondus, developpés and grands battements – everything as it should be. Only it's still not. It's still half-hearted; our bodies move but without any semblance of connection to our hearts. Before the Afton competition it was like we were innocent children, unburdened by care, and now we're grown up and having to face the reality of failure. Humiliation is a bitter pill to swallow. To her credit Helena puts on a brave face and does her utmost to cajole us back to life – but she must feel like she's pulling teeth. I catch the relief on her face as she calls the class to an end.

"OK, well done everyone. That's it for tonight. Shall we set up the party?"

We file out to the changing room and collect the various bags and return to the hall to find Bendrick and Helena setting up a couple of trestle tables.

"My dear danseurs," Bendrick says, opening his arms to us. "Wonderful to see you."

"Good to see you too, Benny." Lucia winks. "We've got enough food to feed the five hundred so hope you're hungry!"

We set out the goodies on pretty floral plates and pour the champagne into union jack paper cups, and with the evening's class put to one side, we all indulge in giggly chatter.

At one point Gloria sidles up to me. "Amy dear, are you okay?"

"Why?"

"You don't look quite yourself."

"Oh Gloria, I've done something awful."

"Is it anything to do with Samantha?"

"Oh, what do you know?"

"Nothing, nothing. But I noted that she left in a hurry from your party and your face dropped tonight when Helena said she wasn't coming. Just call me Clouseau." She taps her nose.

"Ha ha. Yep, Inspector, you've got me. You know Jason?" She nods. "Well, you know Simone Bletchley? The solicitor you recommended?" Her brows knit. "Well, turns out the two are betrothed."

Gloria's mouth drops open. "What? How do you know?"

"I was in her office and there was a photo of her and him and she ended up talking about being engaged, due to get married to a physio, etc."

"Oh dear Lord."

"There's worse. Then, I saw him in the pub with another other woman!"

"The hound!" She thinks for a minute. "So, how have *you* upset Sam?"

"I didn't get the chance to tell her and then I tackled him at the party, not knowing she was standing behind me. She feels betrayed…by both of us…I guess – she won't answer my calls."

"Ah."

"I feel terrible, Gloria. It was the last thing I wanted to do – to hurt her. She had this night with him and was so happy…I should've told her."

Gloria places her plate on the table and puts her arm around me. "Darling, she's probably just feeling hurt, maybe a little humiliated, but she'll come round."

"I hope so, Glo, I really do."

Bendrick taps on a glass to get our attention. "Danseurs, please, may I have a word." We all turn to him. "Thank you so much for this wondrous feast. It's been my absolute pleasure to teach you all, and I'd like to thank you for your hard work, loyalty and passion. You have risen to the challenges," *hmm, doubtful,* "jumped the hurdles," *and then fallen over,* "and proved me proud." *Some folks are easily pleased.* "So I would like to leave you all with a small parting gift. Helena, would you please?"

She walks to the stereo and beautiful classical music rings out. Julay clasps her hands together and she smiles in recognition.

"Oh that's my favourite," she says, as Helena hits the off button.

"What is it?" asks Marion.

"It's the Kingdom of the Shades from La Bayadere," Bendrick answers. "It's the beginning of Act II and the dancers enter the stage on a slope and captivate the audience with a repeated combination of steps. It's a marvellous piece."

"Sound lovely, Benny, but how is this a gift?" Lucia asks.

"Well, this is the piece that will highlight your strengths and with its gentle repetitive steps you'll retrace your learning and grow in confidence. I may have pushed you all a little too hard." Murmurs of feigned polite disagreement rumble. "But I have faith in you all, Dixbury Dancers, and I always have." I see Julay choke back a tear and Marion squeeze her hand. "And so, for now it's au revoir, my beautiful danseurs," he says and then proceeds to bid farewell to each of us individually, kissing the females' hands and shaking Brian's firmly. "Farewell Dixbury Dancers, it's been my enormous pleasure."

As theatrically as he entered all those weeks ago, he now leaves with equal dramatic flair.

"Well," Helena says, breaking the hush he leaves behind. "We'll start work on Bendrick's gift next week. OK?"

"Helena," Julay says. "Are we learning it for a reason or just for enjoyment?"

"Oh, he didn't say, did he? It's for the Dixbury Midsummer festival – they're incorporating another Dixbury Does Talent competition." We all sink slightly. "Oh no, no, no, it's not to compete."

"Not to compete?" I question.

"No, you're going to close the show again! It's not time for competing – it's time for growing and blossoming."

"That is genius!" Lucia says as the room breaks into a buzz.

"Thank you, Helena," Julay says. "This is just what we need – a show piece."

"Don't thank me," she looks to the hall door. "It was all Bendrick's idea."

Chapter 49

If I believed in planets and stars affecting my life I'd be pretty convinced that mine aren't aligned at the moment. Firstly, I know I have to contact Sam, but this evening, after Throwback Thursday at the salon, I just don't have the energy. I'd rather snuggle on the sofa with Joshua and plan how I'm going to see her; procrastination is still the name of my game. And then equally out of synch, and impossible to shake, is that little nagging voice; the one that keeps whispering 'I've fallen in love with a commitment-phobe' and 'if he really loved me he'd…'

"You look deep in thought,' he says, interrupting my thoughts and joining me on the sofa. "Have my culinary skills shocked you into silence?"

"Something like that." I smile. "Nah, I'm just tired. Those blow-drys were thick and fast today and with Karen still off with the flu, we had to do our own shampooing. My poor little hands,' I say, displaying my red cracked hands.

"Aw, poor baby," he says, leaning over to kiss them. "You need some hand cream on them."

"OK, my little metrosexual munchkin."

He chuckles and sits back to face me. "Did your journo get in touch with the estate agents?"

"Yes, she did. I had a call today at work. She's offered five thousand under the asking price. That reminds me I have to contact Steve. I think we should try and bump her up a bit, I mean, everyone starts with a low offer, don't they?"

"Dunno, I've never bought before."

"Do you think you ever will?" It comes out of my mouth before I can stop it and he repays me with a look. "No, no, I'm not being funny, just wondered if having your own property was on your to-do list?"

He sighs and chooses his words carefully. "Yes, Amy, it is on my to-do list. Most definitely."

A small silence passes.

"When d'you think that'll be?"

"This is a real problem, isn't it?"

"No. Maybe. I suppose so. Oh I don't know! I don't want to play games, and if we're not heading in the same direction…I mean, I want our future together…"

"And so do I!"

"But not enough to put your money where your mouth is."

" I choose to be here, don't I? I choose to be with you."

Tears threaten my eyes. "But I don't know if that's enough. After what I've been through, I need more security."

"Amy, you were married, you had security, so you know that even that's no guarantee," he says kindly.

"I know."

He gives a sad sigh. "Look, Amy," he starts, but the doorbell sets Basil off barking. "Hold that thought," he adds, lightly squeezing my arm before he gets up to answer the door.

I yawn and then rest back, closing my eyes. I hear a woman's voice, but it's too muffled to work out what's being said. After a while I realise that the voices have moved to the kitchen. Who on earth is it? I drag myself up and follow the sound to find a twinset and pearls attired woman with greying hair and a sensible handbag perched on one of our kitchen stools, sniffing into a handkerchief. They both look up in mild surprise at me.

"Oh, sorry, what a way to meet," the woman says, furiously wiping her nose.

"Amy, this is Marie, my mum," Joshua quickly says.

"Oh, how lovely to meet you," I say, stepping forward and then having the dilemma of whether to shake her hand or hug her. "Could I make you a cup of tea? Or something stronger?" I ask as she shakes my hand.

"That would be lovely, thank you, tea please," she says with a hint of an Irish accent.

"Joshua?" I ask.

"Not for me, thanks," he says, his doleful eyes communicating that our conversation is temporarily on hold, and whilst I make the tea I'm painfully aware that whatever they were talking about prior to my appearance is also on hold. *I hope it's nothing serious.*

I perform my best waitress service to Marie, make an excuse about needing to lie down and leave them to it. Joshua mouths 'thank you' as I go and gives me a smile.

I'm dog-tired so I take the opportunity to change into, what Joshua calls, my 'lurid lounge suit' (vivid orange velour trackie top and bottoms – just as gorgeous as it sounds) and grabbing my book, I recline on the bed. I hear their voices fade in and out and the kettle boiling a few more times before I nod off.

"Amy, hey, Amy." I awake to Joshua leaning over shaking my shoulders gently. "Wake up a mo. I need to tell you something."

"Eh?" I say, wiping my mouth and pushing hair out of my eyes.

"Sleepy head," he says, sitting down at my side. "There have been some problems at home."

"Uh?" I prop myself up on my elbows. "Like what?"

"My mum and dad have fallen out big time. They've always had quite a fiery relationship, but this time it seems to be worse."

"Oh, I'm sorry. Has she gone?"

"Er, no. That's what I wanted to tell you – I've said she can stay in the spare room, hope that's okay?"

"Er, yes, of course. It's your mum, of course it's fine." I stroke his cheek.

"Thanks." He leans forward and kisses me. "You're a doll." I smile. "Well." He looks me up and down. "A doll masquerading as a Satsuma."

"Very funny. You know you love it really."

"Yep, truth is I love you in anything, Amy Ballerina." He leans over and wrapping his arms around me, squeezes me tightly. "I'm sorry about earlier," he whispers in my ear.

“Shh shh. Let’s not talk about that now. You’ve got your mum to think about.’

“We’re okay though, aren’t we? You and me?”

I nod. “Yes, of course. Shh, come on now, come to bed.”

He pulls away and looks me up and down. “OK, Nemo, I’ll just get my dark glasses.”

“Joshua Milne!” I say, raising the pillow and smacking him squarely on the head. We both giggle until I suddenly remember our houseguest. “Shhhhhh, your mum’ll hear us.”

“We’ll have to be very quiet then,” he says, as he starts to rid me of my orange velour.

Chapter 50

Brian is frying his morning egg and grilling two rashers of bacon when the post plops on the doormat. Padding over he picks it up and in between the bills and junk there's a handwritten letter. He places them all on the table and considers how refreshing it is to receive something personal in the post.

Finishing off his breakfast, he opens the ever-increasing gas bill, moves on to local gutter cleaners and rounds it off with a political party promotion. Savouring the handwritten letter, he notes the Southampton postcode – ah yes, his old school friend, Harry; he'd moved to Southampton – maybe it's him? Opening it, he sees that it's from Harry's wife.

Dear Brian,

I hope this finds you well.

I am sorry to be writing to you under such sad circumstances. Last Wednesday I received a call from the golf club to tell me that Harry had collapsed on the fairway. I jumped in the car to the hospital, it's only a short drive, but sadly by the time I got there he had passed. He'd had a massive heart attack. They assure me that he wouldn't have been in pain. As you can imagine, my world is a little upside down at the moment.

I know how close you and Harry were in your younger days. He often talked
about the things you got up to together and he always spoke so fondly of you.

I've enclosed details of the funeral but as it is such a long way for you to travel from Norfolk I will completely understand if you can't make it.

I wish you all the very best, Brian, and trust that things are well with you.

Yours truly,

Enid.

Brian sits back in his chair, the letter shaking in his hand. *Not Harry - such a lovely man – jovial, trustworthy and a true gent.* Brian considers how he doesn't have a single childhood memory that Harry's not in. How did they end up not seeing each other regularly? It's easy to blame geography - but if two people want to see each other then surely they gap the distance; make the effort and travel? He re-reads the letter, and absorbing the words, a couple of large tears roll down his face. All those years, all the shared times and he didn't get to say goodbye.

Dabbing the tears, he rises, clears the table and then, to distract himself, sets about the washing up and laundry. Try as he might to focus, his mind wanders back to Harry again and again; each time his death becoming a fragment more believable. As it is slowly sinking in, Brian's own mortality looms before him, reminding him that life is not guaranteed from one day to the next. Who knows when a person's time will be up?

Whilst vacuuming, Brian's mind runs film footage style memories of Harry, until he finds his breath becoming short and shallow. Feeling the four walls closing in, he needs to escape. Downing tools he grabs his jacket and heads out to feel the breeze on his face and the earth underfoot; he needs to sense his place on earth – to feel alive. He heads for his favourite spot past the willow-lined lake to the ornate Victorian bandstand in the park, where the bordering beds of sunshine gerberas and tulips usually help to lift his spirits. He drops onto a wrought iron bench and whilst he stares at the wonder of nature all around him, he sharply realises that wherever he might travel in this world again, he will never see his old friend again.

"Brian?" He looks up to see Sam in her jogging gear, perspiring and taking her earphones out. "I thought it was you."

"Samantha, I almost didn't recognise you."

"Yeah, hiding under all this sweat!" she puffs.

"Well you certainly look invigorated."

"Flippin' knackered, to tell the truth."

Brian smiles. "We missed you in class this week."

Her eyes shift away and she moves from one foot to the other. "Yeah."

"Is everything alright?" he asks. "Come, sit a moment."

Sam teeters, not sure if offloading to one of The Dixbury Dancers is such a good idea. Brian looks up at her. "I'm a darn good listener," he says, and pats the bench next to him. Taking in his kind eyes and intuitively sensing she can trust him, she sits and sighs heavily.

"Did you know I was sort of seeing someone?" she starts.

"I had heard a rumour."

"Well, he turned out to be a bit of a rat."

"Oh I see."

"Hmm," she looks out across the park. "He has a fiancée already." Her lips twitch.

"Oh my dear, I'm sorry. Some men are cads, what can I say?"

"And then to make matters worse, Amy knew. And didn't tell me."

"Samantha, I'm sure she wouldn't have meant to hurt you," he says with surprise. "She must've had her reasons."

"I don't know anymore, Brian." Her chin quivers. "She's supposed to be my friend. She was supposed to have my back, not stab me in it."

"I'm sure there's a reasonable explanation – have you talked to her?"

Samantha looks down at her hands. "She keeps calling me, but I just can't face her. I'm so disappointed."

"Do you think you at least owe her the opportunity to explain?" He raises his eyebrows.

Samantha looks up. "I'm scared. Supposing I can't get past it and we can't be friends anymore?"

"Ah, well, you're not going to know until you talk."

"I know."

"We all make mistakes, but I think some people are worth a second chance, don't you?" Brian smiles.

"Hmm." Sam looks out to the rolling greens in the distance. "So, while we're having our little heart to heart, what's happening with you and the lovely Gloria?"

"Ah well, that is a long and sad story."

"Oh no, really?"

"I'm at my happiest with her – but it seems that circumstances have transpired to keep us apart." Sam gives him a questioning look.

"Circumstances? Come on, I spilled. Your turn." She smiles.

"Gloria felt it was all too soon after Stanley's death and, between you and me, I think her daughter applied a little pressure. So we're just good friends, which is fine."

"That's what Gloria wants?"

"It seems so, although I still think there's unfinished business, but maybe that's just me."

Sam shrugs. "If you don't mind me saying, you do seem a little sad."

"I had some rather unsettling news this morning; an old friend of mine, Harry, passed away."

"Oh I'm so sorry."

"I am too." Brian sighs deeply. "He was a good man. Just dropped dead on the golf course. You see, Samantha, it's all so unpredictable, isn't it?" He rubs his chin. "Do you suppose Harry died with unfinished business?"

Sam shivers. "Hmm, there's a lesson here, isn't there?"

Brian stares into the middle distance. "You know, I've spent so much time telling myself that I'm used to the uncomplicated life of being alone. No highs, no lows, just a steady life." His voice withers away.

"Sounds a bit boring, Brian. life *is* for living and all that."

Brian gives a wry smile. "I'm so glad I bumped into you today, young lady."

"Me too." Sam looks around. "Look, I don't feel like running anymore today – it's all I've done for the past couple of weeks and I've had enough. What do you say we stroll over to the café and I'll treat us?"

Brian stands and cocks his arm. "It'd be my pleasure, Miss. Would you care to?"

Sam smiles and takes his arm. "I'd be honoured."

Chapter 51

So, here's my life: Bendrick's left, Sam is still ignoring my messages, our new houseguest is firmly installed in the spare room, I've had no recent battles with Steve and he's even agreed to Leanne Cork's raised offer – yeah, how did all that happen? With all the uncertainty I'm craving familiarity which is why I'm skipping off the bus to the sanctuary of Hip Snips.

"Morning G!"

"Morning babe. 'ow's fings wiv the muvver-in-law?"

I pull a face. "Oh she's alright. Nice enough, I suppose. It's just that thing of having someone else in your house."

"Can't blow off when ya wanna, eh?"

"Ha ha. You have a way with words, Gina." She takes this as a big compliment and wanders off to set up for the day. I'm just collecting brushes and combs when the bell on the door makes me look up. The sight of Sam standing in reception makes my heart picks up speed. I gather myself and quickly walk over.

"Hi. How are you?"

She shakily pushes a lock of wavy hair behind her ear. "We need to talk."

"Yes, we do. Let me just see when I'm free." I move behind the desk and run my finger down the large diary page. "Hang on a mo, I'll see if Gina can cover my first lady, then we could nip out for coffee now. That ok?"

She nods.

I run into the staff room. "G, G, G pleeeeease!"

"Flippin' 'eck, wot now?"

"It's Sam," I whisper, pointing to the front of the shop. "She finally wants to talk. Will you do Mrs Hedges for me, please?"

"Mrs Benson an' 'edges – the walkin' cigarette?"

"Shhhh," I say, checking that said customer hasn't walked in.

"Well, stick thin wiv brown straight 'air – she looks like a ciggie!" She laughs.

"OK, OK, yes, if you like, but will you do it, please? I'll owe you."

"Go on then – I'm keepin' a note of these favours y'know."

"You're a gem." I squeeze her and peck her cheek.

"A soft touch, more like!" she says, grimacing and wiping away my kiss.

"I'll be back in thirty minutes," I call over my shoulder as I grab my jacket.

As we step outside I can't imagine walking the distance to Expresso High in awkward silence, so I suggest the café next door. It's more fry ups than frappucinos, but will suffice as somewhere to talk. Grabbing a couple of coffees we sit on the red plastic chairs at a table near the back.

The atmosphere between us crackles with tension. I have never been more aware that I must find the exact words, and express them with crystal clarity, to avoid losing my friend.

I clear my throat. "Sam," I say, my voice tight. "I'm so sorry."

She blinks and looks me in the eyes.

"Look, let me explain. I went to Simone Bletchley's office and saw this
photograph and it took me a while to recognise who he was – I'd only seen him that time at Dixbury Does Talent. Anyway, I planned to confront him as I wanted to make sure I'd got my facts right before I spoke to you. But through one thing and another I didn't get to see him. Then you slept with him and were so happy and I was trying to convince myself that I must've got it wrong. But then I saw Simone again and she said she was marrying a physio and then..." My voice weakens and disappears.

"So when you found out that he was getting married, you still didn't tell me." Her normally light blue eyes are cold and dark.

"I tried to. That day when we had lunch. But the estate agent called and, to be honest, I didn't think a one-hour lunch break would be the best time. I would've had to run back to work and leave you alone and upset. I couldn't do that."

"So instead you left me to carry on with someone who was
possibly playing me?"

"I actually thought that he should've told you himself. That's
what I was trying to make him do at the party. Looking back I shouldn't have attempted it whilst I was half cut…but hindsight is a wonderful thing." She looks down into her coffee and sighs. "If you believe nothing else," I continue. "Please believe that I'm sorry. Truly." She fiddles with her ring and looks around the café. "So what happened?" I gingerly ask.

"He says he's confused, doesn't know what he wants. He says he's in love with me, and he also says he's going to end it with her."

"Has he?"

She shakes her head. "He says it's not easy. He doesn't want to hurt her."

"Ah."

She looks me squarely in the eyes. "I wish you'd told me."

"So do I, with all my heart." I take a breath. "So what happens now?"

"I don't know. Leaving him to sort things out, I guess. But how can I trust him after this? Ironic, isn't it, initially I had doubts, thought he seemed a bit flaky – but now I really like him. He's begging me to give him time and space to sort it." Sam's shoulders relax a little as she takes a sip of her drink. "And that woman you saw him with in the pub? It was his cousin."

I've been exactly where she is now. Wanting to believe him is, in the short term, easier than facing a pile of hurt and rejection; that tussle between common sense and what your heart's telling you is a tough old battle. For the sake of keeping my friend, if she believes it was his cousin, then it was his cousin.

"Hey, it'll all work out, you know," I say. I reach across the table for her hand and somehow manage to hit the sugar bowl, spraying granules over the table and floor. "Oh for God's sake!" I say, trying to scoop it up, only to find that it attaches itself in patches to the sticky Formica table and leaves me with sugary caked fingers. I waggle them, trying to brush it off.

Sam giggles. "I've missed you, Amy."

"Not as much as I've missed you."

Just then I see Rep-tile Dave sitting a couple of tables along trying to catch my eye. Misinterpreting my actions of shaking sugar off my hands to mean 'come and join us' he's over in a jiffy.

"Hi there!" he says.

"Hi Dave. Dave, this is my friend, Sam. Sam, this is Dave, our friendly Richard Worth rep."

"Nice to meet you," he says to her and shakes her hand. She looks up and they smile. "I was going to drop in," he says, peeling his eyes away from Sam. "Is it worth my while?"

"I don't know, Dave, depends what you're trying to offload today."

He turns back to Sam. "You know Sam, I do my best spiel and offer the best hair care products but this woman never wants to buy. How's a geezer supposed to earn a crust?" Sam giggles girlishly to which I give her a quizzical frown.

Glancing at my watch, I turn back to Dave. "I'll be back in there in five, OK?"

"Okey dokey, I'll just finish my coffee and see you there." He leans towards Sam. "Lovely to meet you."

"You too." She watches him return to his seat.

"Samantha?" I raise my eyebrows teasingly.

"What?" she says innocently, before leaning in conspiratorially. "So is there anything I should know about him?"

"Ouch. I'm not going to be forgiven anytime soon, am I?" I say, cringing.

"It's a long road to redemption, my friend."

"And I'm willing to walk it."

She smiles. "No secrets from now on, okay?"

I sign a cross on my heart. "Promise." I check her expression. "You okay?"

"Eurgh, not really. I'm sad, disappointed, hurt and really pissed off that I might lose my mentor." She finishes her coffee. "But with all that I've been through in the last year, losing my mum and all, I know I'll get through this."

"You're a tough cookie, Samantha."

We both smile. "Anyway," she says. "What about you? What's new?"

"Joshua's mother is staying and it looks like Leanne Cork is buying my house."

"Blimey – guess we all have our crosses to bear!"

"Indeed." I check my watch and puff out my cheeks. "Right, I'm really sorry but I've gotta get back. You gonna be at ballet on Wednesday?"

"Yep, I'll be there."

"Great." I get up to leave. "Are we OK?"

"Pick up the tab and apologise for the sugar explosion and we will be."

I grin widely. "You're the best, Samantha Jones!"

Chapter 52

I open the door and am greeted by the sounds of Radio Two and the aroma of cooking. As Joshua is more of a Radio Six type I'm assuming Marie is in charge in the kitchen.

"Hello?" I call, not wanting to alarm her by suddenly appearing.

"Oh hello Amy!" she calls back. "I'm just in the kitchen."

I go through and plonk myself on a kitchen stool.

"Something smells good," I say.

"Doing Joshua's favourite: shepherds pie," she says as I say, "Lasagne" at the same time. We both laugh nervously.

"Is that his favourite nowadays, eh?" she asks.

"I don't know, now you mention it."

"Takes a while to get to know someone properly, doesn't it? Mick, Joshua's dad, for years I thought he liked mushy peas. I served them and served them, until one night, when he'd had a couple of beers, he told me he prefers garden peas. I couldn't believe it! A lot less effort too, I must say. All that time I'd spent making mushy peas and all the time he liked ordinary garden peas." She shakes her head in disbelief.

Now – this is Marie Milne – a short, tidy looking woman who wouldn't harm a fly, but could win medals for inane conversation. As she talks I can feel my eyes glazing over and the life being drained from me. It's like she doesn't even need an audience – she's quite happy telling herself the same stories she's told a hundred times before.

Just then the object of our love walks in.

"Hi you," he says, kissing me on the cheek. "Mum." He kisses her too. "What are my two favourite girls up to?"

"Your two favourite *women* are discussing peas," I say.

He grins. "Ah. Don't like them myself – not since John Clarkson was opposite me in school and ate so many that he threw up. Bright green…"

"That's enough of that, Joshua," Marie interrupts. "We'll be eating in a minute."

He smirks mischievously at being reprimanded and winks at me.

"OK, I'm going to change," I say.

"Dinner's in five minutes," Marie says.

"What we having?" I hear Joshua ask, as I'm heading to the bedroom.

"Shepherds Pie."

"Oooh my favourite," he says.

*

"Beatrice's husband died, you know," Marie says, spooning some banana liberally covered in custard into her mouth.

"Really?" Joshua says with mild interest.

"Yes. Funeral was a couple of weeks back. Lovely man. Salt of the earth," she says for my sake. "Would do anything for anybody, isn't that right, Joshua?" He nods dutifully. "Poor Beatrice, she's a bit lost at sea at the moment. I mean, you would be, wouldn't you? All those years together." She takes another mouthful of banana. "But, hearsay is that she's fighting off that Bruce Fielding – you know the one who won the marrow competition in the summer? He's always had a thing for her."

"Ah," Joshua says.

"He's a nice enough chap – it's just too soon, I'd say. You know, out of one relationship and straight into the next."

This is a bit close to home. "Different people need different things," I venture.

"True enough," Marie says. "But no one wants to be on the end of a rebound, eh?"

"No, but sometimes it's just right, isn't it?" I look to Joshua for whom the bananas in custard seem to have grasped his full attention. "You can't plan when you fall in love."

"Hmm, you're right enough, I suppose," she says.

Joshua scrapes his bowl. "Mum, that was magic, thanks."

"Always did like your puddings, didn't you? Right chubby youngster, he was, Amy." She laughs.

"Mum," he moans.

"Remember that video of us at Southend?"

"Mum!"

"There we are, me, his dad, Rory and Joshua with my parents and we've all got a chocolate bar. Which one was it, Joshua?" He shakes his head, smiling. "Well, anyway, there he is, this one, he was only about two, walking around, having a bite of everyone's in turn. At the end he had a great big chocolate smile and dribbled chocolate all down his front. I think he even had some in his hair – a right ol' mess!"

They both laugh at the memory.

"Right, I'll just clear up," I say, collecting the dishes. As I head to the kitchen I hear the pair of them chattering about something or other and as I'm heading back for the rest of the plates I hear Marie's lowered tones.

"So, it's there in the bank for when the time comes…"

As I enter the room she abruptly stops. I smile and see something I don't recognise in Joshua's eyes. Guilt? I collect the rest of the crockery and, sure enough, as I reach the kitchen I hear their conversation resume.

Not sure I'm comfortable being excluded from a conversation in my own home…

I reach for the kitchen radio and retuning it to Radio Six I jack it up to drown out their voices, and then proceed to wash up loudly. Very loudly. Plates crash onto the draining board and pots clang on the hooks, whilst I sing badly to Kasabian. It's rare that I drag out the washing up, but tonight I'd rather be here, in my little kitchen, than in the dining room with those two who seem intent on excluding me. *Hmph, let them have their privacy.*

I wipe the surfaces, wipe again, give the cooker a good once over, hang the tea towel up and when I can no longer find another job I put my head around the dining room door.

"Ok, I'm bushed. Thanks for a lovely meal. I'm off to my bed," I say with as much lightness as I can muster.

"OK, night Amy," Marie says.

"I won't be long," Joshua adds.

I nip to the bathroom and get all my ablutions done and then retreat to the safe haven of the bedroom. Crashing into bed I grab my book but, as hard as I try, I just can't concentrate; I'm riled. And I know I won't be able to sleep until I've said my piece.

Forty-six minutes later Joshua enters the bedroom, unzipping his hoodie. "You OK?" he asks.

Can he not see the steam billowing out of my ears? "Truthfully? No."

"What's up?"

"Do you know how it feels to be excluded from a conversation in your own home?" I say in a strained whisper.

"Eh?"

"You and your mother. I came back into the room and you two were clearly talking about something that I wasn't supposed to hear."

"Amy, it's just my mum. She wanted to talk about stuff, that's all. She's old fashioned and thinks that family things are family things."

"And I'm not family," I say matter-of-factly. His face shows fear and uncertainty in equal measures. "Got it," I snap.

"No, you haven't. That's her view, not mine."

"So, what were you talking about?"

"It's my mum's business, it wouldn't be right to talk about it."

"Right." I feel my face taking on a red hue.

"No, Amy," he says, starting towards the bed.

"No." I hold out my hand to stop him. "It's the circles."

"Eh?"

"I am the middle circle of my life. Around me is the tightest circle of the people closest to me. That's you, Sam, Gina and Gloria. Then there's the next circle: friends who are not close, but still friends. The next circle is acquaintances, the next is distant acquaintances and so it goes until the last circle is filled with strangers. Tell me your circles, Joshua."

He takes a deep breath, looks me straight eyes and steadily says, "You, my mum and dad and Rory are in the first circle. And that's why I can't share what one of you inner circlers tell me. Would you like it if I shared stuff you told me with my mum?"

Damn it – he's got a point.

"I feel left out, Joshua. And to be frank, unsupported. Your mum was blethering on about that woman, Beatrice, launching into the next relationship too quickly from the last one and you didn't say anything!"

"Whoa whoa, back up, what?"

"It was fairly obvious she was talking about me!"

"Ok, right, for starters, I wasn't even listening to that conversation!" he says, in spitting whispers. "But, if you think my mother has the guile to indirectly have a pop at you, you don't know my mother! She talks. A lot. But she's not one for scoring points. And, you know, Amy, for your information, she really likes you!"

He marches to the bed and grabs his pillows.

"Oh no, please don't do that." I grab his arm. "I don't want your mother to find you on the sofa." He stops. "Sleep here." I pat the bed. "Please."

He complies, takes off his jeans and climbs under the duvet. He lies on his back staring at the ceiling. With a respectable distance between us, I lie on mine. As the minutes tick by I hear his breath deepen. How can men sleep no matter what is happening? Needless to say, sleep alludes me.

If the reluctance to invest his nest egg gave me the jitters then this isn't making things better. It's testing times indeed. And in the early hours when worries distort and I'm riddled with doubt, I am still stuck with one thought: is lasagne or shepherds pie his favourite meal?

And, as silly as it seems, I think if I don't know this, what else don't I know?

Chapter 53

Marion sits in the visitor waiting area, watching the loved ones of prisoners arrive in dribs and drabs. She thought it would be easier this time – but her insides disagree as the number of trips to the toilet she's had so far today can testify. Pulling at a nail she thinks about the conversation she had with Julay a few days ago.

"Marion dear," Julay had said, waving the blue flimsy envelope with the familiar prison stamp on. "You have to do something. It's almost everyday now!"

"I know," she answered, taking the letter.

Marion had written to Jack, clearly expressing how she didn't want to hear from him any longer, but he'd read that as merely playing hard to get and had continued to bombard her with his prison quota of letters ever since.

"What does he say this time?" Julay asked, raising one eyebrow.

Marion opened the letter and scanned the contents. "Pretty much the same…forgiveness…memories of the past…God is guiding him." She folded the letter back on the table. "I think he thinks he's being romantic."

"It's a fine line between romance and stalking, isn't it?" Julay said.

"Guess it depends on whether you want the fellow or not."

"And do you?"

Looking at the 'Visitor Rules' sign on the wall she still ponders the question; *does* she still want him? Does it depend on whether his transformation is genuine? Or is it too late regardless? Has there been too much water under the bridge? With his letters evoking feelings she'd long since buried, her emotions are certainly in a muddle.

Entering the bare visiting room with its scratched wobbly tables and hard chairs Marion sees Jack immediately. He stands and kisses her lightly on the cheek.

"Mari, I've missed you. Thank you for coming." His skin is even paler than she recalled.

"I thought we needed to talk, Jack."

"Of course, of course. How are you?"

"Fine. How are you?"

"Honestly, Mari, since you came back in my life I've felt a lot better. More hopeful. God is providing." He smiles serenely, links his fingers and flexes his knuckles. "You're looking well, love. Is it that dancing?"

"It could be. We're starting work on another piece for another competition. It hasn't been easy, but now that Bendrick has left us and we're back to Helena teaching…"

Jack looks in her eyes. "Who's Bendrick?"

"The temporary teacher," Marion quickly answers, feeling the familiar stance of being on the back foot. "He took over whilst Helena was recovering from a fall."

Darkness flashes in his eyes. "Did he?"

"Yes."

"And what's he like, this Bendrick?"

"What does it matter?"

"What's he like?"

"Jack, please don't make a fuss."

Jack leans forward but quickly checks himself back in his seat. "Mari," he smiles. "You can't blame me for being jealous. I'm banged up and the woman I love is out and about – it's only natural." He shrugs. "Can't help the way I feel."

He reaches for her hand. It's rough and cold with callouses and her most basic instincts scream at her to run. Maybe he likes to think he's changed, or maybe it is one elaborate ploy to escape prison – but whatever it is, that temperament, that anger, the ability to manipulate and abuse is still there. Old Jack and New Jack are one and the same.

"I've the parole hearing next week," he continues.

"Yes."

"You coming?"

"I'm not sure."

His face drops. "Oh?"

"I just don't think I want to be a part of it."

His lip curls. "You don't care what happens to me, eh?"

"Yes, I do. I do care. I wish you luck, Jack." With that she delves into her bag and pulls out the bundle of letters tied up with string. Pushing them towards him and not quite able to meet his eyes, she rises. "I'll always want what's best for you. But that's as far as it goes."

Turning on her heels, she starts to leave the room.

"Mari, Mari!" he calls desperately.

Hearing his cries, Marion lowers her head and quickens her pace. The warden opens the door and she walks straight out of it without even considering for one moment to look back.

Chapter 54

"Brian," Helena says, placing us in our starting positions. "What I'd like from you is to weave amongst the dancers taking their hands when they are in the arabesque. OK?"

He nods. We are lined up in a zigzag formation with, I note, the more competent dancers at the front. To be fair they are the ones who will enter first and continue the steps for longer, so it makes sense that they should be the more experienced ones. So, we have Julay, Catherine and Sam heading up the line, Gloria and Josie in the middle and Marion, Lucia and I bringing up the rear. I'm happy with that.

"Right, I hope you've all had an opportunity to watch the clip of this dance," Helena continues. "It's beautiful in its ethereal manner."

Lucia leans into me, and whispers, "What the chuff's that?" I stifle a giggle and shrug.

"Like a ghost," Gloria mouths.

"Ooh, have we got ghoulies in this too?" Lucia cackles.

"Shhh," Julay snaps, giving Lucia daggers. Lucia bats it back with a sweet smile.

"So your movements," Helena continues, "must be light, soft, graceful and effortless. It's like you're being swept down the ramp, - I'm still working on getting one for rehearsals – giving the impression of your feet hardly touching the ground. The beauty of this piece is the synchronicity and, for that, the music makes it easy." She smiles at us all. "Are you ready to try?"

We all nod. Things feel different now Helena is back at the helm. There's a security we've been missing. Don't get me wrong, Bendrick was lovely – but you never knew what he'd make you attempt from one week to the next. Helena is a more realistic judge of our abilities – and we trust her.

The music begins – with beautiful melodious strings and a clear even tempo it does help us to keep time. Helena walks with Brian to show him what he needs to do. He takes Julay's hand first and her back leg rises as she executes a beautiful arabesque. As each dancer joins the line from 'the wings' I watch as he partners each one. I hold my breath as I see him take Gloria's hand. As he fixes his expressionless gaze at a point over her head, she can barely reach his eyes. I wonder if he's performing or self-preserving? As he moves to the next dancer I glance back to see Gloria's chin wobble slightly before she shakes it off. I ask myself again why these two are apart? They compliment each other perfectly and have so much in common – why did Fliss have to stick her oar in? It hardly seems fair.

"OK guys, that was beautiful. Thanks," Helena says. "Let's take a moment, get some water, stretch out and we'll run it again."

We trot over to our towels and water bottles and chatter breaks out.

"Who fancies a drink after this?" Lucia asks.

Arms bob up in chorus, "Me!"

"The Swan?" Marion asks.

"Sounds good to me, Mazzy," Lucia says.

"OK," Helena calls. "Let's line up again."

"Blimey, she really did mean 'a moment', didn't she?" Lucia puffs as we return to our starting positions.

Having run through the piece a few more times, Helena decides that after the slow drawn out movements we need something to infuse life – we must jump! She gives us a warm up exercise that has us producing beads of sweat and then sets the grand allegro for the evening. One at a time we are required to diagonally cross the room in a series of steps, small and large jumps and then run back around to the same corner to immediately repeat. With the amount of times we do this I suspect it's not so much about leaping as building stamina.

"Rebound back. You're on a trampoline! Use your plié to spring into the air. Heels down when you land," she calls, like the ringmaster of a show. "You are my birds of flight."

"Knackered old pigeon more like," Marion says, bent over double, awaiting her turn in the line.

"This is when I feel old," Gloria says, swiping an escaped lock of hair over her ear.

"Never," Brian says quietly from behind her. Gloria straightens and allows herself a small smile.

"Weeeeeeeeeee," Lucia shrills as she makes a giant leap. "I'm fly-iiiing!"

Gloria and Brian involuntarily wince as she lands with a thud. "I love her lust for life," Brian says, watching Lucia yank her leotard up at the front and wriggle it down at the knicker line.

"Me too," Gloria says with a soft chuckle. "Brian," she starts.

"Hmm?"

"Are you going for a drink afterwards?"

"Are you?"

"Yes."

He smiles. "Then I am too."

They file around the room and join the queue ready to leap through the air again.

"OK, OK, everybody gather round for a moment," Helena calls. "Now, the piece you've been learning relies heavily on you all being in time. A member of the corps de ballet is only as good as her, or his, fellow corps de ballet-ers."

"This doesn't bode well," Marion mumbles.

"Let me tell you a story about a young ballerina, let's call her Helena." Everyone laughs. "She was on stage and fortunate enough to be given the lead."

"Fortunate? Or maybe she was the best?" Brian says.

Helena blushes. "Anyway, I led and towards the end of the piece one poor dancer in the corps forgot a whole section – it just went! I immediately altered my steps to follow her lead and so did all the others. The audience would never have known. Well except for the part at the end where the music was still playing and we were all finished!"

We all laugh. “So, in a corps de ballet it doesn’t matter who is the best, or who has the highest leg or the most turn out, the point is for the dancers to blend – to shadow one another, to act as one large body. Perfect timing and in formation is the key.

“What information?” Lucia asks.

“No ‘in formation’ like the Red Arrows,” Helena clarifies.

“Gotcha.” Lucia raises her thumb and nods earnestly.

“Right, we are going to try that grand allegro again,” she says to audible groans. “Yes, come on, you’ve all had a breather, so we’re going to do it again, but this time in formation. The first dancer leads to the right and then turns to the left and repeats the steps. As she finishes the first time, the next person joins in and so on.” *I have a bad feeling about this.* “You’ll be a zigzagging line of synchronicity!” *She hopes.*

Helena lines us up with Catherine at the helm. One by one we join the dance. I’m following Marion who falls at the first hurdle by going the wrong way. In the etiquette of the corps de ballet I follow her – I’m her shadow. When the next dancer, Lucia, chooses to go to the right first, it is only a matter of moments before the car crash happens. We trip over each other, apologise, giggle, try to orientate ourselves and continue to the end. In our finishing positions and with the music coming to a close, all we can hear is the sound of Helena’s muffled laughter.

“I’m so sorry,” she says, trying to straighten her face. “Seriously, you know what I loved about that?”

“Our complete lack of coordination?” Marion asks.

“Our flair for failing?” Brian quips.

“That we’re more corpse than corps?” Lucia asks.

“No!” Helena beams. “You carried on like professionals. It fell apart, for sure, but you all carried on. This is The Dixbury Dancers that I know and love! It may be crashing down around your ears but you carry on! So everyone was going in opposite directions, doing different steps, with a couple of minor collisions, but you got to the end. Your finishing stances were those of accomplished dancers. You looked proud and you should be.”

We accept the praise given, have a cool down and then trot into the changing room.

"Helena's fab, isn't she?" Lucia says wistfully, to which we all agree. "And sometimes I just really want whatever she's on."

We all giggle, nodding our heads in agreement.

Chapter 55

The Swan is unusually crowded for a Wednesday night. I remember when Thursday became *the* night to go out and wonder if Wednesday is becoming the new Thursday. Mind you, it's not the young and trendy frequenting our sleepy little pub, more like groups of people grabbing a drink after an evening course – much like us, I suppose.

I buy a round and then, taking a seat next to Marion, I look around the table. With the exception of Catherine, whose Dad picked her up, we've all made it tonight – which is something of a rarity – even Geoff is here, squidged up next to Lucia. I did text Joshua to see if he wanted to join us but he politely declined. "*Can't really leave my mum on her own*," he'd texted. No, quite.

I did eventually fall asleep the other night, but not before I'd stared at him for half of it, his chest rhythmically rising and falling and his curls flopped around his face. I told myself that he's not the kind of man who will let me down – I know that. We're just going through a sticky patch. It'll pass. In the morning we conversed as you do when you've had a falling out but haven't got time to sort it and you've got company. He pecked me on the cheek goodbye and gave me a sad smile.

"What do we think of the new choreography?" Josie asks the group.

"I rather like it," Marion says. "It's slow enough to be able to remember, but not so slow that my legs tremble."

"I'd prefer something a bit bigger and bouncier," Lucia says.

"We're not trampolinists!" Julay says.

"Alright, cool your knickers. Just meant that it's a bit dirgy."

"If we can perfect this 'dirge' we might get the same rapturous applause as last time, and I don't know about you, but I need that," Julay continues. "Were you aware that I was contemplating giving up dancing?"

"What?" I say. "Why?"

"I don't know. With the newspaper and then that diabolical performance I just wasn't enjoying it. Started to wonder if I was foolish still wanting to do this at my age."

"Julay, love," Lucia says. "You can't say things like that. Especially when you've got Marion sitting here." Marion spits her drink. "Sorry Maz, no offence."

"Er, none taken," she says, wiping her mouth.

"I just wish we had more rehearsal time," Sam says.

"Shall we go back to Sunday afternoons? Get a few more in?" Gloria asks. *Hmm, more time apart from Joshua isn't ideal – but it'll only be for a short while.*

"Shall I book the hall?" I ask.

"Seeing as you sleep with the caretaker, why not!" Lucia laughs. "Do we get a discount?"

"No!"

"Whose for another?" Brian asks, holding up his empty glass. Around the table people tell him their order until it gets to Gloria.

"I'm not sure what I want." She frowns.

"Perhaps you could come to the bar and see what they've got."

"Yes, good idea, I think I will." Gloria rises from her seat and we all watch them walk to the bar.

"Is it just me or can everyone else see little love hearts and birds fluttering around their heads?" Sam asks.

"Ah, I think it's just splendid," Marion says with a sigh. "Wish I could be with someone like Brian."

"You will Mazzy," Lucia says. "Top bird like you won't be on the market for long."

Marion's expression suggests it's a first for being called a 'top bird'.

"So, another lime and soda? Or something a bit stronger, a coca cola perhaps?" Brian teases.

Peering over the bar Gloria says, "For that I'll have a sweet sherry please."

"Ooh, madam has expensive tastes."

"The gentleman did offer, did he not?"

They both laugh gently.

"Don't you feel we're back on track?" Brian says.

"You and I?"

"No, no. no, no, sorry, I meant The Dixbury Dancers." Gloria's cheeks flame. "I just meant after all the recent events things seem to be calming down."

"Oh yes, indeed. We've definitely turned a corner," Gloria says, inwardly cursing her misunderstanding. Trying to hide her blush she turns to look fondly at their friends whilst Brian places the order.

Depositing a couple of drinks on the table she returns to the bar for more when Brian catches her arm. "I had some sad news this week."

"Oh?"

"Yes, a friend of mine dropped down dead, heart attack. Made me think about a lot of things, about the things I want, what I want to do with my life." Oh no, thinks Gloria, he's going off travelling, or moving away or something else that doesn't involve her! "And how I'm prepared to fight for the things that I want. I know that you said it was too soon after Stanley, and I understand that, but quite simply, Gloria…well, what I mean is… what I'm trying to say is…it's just that…argh." His eyes burn with frustration.

Gloria places her hand on his. "Take a breath."

He inhales and releasing a long exhale, looks her in the eyes. "I just miss you."

"I miss you too."

Brian smiles with a rush of relief. "So, what do we do?"

"I think we should drink our drinks and then say goodnight."

Brian's brow knits in confusion. "Say goodnight? But…"

Gloria chuckles softly, nodding to the group. "To them."

They both smile and walk back to the table to re-join their friends, just as Marion is saying how costumes still need to be sorted.

"That was fun last time, wasn't it?" I say. "All getting together to make them. Can we do that again?"

"Do you think Helena will let us choose colours?" Marion asks.

"I think we should ask her." Lucia says. Then, across the table she notices Brian knocking back his drink. "Blimey Brian - you part camel or something?"

Gloria covers her snigger with a cough.

"Er, just thirsty, that's all," he says, his eyes wide with innocence. "But I do want to turn in for the night. All those jumps have fair done me in."

"Yes, I'm feeling quite tired myself. I'm going to head out too," Gloria adds.

"Is that right?" Lucia says, looking from one to another. Geoff digs her in the ribs.

With their goodbyes done, we all watch as Brian places his hand on the small of Gloria's back as they head for the door.

"Somebody's getting lucky tonight," Lucia says, curling her lips.

As everyone giggles or tuts, I feel a sense of sadness that tonight that someone, for once, isn't me.

Chapter 56

"Would you like a snifter of brandy in it?" Gloria asks Brian, as she takes two glass coffee cups from the shelf.

"That would be lovely, thank you." He takes a seat on the sofa at the end of the kitchen and switches on a table lamp. He watches her glide around the kitchen, preparing the drinks and arranging biscuits on a plate. Just as he is thinking what a marvellous creature she is, she looks across and smiles, and his heart gently flutters.

"There we are," she says, placing the tray down and passing him a cup. "Here's to the future."

He raises his glass and takes a sip. "Oooh, lovely, this'll warm the cockles nicely." They both smile and continue to chat amiably about anything and everything; all the things that they would've normally discussed excitedly pour out, sometimes even interrupting each other with the sheer joy of being together again. With drinks drunk and biscuits nibbled, the elephant in the room rears its head. "So," Brian says, taking a deep breath. "What we were saying in the pub…"

"Yes." Gloria narrows her eyes. "In these past few weeks I've done a lot of thinking too." She chooses her words carefully. "I thought that not seeing you so much would leave me guilt-free to grieve for Stanley. What I didn't realise is that, although I will always miss him, I've done a lot of my grieving – he was in that care home a long time. I've been a widow far longer than is strictly true." Brian focuses on her eyes, breathing steadily and hoping that the outcome of her words will be in his favour. "And Fliss was going through such a hard time and I felt that having you in my life was just causing her further stress."

"How is she?"

"Oh, she's gone back home. I haven't heard from her so I assume that she's getting her marriage back on track – I hope she is anyway."

"I see."

"Regardless of Fliss, I know what I want and it's really quite simple." Brian's eyebrows rise as she pauses. "It's you."

Brian reaches out to put his arms around her and drawing her close, he kisses her deeply. Her body responds with sparks of passion that have long been missing in her life. Pulling apart, both trembling, Brian questions her with his eyes. She smiles, stands, and gently taking his hand, she leads him upstairs.

*

The bright sun streams in the window as Gloria's eyes shoot open to a ringing. What is that? It's not the alarm, or the telephone…ah, the doorbell. She looks across at Brian who is sleeping through it – she smiles, thinking how she always did suspect he was a little deaf. She kisses him gently on the forehead and then climbing out of bed, she throws on her dressing gown and makes her way downstairs. Probably a parcel too big for the letterbox, she muses. As she throws open the door her jaw hits the floor.

"Fliss! What are you doing here?"

"Charming. Can I come in?"

"Er, yes, of course." Stepping aside to let her in, Gloria's mind frantically races with the thought of Brian's jacket in the kitchen. "Go through to the lounge and I'll put the kettle on," she hurriedly says, and then scoots to the kitchen to quickly hang it up behind the door. Joining her daughter a few moments later Gloria sits down and gently asks, "What's happened?"

Fliss looks around the room, hesitating. "It's over," she says, tears brimming. "We tried, we really did. It's not even about not having babies; he's just not prepared to change his lifestyle for me."

"Oh I'm sorry."

"He says he has a plan. Work until he hits forty and then we'll have enough money to live the life we want. But that's not what I want! What I want is a life with him now. Anything could happen between now and then. We need to live our lives now!" Fliss grabs a tissue and wipes her nose.

"So have you left him?"

"Sort of. I just couldn't bear being there while he packs, so can I stay here for a couple of days please? He's going to a rented flat."

"Yes of course you can, darling." Gloria smooths her daughter's hair. "Let me go and make that tea."

Gloria scurries to the kitchen, her mind in a tizzy. Oh no – what should she do? What's going to happen when Brian wakes up? When he sees that she's no longer next to him in bed? Will he call out for her? Gloria turns tail and taking the stairs two at a time, she rushes into the bedroom.

"Brian, Brian," she half whispers, shaking his shoulders. "Brian."

He jolts awake. "Eh? Everything all right?"

"Fliss has turned up. She's here."

"Oh."

"Look, I know it's wrong, and I will tell her that we're together, but not like this."

He rubs his face. "Hmm, not the best way for her to find out, I suppose. OK, where's my escape route?" he says with a twinkle in his eyes.

"I don't know. Er, how about I shut the lounge door and you come down the stairs and out the front door?"

"Gosh, how exciting, takes me back to my teenage days." He grins.

"I'm so sorry. I just can't tell her like this. I'll call you later, I promise." She leans across and presses her lips to his. As they part she looks deeply into his eyes. "Brian, thank you for a most wonderful night."

"My pleasure," he says, and wraps her in a warm embrace that, feeling the warmth of his body, makes Gloria regret ever leaving the bed in the first place.

"OK, my love, speak later," she says, and blowing him kisses, she leaves him to dress and gather up any incriminating belongings. She rushes back down the stairs, attends to the tea, shuts the lounge door firmly and then joins Fliss on the sofa.

"So, darling, what are you going to do now?" she asks, straightening her dressing gown and feeling like an unwitting player in a farce.

"I'm going to return home after he's gone, dive into work and wait for the rain to pass." Fliss takes a sip of tea. "You know, I'm still not convinced that he wasn't having an affair with Lexy."

"Does it really matter now?"

"Yes, it does. It shows the kind of person he is if he can do this behind my back. He swore blind to me that he wasn't having an affair with her. Can't stand hypocrisy from anyone."

Gloria gulps at the thought of Brian dressing above them.

"Well, it sounds like you've done all you can," Gloria says. "If you've talked through everything and you've both decided it's the end of the road then…" Gloria trails off as a loud thud comes from the hall.

Fliss' eyes are wide. "Mum? Is somebody here?"

"Er, well…"

Fliss rises and marches out of the room, closely followed by Gloria, where they find Brian, standing frozen half way down the stairs, holding one shoe and the other lying on the bottom step.

He winces. "Dropped my shoe."

Fliss turns to Gloria. "Mum!"

"OK, OK, Felicity." Gloria holds up her hands.

"You promised!"

"Yes I know. I know I said that I wouldn't see him anymore. But why? Why should I do that? Why should I do that for you? Or for anybody? It's my life. I don't tell you what to do, do I? I support you in whatever *you* want to do." Fliss' eyes dart from Brian's statue-like figure to her mother. "Fliss," Gloria calmly continues. "You said yourself that you can't wait for Tim to be ready for the life you want – well I can't wait for *you* to be ready for the life *I* want. I know he was your father and you loved him. I did, and still do – but life moves on." She takes a deep grounding breath. "And besides, I've fallen in love with Brian."

"You love him?" Fliss asks.

"You love me?" Brian adds tremulously.

Gloria lifts her chin and looks him proudly in the eye. "Yes I do."

Chapter 57

Rehearsals continue to go well over the next few weeks and gradually we feel our confidence returning. I even manage to think about my legs, arms, body position AND eye-line all at the same time – well at least for a few moments anyway. Extra Sunday sessions have been working well and we've started to find our 'reason to be' once more. Helena has even been giving up her Sunday afternoons to coach us.

"Right, let's talk costumes," she said, at the end of a high intensity class. "I was thinking neutral colours – maybe even some chiffon."

"Brian will look divine in that," Gloria teased and Brian beamed at her like a love-struck teenager. Despite Lucia's regularly goads for them to 'get a room,' we are all chuffed to bits that they are 'official'. I actually didn't believe that Gloria could look more beautiful – but I guess that's the power of love.

"Brian," Helena had continued, smiling. "I'll spare you the chiffon, but I do have the very top for you – a proper leading man's blouson. You can wear regular tights with it."

"Rudy Nureyev, eat your heart out," Lucia had said, winking at Brian.

"And as for you ballerinas," Helena continued. "I'd like you in white or pastel shades. Do you all have a light coloured leotard?"

We'd mentally combed through our ballet wardrobes trying to recall any items that weren't black; we have navy, purple or grey, but not one of us own anything light. Too unflattering.

Catherine raised her hand - something we've told her repeatedly she doesn't have to do with us. "I saw a box in Chappelle the other day full of sale bargains, everything under five pounds. I'm pretty sure they had pale lemon leotards."

"Hmm, that could work," Helena had said.

"A bunch of lemons?" said Lucia.

"That's precisely what you won't be," Helena had firmly replied. "A pale lemon body with a white organza tutu, in the flattering ballerina length, and then a simple chiffon bodice. You'll look heavenly."

"That does sound beautiful," I'd said.

"If you dress the part, you feel the part. Right, I will pop there this week and see what I can find. I know your sizes. I'll also pick up the chiffon – you guys okay to make the little tops?"

We'd all nodded. "It's our speciality!" Julay said. "My house? Next Sunday, before rehearsal?"

We'd all agreed, and that's where we are now, in Julay's front room with a mountain of organza, swathes of chiffon and seven spaghetti-strapped pale lemon leotards. Lucia plucks out the largest size and holds it up to her body.

"Please someone tell me how I'm going to get these," she says, looking down at her ample bosom, "into this? Am I supposed to let them roam free?"

"Good heavens, no dear." Gloria shudders.

"I think the idea of the chiffon overlay is to disguise any bra-straps," Marion says softly. "And any other unattractive features."

"Well I don't have to worry about having any of them, Mazzy" Lucia says, striking a pose.

"No, dear." Marion says, surreptitiously rolling her eyes and busying herself in the mountain of material.

We divide ourselves into groups; top makers, skirt makers and hair stylist – that would be me. "OK, Gloria, let's start with you," I say, beckoning her to Julay's kitchen where I've constructed my pop-up hairdressers. "I think we could just weave two tendrils and fix them at the back, what do you think?" I ask as we face the mirror.

"Do whatever you think, dear. You haven't let me down yet."

Sam wanders in and takes a seat to watch me work. "How's things with the lovely Joshua and the mother in law?" she asks.

"Okay, I suppose. I just feel a bit claustrophobic having another person living with us. Spontaneous sex on the lounge floor has gone out the window, and in fact there's hardly any in the bedroom either – the thought of her in the next room is a real desire dampener." I omit to say how the dynamics between Joshua and I have changed – it's only a subtle shift, but a shift nonetheless.

"Does it look like she'll be leaving any time soon?" Gloria asks.

"Well, she was meeting up with his dad for peace talks last night, so I'm hopeful. Anyway, how are things with Brian?"

"Marvellous," she says, positively glowing. "I feel like I have a new lease of life."

"And you look like the cat who got the cream."

"I am!" She giggles.

"What's happening with your daughter?" I ask.

"Ah, she's coming to terms with her wanton mother." She gives a small sigh. "I don't know if she'll ever be simpatico with Brian, but she's accepted that this is what I'm doing."

"I'm sure she'll grow to love Brian – we all do," Sam says. I nod in agreement.

"I know," says Gloria. "He's such a lovely man. I hope her reservations pass and she finds herself in a happier place. After the divorce, maybe."

"I was going to ask about that," I say.

"Reading between the lines," Gloria says. "I think Fliss might've been right; it seems there might've been something going on with him and his boss. Well – if there wasn't, there is now. Poor Fliss – she's insecure as it is."

"I know looks aren't everything," I start. "But how can she be insecure when she looks as fabulous as she does? Plus she has a great career – she's got the lot."

"Hmm, except love at the moment," Sam chips in.

"Good point, well made," Gloria says. "How are things with you in that department, Sam?"

Sam sighs. "I saw Jason again the other night, only briefly for a chat. It's really difficult. He swears that it's me he wants, but he's just kind of stuck. Anyway, I can't deal with him until he's free."

"Hmmm, it's a tricky one," Gloria says. "Do you think you could trust him again?" *Wow – there's the question…*

"You know, Gloria, I honestly don't know…I really do like him, but wonder if he did end things with Simone whether we'd have a fighting chance." Sam hesitates. "But anyway, confession time, I've been out with another man."

"Samantha Jones! You dark horse!" I say. She smiles shyly and her cheeks tint pink. "Come on, you can't leave us hanging. Spill!"

"Er, Dave."

"Dave?" I ask.

"Rep-tile Dave."

"What? How?" With my mouth open I hit the off switch on my blow dryer.

"That day in the café? You went back into work and as he was leaving, he came back to my table and …" She shrugs happily.

"Ha! I thought he seemed unusually jolly when he came in to see me. Even my serial refusing didn't dampen his mood. When did you go out with him?"

"I've actually seen him a few times. I just didn't want to mention it in case it became a big fat nothing."

"So can we presume it's a big fat something?" Gloria asks. Sam blushes to the tips of her ears. "What's this young man like then?" Gloria looks to us both.

"He's our rep, Gloria – you might've seen him in the shop? He wears slim fitting suits, dark hair gelled back?"

"Yes, I think I have! Oh how marvellous!"

"He's very sweet," Sam says. "It's not thunderbolts and lightening, but I'm enjoying his company." At that moment Josie calls for Sam as her needlework skills are required in the lounge. "Hold on, I'll be back," she says disappearing.

"Well, well," I say.

"Amy dear," Gloria says out of the corner of her mouth. "Should we be encouraging a relationship with a man called 'Rep-tile Dave'?"

"Ha ha. You know, Gloria, he could be an orang-utan with bad breath and a passion for wearing ladies underwear, I'm not interfering – I've learnt my lesson."

"Very wise, dear, very wise."

Chapter 58

We've learnt not to question why and to just go along with whatever Helena asks of us. And so it is that we are all standing in the foyer of the Dixbury Leisure Centre with rolled up towels under our arms and a certain amount of trepidation in our hearts.

Helena breezes through the swing doors. "Evening all!"

"Evening," we chorus.

"Right, thank you for coming. We're going to be here for an hour or so and then on to the hall for our usual rehearsal, OK?"

"I assume we're going to swim?" Marion says, looking around.

"Yes, sort of. Have you all seen Dirty Dancing?" Everyone nods. "What did they do when they had to practise the lift?"

"Ah," I say. "They went to the lake."

"But we're not doing any lifts," Gloria says, puzzled.

"No," Helena continues. "But anything that requires bounce or resistance is great to try in water."

"Hels, I may look like I'm built to float," Lucia says, puffing out her chest. "But I can't swim."

Helena laughs. "Don't worry, we're going to be in the shallow end. Right, shall we?" We nod and follow our leader to the changing rooms.

Ten minutes later at poolside I decide that you can tell a lot about a person by their swimwear. Gloria is in a glorious navy 1950's style ruffled halter-neck, Sam is in your traditional speedo costume whilst Julay opts for a sturdy style with shorts. Brian is the height of decency in cover-all shorts and Marion wears a faded multi-coloured affair. Josie and Catherine are in matching black and I have dragged out my old trusted suck-it-all-in and underwire-me costume.

Thankfully, being the time slot between the after-schoolers and lane swimmers, there is plenty of room to slide into the pool and form a circle around Helena.

"Right, we are going to do some sautés. Put your feet in first and your arms in bras bas and then jump," Helena says. "Let your toes really point as you have more time in the air, so to speak."

And she's right – the water buoying us gives us the opportunity to really stretch our feet and test core strength at the same time. From the small jumps we turn to other steps that are trickier in water.

"Aqua-Ballet – I reckon this could be a winner," Josie says.

"Something you can do in your old age when your knees finally give up," her daughter says with a grin.

"Oi, you!" Josie splashes her with water.

"Now for the main event." Helena grins. "In the competition you *are* doing grand jetés, and this is the place to work on them. Now, I accept that running through water is tough, but just take a couple of steps – it's not about speed – and then grand battement the front and back leg into the splits. Try to get the legs as high as you can."

We're off in all directions, trying to run but only managing to moonwalk and that sets us off giggling. To finish our session Helena instructs us in some synchronised moves, preparing us, as always, for our corp-de-ballet-togetherness. As she watches us performing multiple harmonized relevés I hear her say, "Yes, this is perfect. Busby Berkeley, eat your heart out."

•••

Back in our dance gear in the familiar territory of Dixbury Village Hall we are still buzzing from the adrenalin of splashing around.

"OK, OK, guys," Helena calls us to silence. "Now, as I'm sure you're all painfully aware, the competition is days away." We anxiously mumble. "No need to be nervous – that's not what I want – what I want is for us to run through the dance tonight and keep doing it until you could do it back to front in your sleep."

We take starting positions and the first set piece goes like a dream. We glide across the stage, perfectly in time, lifting our legs in arabesques as Brian weaves his way around us, taking our hands. It's a dream! Then we move onto the second section and slowly we unravel; Marion misses her cue, Julay trips, Lucia misses a chunk of the choreography, Sam ends a pirouette facing the wrong way and I fall off balance. Memories of Afton return.

"Well, that was a pile of poo," Marion says.

"Stinking poo," Sam adds.

"Don't worry," Helena quickly intercedes. "This is what rehearsals are for: to get things wrong. We still have time to fix things. Now, I don't want to change the choreography but if anyone is really worried about a step, speak now…"

One by one our hands shoot up.

"What!" Helena says. "*All of you?*"

"It's the pirouette." "I can't do the retiré." "The posé turn is a pig." "I'm not comfortable with holding that balance for so long." "I can't manage the -"

"Whoa, whoa, whoa." Helena holds up her hands. "Hold it there, guys. What I meant was if there was anything you *really* couldn't do – not something that challenges you. You are all more than capable of performing the steps. Will you be nervous? Yes, probably. Will you be step perfect? Maybe not. But you can do this!"

"But," Lucia says. "That posé turn really is a pig."

"Well, it's a pig you need to crack!" Helena says, to which Lucia pulls a face that makes us laugh. Helena smiles. "Let's go from the middle section and I'll call out cues, OK?"

We run through it time and time again. We even all opt to stay for longer, but it gets to a point where both brain and body decide enough is enough.

"Wonderful," Helena says, as we finally call it a night. "Well done everyone. Thank you for working so hard."

As we file off to the changing room our teacher's expectations weigh heavily on our shoulders. Of course at Afton we wanted to make Bendrick proud, but this time…well, this is Helena! She's the person who took us on when most of us didn't know our fouetté from our fondu and then coached and coaxed us on to the stage; Helena, who always believes that we are winners even when reality proves otherwise.

"I so don't want to let her down," Sam says, echoing my thoughts, as she pulls on her jeans.

"None of us do," Julay says.

"We've put so many hours in that I think we'll go into automatic pilot," Gloria points out.

"Ever the optimist, eh Glo?" Lucia says.

"Well, what's the alternative?" she answers.

And the answer to that is something none of us want to consider.

Chapter 59

With the dinner plates cleared, the three of us are sitting in the lounge; Joshua, uploading photos onto his laptop; me, trying to watch a television crime drama and Marie trying to make conversation with me. *Why do people do that?* I do that thing where I only move my eyes to acknowledge her question – it's universally recognised as the 'I'm only being polite and I would like you to shut up as I'm missing key points of the plot' trick. It fails. After so many interruptions I have no idea who's even in the running for having 'dunnit' and give up and switch off.

"Ah peace and quiet, isn't that grand?" she says. *Hmm, it could be...* "Now then, Amy, I was telling Joshua that I saw his dad last night."

"Oh, how did that go?" I ask with nothing but hope.

"We had quite a nice time, actually. He thinks it's time I went home, and I think he might be right." I look to Joshua to gauge his reaction but he's too busy cursing technology. "So, as I don't want to outstay my welcome – my dear old dad always said three nights was the limit and I've gone well over that – I'll be out of your hair soon enough."

Isn't it strange when that moment of relief comes and you're teetering on the brink of getting what you want you suddenly go all soft and mushy? "Oh you don't have to rush away," I hear myself saying. "It's been lovely having you."

"That's very kind of you. But I'll pack my bags tonight and Joshua'll drive me back in the morning, won't you, Joshua?"

"Eh?" He looks up.

"Your mum was just saying that she's off tomorrow," I say.

"Oh yeah, right, yeah."

"Right, anyone for a cup of tea?" Marie asks, getting up. We all do and she trundles out to the kitchen.

"Psst, Josh," I say, throwing a small cushion at him. "We get the house back to ourselves. Yay!"

"I know!" he says. "And I have plans." His eyebrows move up and down as if controlled by a master puppeteer.

"Oooh, what kind of plans?"

"You just worry about being here for dinner tomorrow evening and leave it to me!" He sees my face drop. "What?"

"Aargh, I've got extra ballet."

"Miss it."

"Any other time I would, but with one week before the show? I can't let them down. Sorry. How about afterwards?"

"Sure, okay," he says evenly. "Let's do something special afterwards."

"Now I thought as it's my last night," Marie says, entering the room carrying the tray. "I thought we'd push the boat out." I look up in hope for some kind of alcohol, maybe a sniff of that little quart of whisky I spotted in her room. "There you go," she says, and proudly presents a plate of chocolate digestives.

•

I idly watch Joshua who has gone back to staring at his screen – I don't know what he's looking at but there's softness in his face and a smile dancing in his eyes. *It's probably a photo of Basil.* With the whole business of his nest egg, the hushed family conversation and his mother's presence, I'm aware that I've metaphorically taken a step back. I mean, things generally between us are fine, but I can't lay myself open to the possibility of being hurt again, not so soon after Steve. So there's a little piece of my heart that I'm keeping safe – just in case.

He wrinkles his nose and tugs his t-shirt down as he sighs at the laptop and I ponder if the measure of a couple is how well they deal with external pressures. Most relationships would be fine and dandy if life sailed smoothly, wouldn't they? It's only when we're faced with stresses that we're tested. With Marie leaving tomorrow will we start to come out the other side? Other people talk about 'working' at relationships, and until recently, I've always felt that ours is effortless, but, in truth, maybe it's peaks and troughs. We do sail smoothly most of the time – our boat has been sturdy - but when the rough waters knock us about a bit, we have to re-stabilise. For fear of sounding like a politician – it is time for us to re-stabilise.

Yes - I'm going to skip out of ballet tomorrow night and, although we won't have a full evening, I'll make sure that we fill our time well. We need to enjoy each other without pressure or future expectations… or his mother in the next room. We need a return to bliss. I like bliss. It worked.

As if he can hear my thoughts he looks up and smiles.

My heart melts.

•

Joshua had turned his attention back to the photographs that wouldn't upload and happily zoned out from his mother's constant conversation. One photo was frozen on his screen; it was of Amy, by the lake, her head back laughing with that ridiculous hat she wears falling over one eye, and with Basil beside her, his backside to camera. Joshua smiled. That day was freakishly warm with the scent of spring in the air, and they'd packed a picnic and spent the afternoon lazing on a tartan blanket, eating, drinking, laughing and just being in love. It was perfect. He wants a return to more days like that.

Damn it, he thinks, he knows how upset she was when he burbled about his cossetted nest egg and then compounded it when his mother insisted on whispering about financial matters. But with his mum finally returning to where she rightfully belongs they'll have a chance to reconnect, won't they? They need time to be together to just 'be'. He looks over at Amy, patiently listening to his mother chat away about something and nothing and his heart swells. Her eyes are slightly glazing over but she's doing her best impression of someone who is hanging on to every word. Why else would she do that unless she completely loved him?

Yes, he needs to make things up to her – it's a shame that they haven't got the whole of tomorrow evening together, but, on the plus side, it will certainly give him more time to work on his plan…

Chapter 60

I struggle past the marauding school children to take one of the few seats left on the bus. Happily looking out over the lush green fields and the low-lying clouds, I try to block out the teenagers' constant effing and jeffing. *Don't they teach non-sweary adjectives at school these days?*

As the bus chugs along I lose myself in thoughts of last night's final rehearsal. It was sadly all slips, trips and missed pirouettes. (The title of my autobiography for sure.) As we were nearing the end our timing was off, our balance was off and in the end we were mightily peed off. How could it all go so horribly wrong? Again?

"This is good!" Helena said as we crashed, slid and bumbled into our finishing positions. *Is she blind?* "This is our last opportunity to practise and it's a well known fact that one *really* bad run through results in a perfect performance on the night! So you've got it out of the way…and you never need to do it like that…ever again."

"To be honest, I don't think we could if we tried," Marion said dismally to consenting voices.

"Exactly. You've made your blunders and learnt from them. Would you prefer to make them on stage?"

"We have before," Lucia said under her breath.

As we turn to leave, Helena had suddenly had a change of heart.

"No, I'm not going to leave it like this. Let's do it one more time!" she said. And so we took to our starting positions for the final rehearsal and tried again. This time, somehow, we held our balances, maintained strict formation, kept our eye-lines raised and, most importantly, papered over the small errors. As we panted, holding our finishing poses, we turned to each other and gave bewildered looks.

"That went OK, didn't it?" I said.

"It wasn't awful," Marion said.

"Not too shabby," Lucia added.

"Wasn't awful? Not too shabby?" Helena exploded. "That was awesomely amazing! You don't know how good that was!"

We all smiled and, feeling like we'd turned a corner, a surge of confidence bubbled around the room.

After cooling down we'd stood around animatedly chattering about how we were going to get to the event. Rather stung by last year's fiasco of the limo breaking down on the way to Dixbury Does Talent, we all agreed it would be safer to make our own way there. Even though we aren't competing, Helena has asked us to be there at six thirty on the dot so that the organisers know for sure that they have their closing act. Fine. Agreed.

I'd left the hall and grabbed a lift with Gloria to be with my beloved as quickly as I could. The thought of our first night alone again after weeks of Marie's company was too delicious. I entered the lounge to find twinkling candles all around, Bublé on the stereo, a silver bucket housing a bottle of wine on a tartan blanket on the floor. Rather worryingly I also found Basil sniffing the cheese on the accompanying cheeseboard.

"Bas!" I said, making him jump. "I don't think that's meant for you." He looked up guiltily and made his way to the corner of the room.

"Thought I heard you come in," Joshua said, entering the room carrying a bowl of hummus and a plate of bread. He kissed me before placing them on the blanket. "Your dinner, m'lady."

I'd thrown my arms around his neck and we'd sunk onto the sofa and it was only hearing Basil creeping back to the cheese that forced us to refocus on supper. It was a beautiful evening together and I made a conscious decision not to revisit topics of contention – we had more pressing matters to attend to…

My phone buzzing in my bag breaks my reverie. Hmm, the estate agents.

"Hello," I say.

"Amy? It's Mikey."

"Hi." I plug one ear to block the teens' rowdy banter. "Sorry, I'm on a bus. I can't hear you very well."

"Right, I'm just ch…left…message…that's what…need…happens…"

"Mikey," I shout. "You're breaking up. What did you say?" He tries again, but the youths crescendo into laughter and I hear nothing. "Can you text me please?" I think he says, "okay," but he sounds too Dalek to know for sure.

I hang up and my legs jiggle in anticipation of his message. What could he want? As far as I know the inimitable Ms Cork is in the process of buying Rose Cottage. Extra questions were posed and answered, the survey was done and I've been nonchalantly browsing the local 'houses for rent' pages online. I do hope he hasn't got bad news.

Thankfully the school kids exit the bus, leaving behind sweet wrappers, the whiff of hormones and a welcome silence. Just as I'm ready to press the bell for my stop, my phone buzzes. Jumping off the bus I try walking and checking my message at the same time – never an easy task. I finally stop dead in my tracks just at the entrance to Hip Snips. NO!!!!!

Gina sees me through the tinted glass and comes to open the door.

"Babe? You alrigh'?"

"Aaargh! No, I'm not. Bloody Leanne Cork."

"Who?"

"That woman who slagged us off in the paper and then was buying my house – she's backed out!"

"Oh no, why?"

"Apparently the survey threw up some damp." I groan. "So that's another thing I'll have to deal with."

"You're living wiv a 'andyman!"

"Not sure he's up to putting in a damp course."

Putting disappointment and house faults to one side Gina and I go about setting up for the day ahead. The customers come thick and fast and it's just before lunchtime, as I'm finishing off Mrs Three Hairs And A Nit that I spot our favourite rep at the counter.

"Dave," I say, smiling broadly.

"Amy." He returns my smile with an abashed look.

"What can I do for you today? Sniffing round after more of my friends?"

He laughs. "Very funny."

"I aim to please."

"So," he says, indicating his briefcase. "Wanna see the latest products?"

"Oh go on then." I nod my head towards the staffroom. "I'm on lunch so you can talk while I eat."

I make us both a coffee as he lays out his latest samples and leaflets. I browse them and maybe it's because I'm getting soft in my old age, but I find myself agreeing to purchase a new shampoo that offers all kinds of delight for grey hair. We spend the next half an hour talking about hairdressing shows and competitions and who's doing what in the world of coiffure. Eventually he is packing away his wares and with his eyes fixed downwards he says, "So did she tell you about me then?"

I grin. As he is usually the epitome of cockiness, it's refreshingly sweet to see this other side of him.

"Yes, she did," I say. "Quite keen, are we, eh?" I can't resist teasing. He looks up at me and I don't think I've ever seen him quite so sincere.

"The truth? – I'm in way too deep."

"Aw, Dave."

"Don't suppose you know how she feels?"

"Dave." I sigh. "I don't and even if I did, I'm sorry, I'm not the person to ask." Been there, done that and not going back there again.

"No, no, that's fine," he quickly says. "I'm coming tomorrow night to cheer you all on and I'm hoping to have some time with her afterwards. Guess I'm going to have to give it my best shot and hope the stars are aligned."

I nod, thinking that's all any of us can do really, isn't it? And that's in relationships and in dance performances…

Chapter 61

"Marion," Julay says, tapping on her housemate's bedroom door. "Big day ahead! If we're going to do facemasks and manicures it's time to get up."

"I'll be down in a minute," Marion says from behind the door, pulling on her dressing gown. "Get the kettle on."

Julay trots happily to the kitchen, places the post on the table and sets the plates and cutlery. Big day indeed, she thinks, as she boils the kettle and turns on the radio. All the weeks of rehearsing; the hours of committing steps to memory, time spent sewing costumes and finally, tonight is the night. If last year's Dixbury Does Talent was important, then closing the summer version of the competition is crucial. It's time that the dancers felt they were on top of their game again – and tonight is their chance to do just that.

"Morning dear," Marion says, entering the kitchen. Rifling through the post she plucks out an official looking letter.

"You know, Marion, I have a really good feeling about today," Julay says, pouring the tea.

"So did I," Marion says, her eyes fixed on the letter.

"What is it, dear?" Julay asks.

"It's from the parole board." She quickly opens and reads it. "He did it, he got parole." She looks up wide-eyed.

"Oh Marion."

*

Sam puffs the pillow and snuggles back down. Just a few minutes more. It's going to be a long day and she needs all the energy she can muster – and she seems to be lacking in that department. Maybe the turmoil of Jason and the tension with Amy is taking its toll on her emotions. It has been a bit of a rollercoaster recently. Still things are well and truly sorted with

Amy so she doesn't have to fret. And last night she finally told Jason that she didn't want to be in touch with him at all. As she's given him space and he's still engaged to Simone, it's definitely time to forget him and what might've been and move on about that relationship anymore, thank goodness. And, she thinks with a wry smile, it is made easier by the presence of Dave. She wonders how her heart can skip from a geeky charmer like Jason to a wide-boy like Dave - but there you go – since when was there any rhyme or reason to affairs of the heart?

Right, ten minutes more and then she'll summon her flagging energy to get up and face this day, and fingers crossed it'll end happier than the last time they danced in public…

•

Brian spits out the toothpaste and looks up at Gloria next to him in the mirror. "Are you nervous about tonight?" he asks. Gloria, her mouth full of toothpaste, shakes her head rapidly. "Me neither," he says. "I doubt anything could be worse than *that* competition."

She spits and takes the towel to wipe her mouth. "Indeed. I just plan to have fun."

"And you will." He takes her in his arms. "You know you look so beautiful when you dance."

"You charmer." She giggles. "But I think you're a little biased."

"I think I am too." He kisses her and they hold each other, barefoot on the bathroom tiles, in a warm, soft embrace. "I never thought I could be this happy," he says softly.

"I didn't think I'd find happiness again either." She pulls away from him. "Wonderful days, eh? And the nights aren't too bad either." She laughs.

He lifts her chin to look in her eyes. "Marry me."

"What?" Her mouth falls open.

He smiles. "You heard me, Gloria, marry me."

•

Catherine fires off another text as she spoons the cornflakes into her mouth.

"Darling," Josie says. "I do wish you wouldn't do that at the breakfast table. Let the twitterers wait until you've eaten."

Catherine rolls her eyes. "I'm not tweeting, I'm texting."
"Potato, patata," Josie smiles. Begrudgingly Catherine puts her phone down and sighs. "So, we have everything ready for tonight," Josie continues. "Costumes, clean shoes, bags packed. We'll aim to leave around six to give us plenty of time."
Her daughter's blank expression stares at her. "You do still want to be a part of The Dixbury Dancers, don't you? I'm aware that we're all a lot older than you, and not at your level. You know you can pull out anytime you like."

"Yes, Mum, I know. I'm fine at the moment."

"Morning you two," Ed says, coming into the kitchen, kissing his wife and daughter on their foreheads.

"Morning," Josie says. "What you got there?" she asks, eyeing the bundle of letters in his hand.

He inspects them one at a time. "Bill, junk, one for next door." He tuts. "Bill, supermarket offers, oh and one for a Miss Catherine Trendell." He passes the white window envelope to his daughter.

Catherine's spots the dance school's address and her eyes widen. "Oh My God! Oh My God!" Apart from trembling hands she is paralysed.

"Open it!" Josie says.

"I can't! You do it!" she says, thrusting it at her mother.

Josie opens it and unfolding the letter she starts to read. Catherine, holding her breath, watches as a tear runs down her mother's face.

•

Joshua jumps out of bed to answer the door. Glancing over his shoulder he sees Amy still fast asleep; he doesn't want to wake her – she's got a big evening ahead. Opening the door he finds his father standing there.

"Pa!" He says and hugs him warmly. "What are you doing here? Fed up with Mum already?"

His father chuckles. “No no no, your mum’s left some things in the wardrobe and asked me to pop over to pick them up.”

“Oh right, come in.”

“Is your young lady around? Your mum tells me she’s a keeper.” He elbows his son in the ribs.

“She did, did she? She’s in bed; she’s got her performance tonight and I don’t want to wake her.”

“Fair enough, leave her be. Just don’t wait too long before you bring her over. Your mother’s very taken with her. Make sure this one doesn’t get away.”

“OK, OK Pa, don’t worry, I’ve got a plan.”

“Have you now?”

“Yep, everything is lined up and ready and tonight, after the competition, I’m going in for the attack.”

“Sounds serious, son.”

“It is, Dad, and I am.”

Chapter 62

"OK, OK, everyone, thanks for getting here so early," Helena says, after she has herded us into the corner of the 'dressing room' tent at Midsummer Dixbury Does Talent. We are the first to arrive and have the white canvas shelter to ourselves. Looking around I have to give credit to the organisers who have created quite a lovely temporary dressing room with full-length mirrors, freestanding costume rails, tables and chairs; pretty much all we need to get ready for our finale performance. "Are we missing anyone?" Helena looks around.

"Lucia," Marion says.

"Ah yes, we'll give her a minute – it's not quite six thirty," Helena says, running her hand through her hair and glancing at her watch.

"Definitely can't do it without her," Brian says, to fill the gap. We all concur. A silence follows that is only interrupted by Helena tapping her fingers on a desk. We all exchange looks; Helena is normally the epitome of cool, calm collectedness. Is our past performance indelibly inked on her brain? Is she stressing that we'll mess it up again? Does she think that we haven't practised enough? That we're not up to scratch? Has she lost confidence in us? And if *she's* thinking all of that, should we be worried?

Visible relief washes over Helena as Lucia makes her usual grand entrance. "Sorry, sorry, sorry," Lucia says. "My Geoff wanted to wish me luck." She smiles salaciously.

"Dear," Marion says, gesturing to the smudged red lipstick mess surrounding Lucia's lips.

"Ha ha, knew I should've fought him off," she says, turning to a mirror, and rubbing it off with a licked finger.

"Right," Helena coughs lightly. "Now you're all here. I er…I have something to tell you."

"Oh no – you're leaving us?" Lucia says, turning from the mirror, still lipsticked up to her nose.

"No, no, it's not that…" She stops to draw breath.

"What is it then, dear?" Marion asks gently.

"Well. Er, I don't really know how to say this, so I'll say…Er…right, you remember when Bendrick was here and you all had a dip in your confidence after the Afton competition?" We all nod. "Well, since then you've all worked so hard, and improved beyond measure. I've never been so proud of you all. I've watched you blossom. You are in such a better place now, and in fact you are so much better than when you almost competed in Dixbury Does Talent…" She trails off and takes another deep breath. "You're not closing the show tonight…"

A chorus of "We're not?" and 'Why not?" fills the tent.

"…Because…" She looks at us, not blinking. "You're competing in it."

A stunned silence fills the air.

"We're what?" I ask.

"Competing," she says firmly. "Look, it was Bendrick's idea. After that newspaper article and then Afton, he saw how your nerves got the better of you. You lost faith in your ability to dance. He thought the best way to build you back up was to give you a focus – a non-threatening focus. I'm partially responsible as I've acted out his plan – but you have to believe me that I only did it because I KNOW you can do it. I KNOW you can win this! You are my fearsome Dixbury Dancers and you have every right to compete here tonight."

"So we're competing?" Marion says, slightly dazed.

"Yes, Marion," Helena says. "And the beauty of it is you don't have time to get nervous. You can all dance this dance beautifully – you would've done so at the end of the show – so now you just have to do it earlier."

"Okaaay," Gloria says with a frown.

"So, Hels, how much earlier?" Lucia asks.

"You're the first up."

The tent erupts. "First up?" "What time?" "How long have we got?" "Oh no, are we ready?" "Aaaargh."

Marion raises her hand and we all stop and turn to her. "And then we have to do it again at the end of the night?" she asks.

"Mazzy, Mazzy," Lucia says. "Keep up, chicken – we're not closing the show – we're in it!" Marion dazedly nods her head.

"And I think it's brilliant," I hear myself say. "We *are* ready for this, people. We *have* practised this dance - we could do it in our sleep. We've never been more ready. I say, let's shut up, warm up and get out there!"

"Yes, spot on!" Julay says. "You know, sometimes, Amy, I don't agree with you – but on this, you're right! Let's do it."

"Er…thanks."

Helena heaves a large sigh of relief. "Right, get into your costumes, plus leg warmers and woollies and let's get you ready!"

As we go through the well-known exercises to warm our muscles the other entrants file into the tent. Surreptitiously we spot a few faces we know and then a few whose acts are quite clear - the top hat and stuffed rabbit being a real give away for one. Our white stiff organza ballerina length skirts and soft floaty tops have turned out splendidly and Brian is simply dashing in his tights and blouson. We certainly look the part. With bodies ready and our minds still catching up, we make our way into the back of the main tent just in time to see the compere open the competition.

"Right," Helena whispers to our huddle. "This is it. You are graceful, beautiful dancers and you're ready for this. Remember, no looking down; you are performing for every single person out there, give them a show. If there's the teeniest error, no one will know, just carry on. Point those toes, elongate those limbs and win them over with your smiles. Do me proud..."

"To start the competition we have a group of ballet dancers who last year unfortunately didn't get to compete…" the tuxedo-wearing compere, apparently called Colin, begins our introduction.

"...Because tonight, Dixbury Dancers, you're already my winners," Helena concludes.

"Please welcome to the stage," Colin continues. "The Dixbury Dancers!"

Chapter 63

Helena didn't manage to beg, borrow or steal a ramp, so we enter from the side of a flat stage, one at a time, exacting our moves perfectly in time to the music. Brian weaves in and out of us, taking each hand in turn as legs are raised backwards in arabesques. When it's my turn I'm sure that the adrenalin forces my leg higher than ever before. We glide gracefully through our steps, not even letting the slightly make-do unsteady stage affect us. The final part of our dance is Helena's slightly more challenging choreography that matches our individual strengths - needless to say, there's no pirouette for me. But around me Julay flies into a grand jeté, Marion's feet skip lightly in spring hops, Brian and Gloria partner perfectly, Josie shows off her beautiful port de bras and, of course, Sam and Catherine effortlessly steal the show. All our practise has certainly paid off.

In our finishing positions the music fades and there is silence. *Oh no! Didn't they like our performance?* From my stage left position I can just about see the judges. The female one is blowing her nose, two of the men are whispering and one is clearly looking for something he's lost. *Hmmm, that's not good.* Suddenly, as if the audience realise we've finished they burst into loud hearty applause. Cheers, whoops and cries fill the tent – in fact at one point I wonder if the top will blow off. We all look to each other and then see Helena at the side of the stage beckoning for us to take our line.

We hold hands and take a long deep bow, drinking up the applause and smiling like lunatics. We did it! We flipping did it! A flawless performance. As we exit the stage a visibly teary Helena tries to hug us en masse.

"Come on guys, debrief," she says, leading us out of the main tent and into the warm evening. We all chat exuberantly, bubbling with adrenalin and relief.

“Oh, I really thought I was going to miss that pirouette,” Sam says.

“Not a chance – you were brilliant!” I say. “And you, Catherine, I’ve never seen you dance so beautifully.” She blushes and Josie puts her arm around her and squeezes her.

“Oh, at one point I’m sure I was wobbling in the arabesque,” Marion says.

“Nonsense,” Brian answers. “All of you were perfectly statue-like. Made my job easy.”

“I think you propped us up a little,” Gloria says, and pecks him on the cheek.

“Guys, guys, did you see my pas de chat?” Lucia says, still insisting on pronouncing ‘par duh shaar’ as ‘pas de shat’. “Not too shabby, eh?”

“Not too shabby at all,” Helena says, smiling.

Standing behind one of the beer tents, we stand before our beloved teacher. “Right, this won’t take long,” she says, drawing a deep breath. “I have never seen anything quite as beautiful as you tonight. You danced from your hearts and souls and made magic out there. I could not be prouder. Whatever the result of the competition, you have to believe me that you’ve won.” Her eyes well up again. “Oh Christ, someone give me a tissue.”

We all giggle and, in lieu of tissues, offer our sleeves.

“What happens now?” Samantha asks.

“Well, you’re free to watch the competition and then wait for the results,” Helena says.

“Or we could all nip in here?” Lucia nods towards the tent. “A nice little bevy might be just the ticket.”

“Not a bad idea,” Brian says.

“Well, put your warm-ups on – and stretch a bit before you go drinking,” Helena says. “I’m meeting Uri in the main tent so I’ll see you in there later, OK?”

Helena goes her way and we all head back to the preparation tent. We give a cursory nod to stretching as we’re all too hyped up; all we want to do is grab a drink and then see what we’re up against.

We enter the main tent just in time to catch the end of the magician's act.

"Not sure he's too much competition," Lucia says, as the poor man struggles to 'mind-read' the judge. A flutter of applause greets him.

"Hmm, we still have quite a few to beat though," I say.

"Oh shit!" Sam says, a little too loudly. "Look who's here." I follow the direction of her gaze and see, standing at the side of the tent, with his trademark ginger hair and specs, Jason.

"What's he doing here?" I ask.

"I'm guessing he doesn't like that I've blocked him." Her lip quivers.

I put my hand on her arm. "Don't worry. You don't have to face him if you don't want to."

"I just…"

"Not talking about me, I hope," comes the familiar voice of Dave from behind us.

"Oh, hi Dave," I say, turning to him. I look back at Sam whose crumpled face has turned ashen. "You OK?" I ask.

"I'm sorry," she says to me and then turns to Dave. "Sorry, I have to, I mean…sorry."

With that, she turns and heads for the exit leaving Dave and I staring at each other. "I'll go," I say.

Racing after Sam I see her dodge behind one of the many tents and catch up with her just as she is bent double being violently sick.

"Oh Sam," I say, and place my hand on her back. As she straightens I think how I've never seen her look so frightful. "Stay there." I duck round into the tent and ask for a couple of serviettes. I take one to the water jug and wet it and then return to Sam who, although no longer vomiting, is a shade of grey-green. I give her the wet napkin and as she wipes her face I say, "Is this the effect all this is having on you? You poor thing."

She shakes her head. "No."

"No?"

She looks at me, her eyes watery and scared. "Oh Amy, I feel dreadful."

"Hmm, I can see that."

She shakes her head slowly. "No, you don't understand, I think I might be pregnant."

Chapter 64

"Pregnant?" I echo.

She nods. "I don't know for sure, but I'm late, I have no energy and I'm being sick."

"Okaaay." I stop to think. "Is it likely you could be?"

She sighs. "I don't think Jason and I were particularly careful that night. Let's just say that neither of us came prepared."

"Ah, I see. Well, look, it could well be nothing," I say, scrabbling my brain. "You know it might just be the stress of all you've been through recently."

"Yep, I know. I'm going to take a test tomorrow. The chemist opens on a Sunday, right?"

"Yeah." I look at her forlorn face. "Oh Sam, come here." I pull her to me. "It'll be okay either way, you know that, don't you?"

Her eyes fill with tears. "I was really starting to like Dave. I can hardly start a relationship with him if I'm up the duff though, can I?"

"Whoa, one step at a time. Find out for sure first, then think about that."

She sniffs and nods. "Jesus, Amy, what am I going to do if I am?"

"I don't know. But you'll find a way. And I'm here, you know that."

She smiles weakly. "Just as I'd finally decided to give up on Jason and think about a new relationship…"

"Come on," I say, wiping a tear from her cheek. "There's nothing you can do about it tonight. Let's go and watch the show and we can both worry about this tomorrow."

She nods agreement and links my arm. Putting my hand on hers we slowly wend our way back to the main tent.

Joining the now seated Dixbury Dancers, we hear Colin Compere announce, "Please welcome to the stage The Toe Tapper Twinklies!" We look up to see ten cute little girls dressed head to toe in turquoise sparkly leotards and tights taking to the stage.

"Oh bum," I say under my breath. "Cuteness overload."

"Hmm-mm," Sam agrees.

Sitting down we watch the little darlings shoe shuffle their way through the classic, Chattanooga Choo Choo.

"Ah, I see what they're doing," Lucia says, leaning into Marion. "Very clever. Adorable youngsters dancing to something for the oldies." She looks to Marion and pauses. "No offence."

"None taken, dear." Marion rolls her eyes. "You do actually know I'm not old enough to remember this song, don't you?"

"Maz, it doesn't make any difference to me whether you're twenty-five, fifty or one hundred, I'd still love ya." She exuberantly throws an arm around Marion who reluctantly giggles and nudges her away.

I turn to Gloria behind me. "Did we miss anything?"

"Erm." She checks her programme. "We've had the magician." She grimaces. "A clown act, a comedian of sorts, a singer and now these little loves."

Finishing with jazz hands the tapping twinklies beam huge gap-toothed smiles and exit the stage for the compere to reappear to announce a twenty-minute interval.

"Beer!" Lucia calls and exits with half the troupe. I look at Sam who's furtively looking towards Jason.

"Do me a favour, Amy," she says. "Tell Dave that I'm just sorting out something and I'll see him afterwards, would you?"

"You sure?"

"Yep. See you in a bit."

With that she wanders off in the direction of Jason and leaves me looking around for Dave. I wander through the crowd and spot Joshua at the back who raises his thumbs and then mimes that he's heading to the toilet. *Hmm, too much visual information.* Then I hear a familiar voice calling my name and turn to see Bendrick. A huge wave of fondness washes over me as I take in his multi coloured striped trousers, white filled shirt and jauntily worn fedora. He holds out his arms and envelops me in frills and sweet aftershave.

"Dear Amy," he says, finally releasing me.

"Bendrick, how lovely to see you!"

"My dear child, I wouldn't have missed it for the world! And I must say The Dixbury Dancers' performance was magnifico!" He makes an 'O' with his finger and thumb.

"Thank you. It was you who set all this up though, wasn't it? You wily devil," I say with a smile.

He grins. "I only hatched the plan because I KNEW you could all do it. And, by George, you did!"

"We haven't won."

"A minor detail." His eyes sparkle. It's then that I notice the slender handsome man standing slightly behind him. "Oh, how rude of me," Bendrick says, stepping aside and ushering the man forwards. "This is Lawrence."

"Nice to meet you," I say, holding out my hand.

"You too," Lawrence says. Turning back to Bendrick, he touches his arm gently and says, "Would you like a drink?"

Bendrick smiles at his companion. "Yes please. The usual." Lawrence wanders off and Bendrick's gaze follows him.

Hmm, that might explain why Julay and he didn't become an item…

"So, how's life?" I ask, jolting his attention back to me.

"Good, good. I do miss you all, but, to be honest, it's quite lovely just taking things easy. I'm quite happy." His gaze returns to the back of Lawrence.

"Yes, I can see that." I squeeze his arm. "I'm very happy for you."

"Thank you, dear." He gives a happy sigh. "And, I tell you this, if you and the rest of the ballerinas win this competition that'll be the cherry *and* the icing on my cake."

"Look who I found," Brian says, returning to his seat with drinks in his hands. Gloria looks up to see Fliss.

"Darling, I didn't think you'd come!" Gloria says, rising to greet her daughter.

"I was here at the start." She kisses her mother's cheek. "And you looked stunning up there."

"Thank you. Not bad for an old girl, eh?"

"Not bad at all. I hope you guys win," Fliss says, looking to them both. "You deserve to."

"What, and beat the little turquoise toe tapping twinkle children?" Brian says jovially.

Fliss laughs. "They can win another year. They've got time on their side." She looks at Gloria and Brian. "I mean…sorry, I didn't mean it like that."

Brian chuckles. "Will you join us, Felicity?" he says, offering a seat.

"Thank you," Fliss sighs and smiles. "That would be lovely. And please Brian, it's Fliss."

Samantha takes a deep breath and steps in front of him. "Jason…"

"Sam, hi! Just the person I was looking for," he says, his lips twitching. "How are you?"

"Fine. Why were you looking for me?"

"Can we…?" He nods towards the exit.

"Sure."

They walk outside and stand in front of a stall selling falafel and vodka. Not a likely combination on any day, Sam thinks, but especially not today.

"Would you like a drink?" Jason asks.

"No, I'm fine, thanks."

"So," he starts. "Right. Now, I know I've made a mess of things, but I'm putting things right. I've called it off with Simone. She's hurt but I just couldn't marry her when I have these feelings for you. So, I'm free and I'm absolutely committed to making a go of things with you."

"Well that's romantic."

"Sorry, I didn't mean it like that." He sighs. "I've rehearsed this a thousand times but I'm so scared I've lost you I can't think straight. Look, you can walk away from me – I wouldn't blame you if you did – but I'm here, I'm single and I'm deeply besotted with you. I will do anything to make you see that I'm not that man who's unfaithful; I'm not a player, I am just Jason who wants to spend the foreseeable future with you."

Sam's stomach jolts, forcing her to wonder if she will throw up again, but a hard swallow luckily dissipates it. She looks at his strained face imploring her to believe him. How many times has she wanted to hear him say this? Before she knew of his deception she would have been dancing on air at these declarations. But now? She was enjoying the uncomplicatedness of dating Dave; she'd be surprised if he has any skeletons in his cupboard. He's more of a 'what you see is what you get' kind of guy. It's true enough that her heart doesn't miss a beat and her loins don't fill with lust for him, but he's sweet, kind, funny and caring and he definitely wouldn't hurt her.

"Sam?" Jason says, his brow knitted with concern.

She looks at him closely. She adores the sight of him, the geeky awkwardness, the buttoned up shirt and Campers boots, the soft ginger hair and smooth broad hands. Her whole body responds to his presence. Especially now he's standing before her, offering himself completely. OK, they met at the wrong time, and he definitely shouldn't have slept with her that night - but some relationships do start from the ashes of the one before, don't they? And, to give him his due, he didn't plan to become entwined with her whilst still with Simone. If it's passion or love or whatever, sometimes it's just meant to be. Would they be able to wipe the slate clean and start again?

With her heart weakened, she takes a step forward, puts her arms around him and softens into his warm body. She then pulls back slightly. “Before we take this any further, there’s something I need to tell you…”

I stumble out into the daylight, still on my quest to find Dave. I’m brought up short by the sight of Jason and Sam kissing passionately; their bodies seemingly moulded together, oblivious to their surroundings. *Ah, not quite what I was expecting.* It’s as I’m turning away that I spot Dave, his face a maze of disappointment, rooted to the spot, staring straight at them.

I move towards him, but in quite a manly fashion, he throws the scrunched up remains of his falafel to the ground and goes to storm off. He then stops, turns back, checks no one caught his littering, retrieves the wrapper, deposits it in the bin and then lamely slopes off in the direction of the car park.

My heart hurts for him. In fact, I kind of wish he had his crappy plastic briefcase here so I could buy some of his hairdressing products; it might cheer him up a little. I look back to see Jason and Sam still locking lips and, with a small sigh, I turn on my heels and return to the main tent.

Chapter 65

I take my seat just as Colin Compere introduces Anna Jones, who turns out to be a ten-year-old classical guitar prodigy. She takes to the stage with the light bouncing off her thick glasses and a metal clip holding her frizzy hair off her face. As she sits and begins to play, her long slender fingers effortlessly pluck the strings. The tent falls silent as people drift away to the soft sounds of Cavatina. As she finishes I'm sure I hear a gasp before the audience erupts into applause.

"Well that's us well and truly buggered," Lucia says, sinking in her seat.

"It's not over 'til the fat lady sings," Gloria says.

"Well, don't look at me - I'm not singing!" Lucia replies.

"These youngsters may have the 'aaaah' factor, but you guys had the 'wow!' factor tonight," Helena says, smiling encouragingly.

"Who's on next?" Josie asks, leaning over to read Brian's programme. "Oh no! The Gymnastinas! They sound like kids too."

We all groan.

"Not being funny," Lucia starts. "But if we were all wrinklies we might stand a chance – the public like youngsters and oldies. We're somewhere in between," she says, looking around at us.

"I'll stop with the anti-ageing cream pronto," Josie says dryly.

Joshua appears beside me and kisses my cheek. "What'd I miss?"

"The winning act." I sigh.

"No I didn't, I saw you guys," he says, and smiles sweetly.

Lucia high fives him. "Nice one, Josh!"

We continue watching the competition and groan with despair as, after the gymnasts, the opera-singing winner of the Afton competition, Beth Underwood, appears.

"Cute talented children and a note-perfect singer – call me a taxi now," I whisper to Joshua who, in return, squeezes my hand.

For the remaining twenty minutes we sit through an array of acts: a juggler, an impressionist, another group of children dancing, a group of people dressed in onesies forming a (very small) human pyramid and a wannabee Oasis act consisting of four teenage boys.

"Ladies and gentlemen, boys and girls," Colin Compere says, walking onto the stage. "There will be a fifteen minute break whilst the judges deliberate. Hope none of the acts are found guilty…" Not a titter. "So please have another drink, or try some of the delicious local foods in the surrounding tents and we'll see you back here to announce the winner of the 2017 Midsummer Dixbury Does Talent!"

As the polite applause peters out, Lucia says, "Another beer!" and once again heads out to the beer tent.

"Has she got shares in the brewery?" Joshua asks in awe, watching her head out.

"Ha, yep – that's our Lucia." I laugh.

"OK, guys," Helena says. "We have to be at the side of the stage when they
announce the winner. So meet you there in about ten minutes, okay?" We all nod agreement.

We chat and joke and on the surface all seems fine, but, in truth, don't we all know that it's impossible to win? Our minds may well understand the ridiculous odds stacked against us but that doesn't stop my heart from holding hope. There's still a flicker of a wild chance that the judges have a penchant for ballet, isn't there? Maybe our performance caught their imagination? Made them *feel* something? Can we beat the oh-so-talented-crowd-pleasing children? Probably not in this lifetime.

Gathering at the side of the stage we find ourselves next to the classical guitar-playing child star.

"Oh dear," Gloria says to me in hushed tones. "When they hail her the winner everyone's going to be looking this way. So smile widely and clap her enthusiastically."

"I'll clap her round the ear," Lucia says.

"Shh," Marion says, as the compere takes to the mic.

"Well, ladies and gentlemen…" he begins, but just at that moment, everyone turns to the sound of a loud scuffle breaking out at the back of the tent. Craning my neck it looks like two younger men up against an older dishevelled man. I hear one of the young men say, 'Aw, give it up grandpa,' at which the older man flips out and swings wide, missing his targets completely. A tussle erupts with punches flying. The old man turns out to be no match for these young guns and with a couple of blows to his face and some school playground bundling he's on the ground. A few bystanders wade in to break it up and the two youngsters eventually walk away backwards, pointing their fingers and swearing threats. The older man, who I can now see clearly, red-faced, dripping sweat and spitting blood onto the grass, struggles to stand up straight, but as he does I hear a small gasp beside me.

"Marion," Julay leans in and whispers. "Is that who I think it is?"

Marion with tears creasing the corners of her eyes, stares blankly and nods. "Didn't take him long, did it?" she says gravely.

Watching Jack stumbling around, trying to get his bearings, we then see a tall, well-built man approach. "Come on, let's get you somewhere else and calm you down," he says firmly.

"Oh sod off," Jack slurs.

"Sir, I'm an off duty police officer and I'm requesting that you come with me." Incredulously, even in the light of this new information, Jack continues to takes a swing at the officer, who, with well-learnt self-defence moves, neatly pins him back to the ground. "Sir," the officer says. "Assaulting a police officer isn't clever. Let's take a trip to the station, eh? You can cool off there."

In a surreal moment it almost feels like we should applaud this display. What are the chances of an off duty copper being around just when you need one? The shocked crowd buzz at what possibly is one of the most dramatic events to happen in Dixbury for a long time.

"That should've been our act," Lucia says, with her eyes still fixed on the policeman and Jack.

"Well," Colin compere says above the hubbub. "You can't say it's dull around here, can you, folks!" He shakes his head in disbelief. "Oh and a big thanks to our local bobby there," he calls after the officer who raises one arm whilst steering Jack out of the tent.

Julay puts her arm around Marion. "That's not good for his record, hmm? Just out on parole and trying to punch a police officer."

"Do you think he was looking for me?" Marion asks, slightly trembling.

"I don't know, dear, but I think a conversation with that parole liaison officer woman might be a good idea, eh?"

Marion nods. "Absolutely. First thing Monday morning."

"So, where was I?" Colin tries to settle the crowd. "Yes, so, ladies and gentlemen, boys and girls, I think you'll agree that this year's competition has been fierce. Rarely have we had such talent under one roof, or should I say under one tent." Tumbleweed again. "I think we can all agree that whichever act wins, Dixbury most definitely does have talent!"

"Get on with it, Col," Lucia murmurs.

"So it was a particularly difficult decision for the judges to make and they just couldn't decide! So, after lengthy discussions an unprecedented move has taken place; ladies and gentlemen: the judges wish to split the competition into two halves." The audience 'ooh'. "Yes, there will be two winning acts tonight – the Under Eighteens and the Over Eighteens! The Unders will take the trophy and the Overs will receive a hamper of goodies courtesy of The Jolly Pig Company." Hearty applause breaks out.

"I think the competition just got interesting again," Sam says.

"Yesssssssssss," Lucia says.

"Even splitting the acts into two categories the judges still had a hard job to do," the compere continues. "And I'm sure you'll all agree that all the young people who've performed this evening have been amazing." The audience claps again. "But there can be only one winner and so without further ado…the winning act of the Under Eighteens Midsummer Dixbury Does Talent 2017 is…Anna Jones!"

As instructed by Gloria, we smile widely and pat her on the back. A tiny part of me sighs – we were supposed to be holding that shiny silver trophy, but how can I begrudge this young slip of a thing as she blushes and stumbles up onto the stage? As with the rest of the audience I clap her wildly.

As a hush falls, Colin continues, "And now, the Over Eighteens…"

"Very much over eighteen," Gloria says.

"You and me both," Julay says.

"Shh," Lucia says.

"Again, the judges found it a difficult decision to make. They felt that the standard of entrants has been exceptionally high and that all the acts were potential winners. But in the end, and after much deliberation, they were unanimous in their decision." He consults his notes, looks around the room and then coughs.

"C'mon!" whispers Lucia.

"Ladies and gentlemen, the Over Eighteens' winning act of Midsummer Dixbury Does Talent 2017 is…" We surreptitiously reach for each other's hands and hold our breath. "The Dixbury Dancers!"

We gasp, dissolve into congratulatory tears and hug each other in the manner not dissimilar to Miss World contestants.

"Come on, guys," Helena says, beckoning us forward. One by one we take to the stage, our smiles as wide as miles, whilst the audience continue to cheer and whoop. Filing past Helena, Lucia she grabs her hand and drags her onto stage with us. Helena's attempt to escape is futile as I'm sure Lucia was a weight lifter in a previous life.

Colin Compere holds out the enormous wicker basket stuffed to the brim with goodies, and looks for whom to present it to. We all turn to Helena who shakes her head defiantly. Again, Lucia comes into her own by taking Helena's shoulders and thrusting her into the middle of the group.

"Take it, dear," Gloria says in Helena's ear. "We may be the dancers, but you are the creator."

Wiping a tear, Helena accepts the hamper to our applause. She looks to Colin Compere.

"Excuse me, could I say a few words, please?"

"Certainly,' he says. She places the hamper on the floor and takes the mic.

"Ladies and gentlemen, I won't keep you long, I know you're eager to get to the bar." People titter. "But I just really want to thank these glorious dancers up here. I have been teaching for many years and I have never seen such dedication and commitment from a group of people. They've been through some tough times and have come out of it smiling, and winning! They insist that I take a bow here too, but, in all honesty, tonight belongs to them." She sweeps her arm gesturing to us. "My fabulous Dixbury Dancers!"

Chapter 66

We skip off the stage, back to the dressing room tent, literally dancing on air. OK, so we're not holding the trophy, but we are holding renewed confidence, a sense of pride and a flipping good hamper!

"What we got then?" Lucia says, foisting her nose into the large basket. "Beer!"

Josie giggles. "How *are* we going to divvy it up?"

"Let's take everything out and see what everyone wants," Helena says unpacking the items onto a table. A delicious selection of cheeses, wine, beer, cured meats, olives, crackers, pates, chocolates and the like, lay out before us, but for me, one item stands head and shoulders above the rest.

"Okay if I have this, guys?" I ask, picking up the waxy paper parcel encasing a pork pie.

"Bleugh – with pleasure," Lucia says, gesturing her fingers down her throat.

Then we go round the circle one at a time selecting products, chatting and giggling and generally enjoying our prize.

"Excuse me," Colin Compere interrupts. "Would you mind awfully?" He nods over his shoulder. "The press are here and would like a quick interview and photo."

"Certainly," Helena smiles brightly and turns back to us. "Shall we?" We move out into the warm night air to see our least favourite journalist standing there with her oversized camera.

"Oh Lord," Gloria says under her breath.

"What the ?" Lucia says.

"Hi," Leanne says, shifting nervously. "Could I have a photograph please?"

"You gonna write anything to go with it?" Lucia steps forward, squaring up.

Leanne nods dumbly.

Helena steps in front of Lucia. "Could you tell us what you'll be saying please?"

"Er, something along the lines of tough competition, shock deliberation by judges of splitting the contest into two categories, an unrelated altercation under the Big Top…" she exhales. "And that The Dixbury Dancers are the deserved winners."

"You sure you're going to write that?" Lucia asks.

Mental note: never get on the wrong side of Lucia.

"Hmm-mm," Leanne nods.

Helena touches Lucia's arm and then turning back to Leanne says, "Then yes, that'll be fine, thank you."

After a few photographs and a quick interview we all mill around the preparation tent picking up our belongings and getting ready to leave. I watch Leanne in the corner of the tent putting her camera away.

"What you thinking?" Sam asks, following the direction of my gaze.

"Talking to her about the cottage; see if we can come to some kind of a deal."

"Guess it wouldn't harm?"

"Hmm." I shrug and turn back to Sam. "So, what's happening with you and Jason?"

She flushes. "I told him I might be pregnant and he was really thrilled. Well, shocked, but then thrilled. That's got to be a good sign, hasn't it?"

"Absolutely. What about Dave?"

"I went looking for him but couldn't find him. I'll contact him and explain. I feel bad, but if I'm not ready to let go of Jason, it wouldn't be fair on Dave."

"Fair enough. As long as you're sure."

"Yeah, I am. Well, I think I am." She laughs. "Anyway, Jason's going to be with me tomorrow when I take the test."

"Aw that's great. You'll let me know, won't you?"

"Of course. See you." We hug goodbye and watching her wander out of the tent to a waiting Jason, I reaffirm to myself that, whatever happens between them, my one and only job is to support her; the rest she can deal with herself.

Heaving my bags onto my shoulder I head for Leanne when, from out of nowhere, Joshua appears at my side.

"Come on then, Amy Ballerina, you have a date with destiny," he says, guiding me away from my chosen course and towards the exit.

"Hang on, I haven't said goodbye to everyone."

"Oi! Dixbury Dancers!" he shouts over his shoulder. Their heads bob up. "Amy says goodbye."

"Bye Amy," they collectively say. As he is whisking me out of the tent, I'm sure Leanne is about to greet him but as he's steering me by the elbow at breakneck speed, the moment passes. Before I can blink we are buckled up in Sheila Skoda.

"Joshua Milne, where are you taking me now?" I ask, looking over at him.

"Paradise." He grins.

"You mean the end of the world place?"

"Edge of Heaven."

"That wasn't what we called it."

"Woman, I have no idea what we called it." He laughs.

"Me neither."

He pulls away and we head out along the narrow twisting country lanes, leaving Dixbury behind us.

"I prepared music," he says, and clicks the CD button. 'We Are The Champions' fills the car.

"Ha ha, you really do have faith in me, don't you?"

"Always." He reaches over and rests his hand on mine.

I hum along, looking out of the window at the pale moon hanging between the telegraph wires and think how ridiculously happy I feel. As if he can read my mind he squeezes my hand. I lean across, kiss his cheek and then settling back in my seat, we speed off into the night.

Almost the end...

Epilogue – Two Months Later

Of course, driving off into the night isn't the end of the story, and now, sitting here in the changing room, getting ready for tonight's class, I think how things have panned out.

Helena announced that now we've won Dixbury Does Talent, we automatically qualify for the regional heats, and has started rehearsing us relentlessly. We're attacking something technically advanced and my little legs wobble at the thought of it. But we have faith in her, her choreography and in each other, so we'll give it our best.

Marion made that call to the parole liaison officer and a few days later received a call telling her that Jack's attempt to assault a police officer, not surprisingly, violated the terms of his parole. Marion took a huge sigh of relief as he was swiftly returned to reside at Her Majesty's comfort. Marion is currently seeking the services of Simone Bletchley.

Buoyed with the success of the competition Julay stopped talking about quitting dance - in fact, she seems to have thrown herself into the new rehearsals with aplomb. She continues to keep a quiet eye on Marion and together, on nights when they're not dancing, the pair can be found singing their hearts out in a local choir.

It seems that when Lucia is happy, she eats, and judging by the weight she's gaining I'd say she's very happy. Geoff appears to be the calming influence to her fiery character and I have every hope that theirs is a love story built to last.

Next month the Dixbury Dancers will be one less as Catherine heads off to dance school. We're all so proud of her and will be following her, sure to be, dazzling career with much interest. Josie gets choked every time it's mentioned and we've all taken to carrying tissues for such moments.

On the morning of the competition, standing barefoot in the bathroom, Gloria did indeed say, 'yes' and since then, we've all been pestering the happy couple to let us perform at their wedding. They keep evading the issue and I suspect they might just keep it an elegantly private affair.

The day after the competition, in another bathroom, Sam and Jason stood looking at each other with the pregnancy stick on the side. He told her he thought he was in love with her and she smiled. After the allotted time they looked at the stick…and nothing had changed. She wasn't pregnant. She told me that her first thought was one of relief, and her second was of Dave.

And me and Joshua? Well, we arrived at our special plateaued spot. He switched off the engine and we sat for a moment to drink in the vista. The sky was a montage of swirling blues with a liberal sprinkling of the brightest stars illuminating Dixbury below us.

"Come on," he'd said, as he got out of the car and opened the boot. I stood on the precipice and breathed the cool air with the gentle breeze tickling my skin. Joshua laid the tartan blanket on the ground, opened the picnic hamper, switched on the radio and patted the space beside him.

"Oooh hang on, I have something to add," I said, moving back to the car for the pork pie.

As I placed it amongst the many nibbles he'd said, "That's my girl!" and went to kiss me.

"Don't you be getting any ideas, matey," I said, pushing him away. "I'm starving!" He gave me a devilishly wicked grin and then handed me a plate and napkin.

We feasted on delicious snacks and sipped sparkling wine from glass flutes. We talked about mundane matters such as Basil's impending annual vaccinations and getting the rising damp treated, but inevitably the topic returned to the success of The Dixbury Dancers.

"Proud of you, kiddo," he said. He didn't need to say anymore.

Wiping the doughnut sugar crumbs from my mouth, I reclined, groaning, holding my stomach.

"Urgh, I'm stuffed." I said. "That was delicious, thank you."

He leant over. "You're more than welcome." He looked into my eyes and then started kissing me, passionately yet gently. My body yielded, moulding to the shape of him and just as I was thinking that this couldn't be any more perfect, he suddenly pulled away.

"What is it?" I asked, sitting up.

He lifted one finger and then ferreted in his jeans pocket. My eyes popped as he produced a small velvet box.

A SMALL VELVET BOX!!!

"Here," he said, passing it to me. I smiled, chewing my lip in anticipation. "Go on, open it."

Romantic setting, with the man I love, and I was opening a box...

As I slowly pushed open the lid, disappointment hit me like a ten ton truck – it was a key; a door key! I swallowed hard and gave him a confused look.

"Don't you recognise it?" he asked.

"Er." I studied the key in front of my eyes. "Oh! It's my house key, well, your house key." He beamed broadly. "You're giving me back my house key?! Are you leaving me?!"

He laughed and then reached for a scotch egg.

"Amy, this is a scotch egg. And this," he pointed to the key, "is a nest egg."

"Sorry? What?"

"I've been an idiot - " he started.

"Well.."

He gave me a mock warning look. "...I was scared, okay? I've been burnt before and no matter how much I love you, I just couldn't bring myself to put that commitment into bricks and mortar." He looked deeply into my eyes. "But now I can."

"Oh I see." I thumbed the key. "What changed your mind?"

"I think it was the orange velour." He ducked too late to miss my playful smack to his torso. "Ow! Ha ha, alright alright. Truthfully? I gave myself a good talking to and agreed with myself that you and Basil are my future."

"Aw, so you're buying into Rose Cottage?" I reached up and placed my arms around his neck.

"I am. I'm buying into us."

I happily sighed. "Hang on a minute, what would've happened if Leanne Cork hadn't pulled out?"

"Well…," he said, scratching his chin. "I might've had something to do with that…"

"Josh! What did you do?"

"I might've accidentally on purpose bumped into her and just happened to mention a few problems with the house – I mean, the survey did say there was a damp problem, but I might've made it sound a little bit worse…"

"Joshua! How terribly underhand - I love it!"

We laughed and brushed lips gently, tantalisingly lingering before he said, "So, we okay here?"

"Well now you ask, there is one more thing…"

"Go on."

"Tell me the truth, is lasagne or shepherds pie your favourite?"

He threw his head back with laughter. "You're still thinking about that?" He pulled me close. "I don't give a toad's winkie if I eat lasagne or shepherds pie as long as it's with you!"

"A toad's winkie? Please don't ever say that again." He laughed and crossed his heart. "Hey, do me a favour?" I said.

"Hmm?"

"Dance with me?"

He stood and helped me up, and then put his arms around me as we swayed to the strains of a slow song on the radio. With the warm breeze, the starlit sky and being pressed against the man I love, I decided we should call this place, 'Simply Heaven'.

"Amy," he said, his cheek pressed to mine. "Do *me* a favour?"

"What?"

"Stay with me forever," he whispered.

I pulled away to look at him and his eyes twinkled.

I shrugged happily. "Not a problem."

He then took my face in his hands and kissed me tenderly until my toes tingled. A blast of heavy gangsta rapping from the radio made us giggle and break apart.

"Come on Amy Ballerina," he said, pulling me back in. "We can do this." And taking me in his arms again, we continued our dance.

The End.

Acknowledgements

Thank you, thank you, thank you…

Malcolm, Ruby, Beattie, Viv, Jeffery, Laura, and Phil for all your help and support.

Joyce Munton for championing my efforts.

Matthew Talbot for always (and freely!) offering your insight.

MH Ferguson for editing and your unwavering support.

Penny Henderson and Liz Ireland for the use of your words. And to all the dancers in my classes who continue to inspire.

To Nicky Gibbs for teaching and for always believing that adults can dance ballet!

And to all the people who read Dixbury Does Talent and have been nothing but supportive and encouraging. Your kind words have meant the world to me. X

Thank you so much for reading and, if you are interested, the other books I have also enjoyed creating are -

Dixbury Does Talent

Snapshots

Hope to see you again for the final instalment of The Dixbury Trilogy!

26513137R00195

Printed in Great Britain
by Amazon